M000307832

We've all seen them. We've all received them, but how many of us were actually aware of the miracles that happen all around us every day. Obviously… (this) is one of those few books that pulls you in and doesn't let you go. It is inspirational. It is enjoyable. It is loving. I hope this is only the beginning of many more books to come. The largest bit of praise I can give this author is that my husband will study manuals, but does not read for enjoyment. He started to read this book only to humor me. He kept reading only because he couldn't put the book down. It's that well written. It's that gripping. It's that enjoyable! Judy - Bellevue, Ohio

…After reading the foreword to "When the Angels Cry: The Story of Arielle," it is obvious Mr. Braun has taken his own experiences and has woven them into a fascinating story which captures the reader from the first paragraph. The author's explanations of angels and their purpose in God's plan are so real and relevant to our lives that it makes you wonder why you had not thought of it exactly that way yourself before reading it in his book. Not only is Mr. Braun's insight germane to the characters, his words can be applied to our lives today. This is a novel that will keep you thinking long after you have read it, I feel I must warn everyone that you will not be able to put this book down once you start reading it. So make sure you are in a comfortable spot, with no distractions, once you begin. This book should definitely be on Oprah's must-read list! Cyndy Salins-Kentucky

This book is a fun and intriguing read! So many exciting twists and turns, starting with Arielle's timely and mysterious arrival on her lonely mother's doorstep. Her spiritual visits with curious clergy were always a surprise…. I could hardly wait to see what fascinating events the next page or chapter held. I'm excited to see what this author does next. Dianne N.-Nebraska

Reading this book only confirmed my belief in Angels. I could not put this book down and only wished it did not end. This book will make you think of things that have happened in your life. I am hoping Tim's next book is coming soon. Sandra E. Troyer, Massillon, Ohio

Electrifying, gripping and stimulating, from the foreword to the end. Arielle is captivating; I could not put this book down. I am looking forward to more creative works from Mr. Braun. Pat Moore-Florida

This is a fascinating book that you can't put down. It has thought provoking twists and turns that keep you captivated! If you read it with an open mind, it has a deep and inspiring message. It is an absolute MUST READ! P. Schaffer-Iowa

WHEN THE ANGELS CRY
THE STORY OF ARIELLE

❦

A novel by
Timothy M. Braun

www.whentheangelscry.com

Sangre de Cristo Publishing, Inc.
Cripple Creek, Colorado

ISBN: 0982815816
ISBN-13: 9780982815816
Library of Congress Control Number: 2009914243

Printed in the United States of America

Photo courtesy of Victoria R. Burke and Isabelle Guzman-Burke of Cripple Creek, CO.

Cover design by Matthew Bowen of Brownsburg, Indiana,
www.magnumopusbookcovers.com

Published by Sangre de Cristo Publishing, Inc., P.O. Box 1003, Cripple Creek, CO. 80813

Dedication

This book is dedicated to my wife, Anita, for this book would not have been possible without her love, support, words of wisdom, and her belief in me throughout the long road to publishing.

A Special Thanks

To all who helped save my life in Stanton, Arizona in March of 2008, especially Carol Roe, and Carolyn and James Plunk.

Acknowledgements

Thanks to all the members of "Writing Above the Clouds" writer's critique group, especially Sandi Sumner, author of *Women Pilots of Alaska*; Leah Persons, Kari Wainwright, Natalia Brothers and Kathryn Veres, who gave me immeasurable guidance and support. Thanks to my cousin, Kathy McHugh, author of *Passing on Hope;* my mother, "Jo" Braun, and Julie Casey for their editing help, Matt Bowen for the cover work, and the numerous people who gave me inspiration, criticism, and suggestions. Also thanks to Vicki Burke and my little angel, "Izzy," for the cover photo, and all those at Colonia del Rey RV Park in Corpus Christi, Texas for their encouragement.

This story was written for all those who've had something special touch their lives, but aren't quite sure, and all the little angels without wings.

ᏠᏠᎮ

Psalm 91:11

For he will command his angels concerning you to guard you in all your ways.

FOREWORD

I believe everyone has experienced coincidences in their lives that have left them wondering how lucky they were—but could those experiences have really been divine interventions, veiled as coincidences? We have all had incidents that, as we look back, we question, could it have been?

As I look back on my life, I vividly recall several such situations where I was faced with a horrible set of circumstances, some in which I probably would have died or been severely injured, which somehow turned out for the best or at a minimum, okay: the time I fell asleep driving, only to wake up at the last moment before crashing into an abutment; the time (in what I call "my stupid years") when I almost drowned trying to swim across a lake to prove a point, but just as I gave up and started to go under, somehow found the strength to continue. I still remember how peaceful I felt at the prospect of giving up.

There was the time in my early twenties when I was fueling the lawnmower and suddenly realized I was also smoking a cigarette. I immediately threw the smoke away. Seconds later, as I finished fueling, the plastic nozzle of the gas can flipped up and sprayed gas all over my face. My neighbor rushed me to the hospital, my eyes blinded and burning from the raw gasoline.

When I was three years old, I was sleeping over eighteen hours a day; doctors discovered I had a dislocated heart which was pushing against my ribcage, not allowing it to pump needed blood. My parents were told there was a common operation for that type of condition, but the mortality rate was fairly high. If I didn't have the operation, I would have been lucky to live a couple of more months. There were no good options. My parents were referred to Doctor Berman, a heart specialist, who had developed a brand new type of operation. I was *the* guinea pig for this procedure. Of course it was successful, and is still used today. A girl my age, who had shared the same hospital room with me, had the old type, standard operation. She passed away days later.

I ponder many of these times in my quieter moments. The years have taken a toll on my memory, but certain things have remained and probably always will.

On March 9 of 2008, my wife and I were vacationing in a private RV park in the desert of Arizona, about an hour north of Phoenix. I was going to set up a small dredge in a stream that had recently started to flow due to some heavy rains. It was nine o'clock in the morning and I had eaten a good breakfast of bacon and eggs, compliments of my wife, Anita. I was able to borrow a four-wheeler from someone at the RV park where we were staying, and a friend decided to ride down to the stream with me on his ATV. He could stay only a few minutes, but wanted to see me set up the dredge. To get to where I wanted to search for those little gold nuggets, we had to negotiate a steep hill down to the creek bed and then carry the equipment about forty yards.

Finally there and the equipment pieced together, I put my waders on and was trying to start the dredge's engine. I suddenly became very warm, followed by profuse sweating. The sun had come out, and I thought the waders, which were chest-high and insulated, were causing me to overheat. Within another minute, I felt nauseated and soon after that, lost my breakfast. I sat on a boulder in the middle of the stream thinking I must have eaten something bad.

My friend told me I didn't look very good, kind of ashen white, and thought maybe I should go back and lie down. I continued to sit there for a short time, considering what to do, but finally decided he was probably right as I continued to sweat profusely. He told me he had to get back—he had an appointment. I tried to get up, but all my energy was sapped. I asked him to stay a few more minutes. I found I couldn't even take my waders off; he had to help. I could barely even put my boots back on and left the laces untied.

We left all the equipment where it was. It took every ounce of energy I had to get back to my four-wheeler and make it take me up the hill to my RV. Once there, I lay down on the couch. My friend went and summoned a nurse practitioner who happened to be staying at the park, a friend of theirs. She brought her blood pressure cuff, but couldn't get a reading. They called for an ambulance—I was in full cardiac arrest.

The lights were dimming; my arms and legs went numb. I could barely see anyone. My wife stood at my feet. I could see the concern in her eyes and I tried to tell her I loved her, but the words wouldn't come out. I heard someone say they hoped the ambulance arrived quickly. I then realized I was dying.

Could this be it, I asked myself? Is this the way it all ends? It was a peaceful way to die—no pain at all. Minutes later, when all I could see was faint light, I heard someone say into my ear, "This is going to hurt a little," then *WHAM*. The paramedics shocked me with a defibrillator. Within seconds, warmth began returning to my extremities and my sight gradually returned. I felt great. I wanted to get up and tell everyone, including the paramedics, "Okay, you can go now." I realized there and then my life had taken a significant turn, I was no longer that invincible person.

A life-flight helicopter flew me to a heart hospital in Phoenix where I stayed for five days and had a defibrillator/pacemaker implanted. Through the medicine-induced fog, I remember one of the first things my cardiologist at the hospital said to me, "Do you know how lucky you are?" I did not, and I didn't understand what he was trying to say.

Later, I found I had joined the "Eight Percent Club;" only eight percent of patients having a cardiac arrest outside of a medical facility survive. My heart had taken a beating (no pun intended); it was enlarged and only pumping about thirty percent of what it was supposed to. I heard talk of a heart transplant.

I relate this story because: 1) If I had never met and been friends with that certain person in the RV park—I'd be dead. 2) If he hadn't accompanied me to the stream, I'd be dead. 3) If I hadn't borrowed the four-wheeler, I would never have made it to the top of the hill—I'd be dead. 4) If the nurse practitioner hadn't been there to immediately know what was wrong—I'd be dead. 5) If my neighbors hadn't been friends with the nurse practitioner—I'd be dead.

If each of these obstacles that were overcome hadn't come together, I wouldn't be here to write this novel. Was it a miracle or just a tremendous set of coincidences? I know what I believe; you must find your own beliefs. Which brings us to our story.

I NEVER remember my dreams. My wife wakes up almost every morning and relates this or that about her dreams from the previous night's sleep, and they're usually pretty funny. I always draw a blank—except for one morning about a month after my cardiac arrest. The book you are about to venture into was given to me in that dream. As soon as I arose that morning, I grabbed a yellow legal-sized pad and wrote three pages of notes describing the different chapters and characters, and even part of the title. The following story is from those notes. I hope you enjoy it.

Consider retracing your own life's experiences and ask yourself…was it just a coincidence or was I the recipient of something more miraculous?

CHAPTER 1

Anguish

Rebecca stood clutching her son's teddy bear to her chest, crying softly into it as her baby's tiny coffin was lowered into the damp earth. The snow-white lilies she had placed on top of the casket fell into the concrete vault to lie eternally with her child.

Her husband wrapped his arm around her shoulder, hugging her to him, sharing his grief. The small crowd filed past the couple paying their respects and began to drift away.

The day was cloudy, cold, and threatening rain again. A slight breeze wafted through the air as the few crimson and gold leaves left on the maple trees came loose and gently glided to the ground. Flowers, planted in the cemetery at the start of spring had turned to seed, leaving the shells of life protruding from the ground. The deep green foliage that once lined the streets and surrounded headstones had also given up its color to the frost.

Rebecca looked toward the sky. The chill in the air made her button up her coat and lean even closer into her husband. *Fall—the death of nature for the year. This is a perfect day to bury my innocent one.*

ⓒ⅏ⅇ

Tyler had barely celebrated three months of life when Sudden Infant Death Syndrome took him from them.

Rebecca had gone in to check on the baby for his two a.m. feeding. He was cold to her touch. Panicking, she picked him up, repeatedly called his name and jostled him; she couldn't believe or accept what she knew was true.

She hugged him to her, screaming for her husband. Craig bolted from bed and was immediately at her side. He pulled the baby from her arms and began compressions on his tiny chest. He started giving breaths to Tyler's little body while Rebecca frantically called 9-1-1.

It was all in vain. As soon as the paramedics arrived and checked the baby, the parents were told there was nothing they could do. The infant had been without oxygen for too long. Rebecca cried and pleaded with them to fix her child, but all they could do was call the coroner and try to comfort her. The paramedics ended up taking her to the hospital where she was given a sedative.

CRSO

After the graveside service, Rebecca and Craig went to her sister's house and accepted condolences from their family and friends. She listened to each person tell her how sorry they were, but she didn't hear any of them. How could she? Her mind was somewhere else—with her son.

When they returned home, Rebecca stepped across the threshold the same as she had done a thousand times before, only this time she felt as though she had entered someone else's residence.

The house hadn't changed, the smells were the same, all of the furniture was still where it had been just yesterday, or a week ago; but now, it felt empty. She wandered throughout the house until she arrived at Tyler's room, looking but not seeing, touching but not feeling. She was numb. She wanted desperately to enter that room, pick up Tyler, and shower him with hugs and kisses, or even hear him cry. Not today, not ever again.

But something held her back, tugging from behind, pulling on her, saying, "Don't do it. Don't go in there. You may never come out." She bristled at the thought, rubbing the goose bumps on her folded arms.

CRSO

A week after Tyler's death Craig tried to console Rebecca by trying to get her to talk about him. Settling into bed, Craig caressed her shoulder and asked, "How do you feel tonight, Hon? Do you want to talk?" Rebecca refused to discuss the tragedy. She rolled away and faced the wall.

"Not tonight," she replied. "Just hold me." She felt comforted by his embrace, but discussing Tyler made her miserable. It was okay with her when he just held her. She sensed he hurt too, but talking about the death of their baby just made all the pain come back again, and she wasn't ready.

CRSO

Soon after giving birth, Rebecca had secretly wished she could have another child. She imagined it would be great if Tyler had a brother or sister around the same age he could play with. But there was a problem, due to her prior history of miscarriages, her doctor had told her when Tyler was born she shouldn't become pregnant again; it could be dangerous for her. She had a tubal ligation, something she never told her husband and had also made her doctor promise not to tell him. She hadn't intended to keep it from him this long, the time just never seemed right. She thought about adoption, even going to visit several adoption agencies on her own.

As they lay in bed one night before their baby's death, Rebecca rolled over to Craig and stroked the hair on his chest. "Hon, what would you think about adopting a baby?"

Craig, half asleep, opened his eyes. "What?"

"I mean, if I couldn't have another baby, what would you think about adopting? Maybe a little girl? Tyler would have someone to play with."

"Why are you asking me this? Don't you want to have another baby?"

"No, no, that's not it at all. I'd love to."

Craig sat up. "Well, what is it then? What brought this on?"

"The doctor, he said…" She stopped.

"He said what? I know you Rebecca; you're trying to tell me something. Spit it out."

With her head still down, she slowly looked up at him. Her eyes were moist. "I can't have any more children."

Craig reached over and turned on the lamp next to the bed. He stared at her for several seconds, rubbing his face, his eyes demanding answers. "I think you better start at the beginning."

Rebecca explained what the doctor had told her and what he had recommended. And what she had done.

"Why didn't you tell me? What in the world would make you keep this from me?"

"I didn't intend to." Rebecca put her hand in his. "It just never felt like the right moment. It seemed like there was always something else happening, something else to discuss."

"Still, you should have."

She lowered her head and her voice. "I know. I…, I was too ashamed to tell you."

"Ashamed? Why?"

"I felt like I wasn't worth anything anymore, a half a person. I couldn't have any more babies, and that's all I wanted, one more baby. But there wasn't anything I could do. I felt so worthless." She started crying. "I didn't know if you'd want me anymore."

Craig put his arm around her, bringing her close to him. "Becca, those are your hormones talking, not me. Don't keep things like that from me, okay?"

"I promise." She wiped her eyes with a corner of the sheet and waited a few minutes before asking him again. "Now, what would you think about it?"

"About what?"

She rolled her eyes. "Adopting."

Craig rolled back over, away from Rebecca. "Let's talk about it some other time. I want to get used to being a father to one child first."

They never did discuss it again, and now it was a moot subject.

ভিপ্ত

The sun cast shadows through the living room windows as it made its way from east to west; Rebecca barely moved as the days rolled from one to the next.

Looking through Tyler's photo album, she wondered which one of them he would have looked like—her, with dark brown hair, brown eyes and soft, beautiful features noticeably of French-Canadian decent or Craig with blond hair and a tall, muscular build. She always teased Craig that she hoped Tyler would have her brains and personality and his looks.

Rebecca had one more month of family leave left and the thought of going back to work was dreadful. Everyone at work knew about her son, and they would all be taking her aside and telling her how very sorry they were, constantly reminding her of a son she missed so much. She didn't want that, as a matter of fact, she despised all the drama and false sorrow. She was an emergency room nurse and many of her co-workers had come to Tyler's funeral. She was used to death. She lived with it daily. But, this time it was different, personal—she had never experienced the death of a loved one—not as an adult, anyway.

When she was ten years old, her older brother, Steven, died from an accident at a local privately run swimming pool. Her parents had paid for a family membership and the three siblings went there each day to cool off and play with their friends during the worst heat of the summer. After finishing chores around mid-morning, they all changed into swimsuits, hopped onto their bicycles, and raced each other to the pool. Of course, Steven always won the race, but occasionally Rebecca would beat Sue, brag about it to her friends and taunt her sister the rest of the day.

One day towards the end of the summer, Steven was horsing around with two of his buddies. He dove off the side of the pool in a place where he wasn't supposed to, and broke his neck. He was under water for over a minute before he was missed. That was almost sixteen years ago and she remembered it as if it happened yesterday. She still occasionally thought about Steven—who he might be, and what he would have been like. A handsome boy as a teenager, he had been very popular. Losing Steven pierced her heart, a wound that never healed. He was more than a brother to her, a soul mate who protected her and stood up for her. There was a little, dark, empty room inside her that held the emotions she felt on that dreadful day.

ᏝᏎᎦᏬ

Rebecca returned to work when her family leave came to an end. As much as she loved her job before, she now found it cathartic on the road to forgetting, and accepted every overtime shift offered to her. She was constantly tired, but reserved her Mondays off as her day to reenergize. Inside, Rebecca knew she was clinically depressed and it was certainly more than the ebb and flow of hormones associated with postpartum depression. If only Tyler were still with her, she would welcome the baby blues.

She set the photo album aside as she heard her husband come through the front door.

"I see you're still in the same place as when I left this morning. Are you ever going to get dressed today?" Craig put his coat down as he entered the living room. "We've got to talk about this sometime, Becca." He crossed the room and sat down next to his wife, placing his arm around her. "Tyler is gone; you've got to let him go. You can't keep spending all your time on the sofa hugging his teddy bears, crying, and staring at his pictures. Why not let me make an appointment for you at the therapist, or, at least call your mother and talk with her."

"No!" she said as she shrugged off his arm. "I told you I'll handle this—my way."

"How about I call your mother and ask her to take you out shopping for a day?"

She glared at him. "I told you, no! Leave me alone." She stormed off to their bedroom and slammed the door.

സ്ക്രൂ

A week later, Craig returned home from work and found Rebecca in the kitchen fixing supper. She still had her house robe on, open, revealing lingerie he had bought for her last Christmas.

"Hello, sexy," he said putting his arms around her inside the robe. He tried giving and receiving a long kiss.

"Craig, not now." Rebecca pulled out of his embrace, turning from him after a short peck.

"Becca, come on. It's been over five months since Tyler died. There's nothing we can do about that. Sooner or later you're going to have to deal with it."

"I am," she snapped back.

Holding her shoulders, Craig turned her around to face him, his blue eyes pleading with her. "I still need you. I still want you. Sex isn't just about making babies; it's also about expressing our love to each other, and we still need each other. I love you, Becca."

"Craig, I don't want to even think about sex right now—I'm just not interested. And I am dealing with it—-in my own way. I don't want to talk about it. Now please, just leave me alone." She pulled from his grasp.

He followed her down the hallway as she walked away from him. "Why do you keep denying you need help? You know you're still depressed. You need to see someone, a doctor or psychologist. Maybe join a grief support group or visit a counselor. You can't go on like this."

He grabbed Rebecca and hugged her, but she wouldn't look at him. Her arms hung limp at her sides. After a short pause he put his finger under Rebecca's chin and lifted her head up to face him. He looked into her eyes, took her hand and said, "*We* can't go on living like this." He kissed her hand.

Rebecca looked back down at the floor—she didn't respond. Craig ran his fingers through his hair, and then stared at the tears flowing from Rebecca's eyes; his face reflected the rejection he felt.

"We need to resolve this one way or another—tonight," Craig said as he slowly dropped her hand. "Are you going to get help, or not?" He seemed determined to confront the problem whether she wanted to or not. "I'll be back in a while. Make up your mind how you want this day to end." Rebecca watched as he walked away, then went to the bedroom and lay down.

CRSO

Craig returned an hour later. He was glad he had taken the time to cool down and gain some insight as to what he was going to say to Rebecca. He didn't want to leave her, but he couldn't continue living with someone who desperately needed mental help, but refused to get it. He was going to tell her. It was up to her to get some help or he would move out.

The confrontation didn't take long. When he tried to talk to her, Rebecca just lay on the bed and refused to talk, just as before. Silently, he pulled a large suitcase from the closet and packed his clothes and toiletries. Twenty minutes later he headed for the front door.

"Call me when you decide to get some help or want to talk," he yelled down the hall to the bedroom. He turned on his heel and walked out the front door, slamming it behind him.

In the following days, Rebecca's mother, sister and father tried to intervene, talking to both her and Craig, individually and as a couple, but Rebecca couldn't be reached in her stubbornness and the darkness surrounding her.

CHAPTER 2

The Mystery Child

"I know it was partly my fault," Rebecca told her mother over lunch at Richard's Delicatessen, "But it's mostly his." She took a bite of her personal veggie pizza, heaped with green peppers, and sipped at a strawberry smoothie. "Look, I know we've been separated almost six months, but Craig's the one who has to apologize before I'll seriously talk with him about getting back together. He walked out on me, not the other way around. And he left me just when I needed him most."

Alice, Rebecca's mother, was in the middle of consuming a chicken salad with all the trimmings, topped with Italian dressing. She looked up and pointed her fork at her daughter. "That's bunk. I know you believe it, Becca, but you bear a large part of the responsibility for this mess. It almost seems like you intentionally alienated your husband. He consoled you for over five months, and you just kept ignoring him. What did you expect?" She took another bite. "He's a good man. You need to call him."

Rebecca put down her pizza and adjusted herself in her seat. Her face looked flush. She leaned forward and looked directly at her mother. "Mom, you don't..."

"Men are different," her mother continued as she dug into her salad and acted as if she hadn't heard her daughter. "You just can't push him away all the time without a good explanation when you seem to him to be as healthy as a horse and are just being obstinate."

"I know, Mom." She folded her arms on the table. As she continued, her voice rose. "But I'm learning to live with my losses without anyone's help, including his." She wiped her mouth with a napkin and scanned the room to see if anyone was listening. She noticed an older woman across the room glance in her direction. She lowered her voice to an icy whisper. "I needed Craig when Tyler died. He wasn't there for me then, so I sure as heck don't need him now."

Alice shook her head slowly. "He was there for you, begging you to get help. You never told Craig you needed him. What did you expect him to do?" She finished her iced tea with a long swallow. "Instead of listening to Craig, trying to understand him, you chose to work sixty hours a week." Her voice rose. "Then, on top of that, you still took nearly every extra shift offered to you. You just wanted to push everything into a little box so you didn't have to remember or talk about Tyler's death. I know you like the back of my hand, Rebecca Jean. You probably went home and wouldn't talk to your husband either. That only works for so long, my dear. I know what I'm talking about. Something had to break. And it did."

"I don't want to talk about Tyler," Rebecca said, not looking at her mother and taking a drink from her smoothie. Her voice again returned to an icy whisper, as she looked her mother in the eyes. "Just how do you know if we talked or not? Have you been speaking with Craig?"

"What, knowing *you* isn't enough?"

"Answer my question, Mom."

Alice raised her eyebrows and looked off in the distance. "Maybe. I might have off and on." She looked back at Rebecca. "But I haven't heard from him in awhile now."

Rebecca grit her teeth. "Mom, you had no business..."

"Becca," she said in a stern voice, "I'm trying to help you. The last time I talked with your husband, I believe he was hinting around that he might file for a divorce.

Maybe it was more than a hint. He might have been trying to tell me something... something he wanted me to pass on to you."

Rebecca stopped chewing and shook her head. "He wouldn't do that... not without talking to me first."

"You've been impossible! You won't talk to anyone; won't take any advice. My suggestion to you is if he calls you again, talk to him—or better yet, call him."

Rebecca wouldn't budge. Taking another bite from the pizza, her mouth full she said, "Not until he comes to see me first and apologizes."

Alice threw her hands up. "Do it your way, Rebecca. You always have. But remember, the Lord works in mysterious ways, and He may be working something out at this moment. Don't push Him away too."

"I wouldn't do that, Mom, but it would take a miracle for me to take Craig back right now. I just don't have the need for him or anyone. I'm doing fine by myself."

Alice finished her chicken salad, "Okay, do what you want. As I said, you always have." She picked up her brown eel-skin purse off the floor and pulled out her wallet. She paid for their meals, leaving the money on the table. "Are you ready to go?"

"Definitely."

As they left the restaurant, Rebecca gave her Mom a hug. "Thanks for listening, Mom. I always feel better after I talk with you, whether we agree or not." She patted her on the back. "I have to run. I'll talk to you tonight."

"All right. Love you."

"Love you too. Tell Dad I said hi."

On her way home, Rebecca stopped at a local church where she found solace from the torment of her loss. These visits had eventually replaced the trips to the cemetery she'd made daily for the first few months after Tyler's death. Sometimes for hours on end she would stand and stare at Tyler's headstone. Now, going to the church most nights after work to say a few prayers for him and then speaking to him silently for several minutes gave her the peace and tranquility she sought. In church, she always pictured him sitting on Christ's lap with a dozen angels surrounding them.

A few weeks after Tyler's death, Rebecca remembered and recognized the horrible things she'd said to God when her son died, and confessed. She knew He would forgive her, but she had a hard time forgiving herself. She still found herself apologizing to Him and crying each time she prayed.

This time she felt peculiar as she stood up from the pew to leave. It was nothing she could explain or put into words, but she felt as though a hundred pounds had been lifted off her shoulders. She felt alive, a reckless abandon, a freedom she hadn't felt in months. She felt forgiven. It felt good.

⊗⧢⊙

Early the next Saturday morning, Rebecca was preparing to work another extra shift when the phone rang.

"Becca."

"Hi, Mom, you're up early. What's up?"

It was a crisp, fall morning in early October. The sun was just breaking over the horizon and not a cloud was in the sky.

"It's supposed to be such a beautiful day, I thought about going to the farmer's market this afternoon. Your sister said she wanted to go, and we can all have lunch at that deli again. Want to come?"

"Sorry, Mom, I was just leaving for work. They're paying me double-time and a half today. I couldn't turn it down."

"Well, if you ask me, you're still working too much overtime. Stop and smell the flowers once in a while."

"Mom, I love you, but please, I didn't ask. I'll take a rain-check for a little shopping next week though."

"Okay, I'm going to hold you to it. I didn't want you to be alone today, this being Tyler's one year anniversary and all."

"Bye, Mom."

Rebecca put her coat on over her nurse's uniform, grabbed her purse and keys and opened the front door. When she stepped outside to leave for work, she looked toward the sky, stopped, closed her eyes and took in a deep breath of the crisp, cool air. Aw, smell that fall air; Mom was right, she thought to herself as she twisted around to pull the door closed to lock it. She noticed Ethel, the woman next door who always seemed to have her nose pressed against her window, watching the comings and goings of her neighbors. Rebecca gave her a short wave, wanting her to know she saw her too.

Something rubbed against Rebecca's leg, startling her. She looked down. The neighborhood Ragdoll Siamese cat she often fed, purred and pushed against her leg again. It was a pitiful sight; its long, multi-colored hair all matted down and filthy, its cry begging for something to eat.

She bent down to pet the little fur-ball. "I'm sorry, Ragamuffin, I don't have time to feed you this morning. You'll have to wait until I get home tonight."

Something else caught her attention as she started to stand up. There, down the walkway on her bottom step was a large brown wicker basket, a pink knitted blanket loosely covering the top. She let the screen door bang closed behind her—the heavy wooden door remaining ajar. She walked down the three steps, and bent over the basket.

"What have we here?" she said aloud. There was a note, folded and pinned to the top of the blanket, which she removed and opened. In beautiful script handwriting, it read: *REBECCA, I AM A GIFT FROM GOD. PLEASE TAKE CARE OF ME.*

Cautiously, half expecting something to jump out at her, Rebecca slowly pulled back part of the blanket revealing the face of a tiny, sleeping baby. "Holy..." Rebecca sucked in a breath. Her heart pounded. "Who are you?" Rebecca asked in a whisper. The baby, probably six weeks old, was wrapped in a pink and blue receiving blanket, sound asleep. Rebecca tucked the note in her coat pocket and carefully looked around the neighborhood. She didn't see anyone, and surprisingly Ethel wasn't peering out her window. She just knew someone had to be watching; no one would leave a new baby on a doorstep like this and walk away. What if she hadn't been going to work so early? It could have frozen to death before being found, or a dog or other wild animal could have gotten to it and done something horrible.

She gently picked the basket up and went back into her apartment looking over her shoulder. She pulled the blanket back and saw that the baby was now wide-awake, staring up at her with large, sky-blue eyes. Golden blond hair capped the infant's head and wisps curled on its forehead. Rebecca's heart skipped a beat as the baby gave her a happy toothless grin. She couldn't resist smiling back, kissing the top of the baby's head as she lifted the little swathed bundle carefully from the basket. Holding the baby gently to her shoulder she walked back to Tyler's room. She stopped as she breached the doorway.

An avalanche of memories revisited, flooding Rebecca's being. All her maternal instincts returned, warming and filling her veins. Gently lying the child down on a changing table, she unwrapped the blanket from around the tiny baby, discovering a naked little body. A baby girl!

Still hoping someday to adopt a child, she had kept all of Tyler's furniture, toys and clothing. She dressed the infant in a disposable diaper, a t-shirt and a sleeper to keep her warm. Retrieving a bottle and the last of some formula powder from a cabinet in the kitchen, she mixed it with water and warmed the formula in the microwave, pouring it into the bottle.

Cradling the child in her arm, the baby eagerly gulped the milk, her miniature fingers caressing the bottle as she suckled and emptied it. She lifted the baby to her shoulder and patted her back until she let go of the extra air with a loud burp.

What a sweet little girl. Who would abandon this child and why leave her on my doorstep?

As she held the infant, this helpless creature, all the feelings and emotions she had suppressed since Tyler's death returned with the ferocity of a thunderstorm. Rebecca cried, tears steaming down her face as she recalled holding Tyler the same way. She wiped her eyes with the corner of the baby's blanket.

The baby's stomach full, her eyes no longer able to stay open, the infant fell sound asleep. Rebecca gently placed her back into the basket.

Wiping away her own tears again, she watched the infant doze for several minutes, and then decided to make up the crib. But first, already running late for her overtime shift, she was either going to have to call in sick or call the police and turn the baby over to social services.

What should she do? Should she really keep her? What gave her the right? What would she tell everyone? What about her mom and dad, her sister, and especially that pesky, nosey neighbor?

The thought of turning her over to social services made her cringe and gave her goose bumps. How could she do that to this child? The idea of the infant being passed from one foster home to another sickened her as she recalled some of the foster children with questionable injuries brought into the emergency room where she worked. The last child, a three-year old boy had more than twelve cigarette burns on his back and chest. These were found when he was brought in with a broken arm that his guardian claimed he obtained from falling down a stairway.

The note. That was it! The note that accompanied the infant, she decided, gave the baby to her, no one else. It would be her proof—to herself—of legal custody. She knew it would never stand up in court if it ever came to it, but to her it was enough to make a decision. Besides, it was her doorstep the child was left on and the note had her name on it, so the person who abandoned her there must have wanted only her to take care of the baby. That had to count for something. And if the mother ever came back and wanted the baby, well, she would deal with that then.

Rebecca finally called the hospital and told her supervisor she didn't feel well and would not be in. She didn't approve of lying, but this had to be one of those rare exceptions. There were greater concerns right now and she didn't see any other way at the moment. Explanations, those that made sense, were not immediately available and in addition she did not wish to compound her lie.

She went to the living room window and peered out from the side, hidden by the curtain. Could someone still be watching? For almost twenty minutes, she went from room to room, looking out every window searching for something out of place, a strange car parked in the street, someone who didn't belong. Nothing.

CRISO

The telephone rang and Rebecca jumped. She hesitated to answer it. Could it be the hospital? Should she try to sound sick? Turning the ringer down so as not to wake the baby, she let it ring several more times before deciding to answer.

"Hello," she said weakly, coughing a few times. She was barely audible.

"Becca, are you all right?" It was her sister and she sounded concerned.

"Oh. Hi, Sue," she said in her normal voice. "Yeah, I'm fine."

"What's wrong? I tried to call you at work. Mom told me you couldn't go shopping with us today cause you were working overtime, but the hospital said you called in sick."

"Yeah. I did. But I'm not sick," she said cautiously.

"What's up? That doesn't sound like you."

She paused. "Sue, something really strange has come up." Rebecca thought fast. "I was getting ready to call you. I have a situation and I can't discuss it with anyone else right now, especially Mom. Can you come over?"

"When?"

"As soon as possible. Right now."

"Becca, I've got the baby, I've got to go shopping with Mom later, and I'm really kind of...."

Rebecca pressed. "Please, Sue. This is really important. I wouldn't ask you otherwise."

"Becca, what's wrong with you? You're worrying me. What in the world could be so important? Why can't you just tell me over the phone?"

"I don't want to...I can't discuss it over the phone."

"That bad, huh? Who'd you kill?"

"I didn't kill anyone, Sue! And it's not bad. I just have to be very careful. You'll understand when you get here."

"Well, okay. Let me get Christina ready. I'll be over in about an hour."

"Thanks, Sis. Hurry."

CHAPTER 3

Decisions

Sue was standing at the door ringing the bell while juggling her two-month old daughter wrapped in a blanket in one arm, and the diaper bag with all the baby necessities and toys in the other. *"C'mon Becca, hurry it up."*

The door finally swung open. Before she would even step aside and let her in, Rebecca demanded, "You have to promise me you won't breathe a word about this to anyone. Your word of honor. Okay?"

"No 'Hi Sue, thanks for coming over' or 'Gee, you look great today, Sue' or 'Let me help you with all that, Sue'?" She took a breath and waited for Rebecca to respond.

"Hi, Sue. You look great. Thanks for coming over. Let me help you with that," Rebecca parroted in a hurry as she looked out around the neighborhood. "Now promise me." She took the diaper bag off her sister's arm.

Sue watched Rebecca scan the neighborhood as she held the door open. "Breathe a word about what to whom? What in the world is going on?" she asked loudly, as she pushed past Rebecca with a look of annoyance. "Who or what are you looking for? You're acting way too weird."

"Shhh! Quiet down!"

Sue turned around, looking at Rebecca, half questioning, half aggravated. "Of course I won't tell anyone. Don't you trust me? What's with you anyhow? Who're you plotting against and why are you shushing me?"

"I'm not plotting against anyone. I've got a bizarre situation and I don't know what to do. I need you to help me with some decisions."

"You? Madam Hardass; Miss *Always-my-way*. You want *me* to help *you*?" Sue scoffed as she pointed from herself to Rebecca.

Rebecca grimaced. "Yeah, I do," she said in a hushed voice. Her face flushed a dark pink.

Sue's manner turned to a combination of concern and curiosity in a half-hearted smile. This was so unlike her sister. She spread a blanket on the floor and placed Christina on it. Rebecca set the diaper bag next to her. "I'm sorry, Sis, I didn't realize how upset you are. What's going on? What do you need help with?"

CR80

As soon as Sue had her daughter situated on the blanket between two stuffed teddy bears, Rebecca wiggled her index finger at her, "Come on."

Sue got up and followed. They went down the hallway where Rebecca quietly opened the door to Tyler's room. Sue sniffed the air. A smell of fresh baby powder greeted her. *What is that from? That smell couldn't still be here from Tyler.*

Sue entered and followed Rebecca cautiously across the room. *What is going on?* She knew her sister hadn't been quite the same since the death of Tyler, but could she be completely losing it now?

"Where're we going?" she whispered, and then wondered why she was whispering.

As Rebecca tiptoed across the room, she motioned for Sue to come with her. A blanket was hanging over the side of the crib; Sue couldn't see the sleeping infant until she looked directly down into the baby's bed. She gasped as she looked over at Rebecca. Her eyes were the size of half dollars.

"Whose baby is it? Where'd it come from," she finally whispered staring at her sister. "Did you take the day off work just to baby-sit someone's child?"

"No, no, no. That's just it," Rebecca replied. "I don't know whose baby it is or where she came from. It's a little girl and I don't even know her name. Right now, I don't know anything about her."

"Well, where'd she come from?"

Rebecca looked at her sister out of the corner of her eye. "You're not going to believe me."

"Try me."

"She was in a basket, wrapped in a blanket on my doorstep this morning as I was going to work."

"Yeah, right." Sue scoffed again. "Just like a gift basket. Did it have a bow on it also? I heard the stork dropped off a couple of other kids this morning too."

Rebecca pointed to the basket sitting in the corner of the room. "I'm telling you, she was on my steps this morning, in that basket, when I was heading out to work. She was just there. I know it sounds crazy, but that's what happened. I told you it was bizarre."

"Please, tell me you're kidding." Sue looked around the room then at Rebecca with a big smile. "This is all a big joke and I'm on Candid Camera, right? I'm being punk'd."

Frustrated, Rebecca shook her head. "No, I'm not kidding and you're not on Candid Camera. That's why I need your help. I don't know what to do."

"I'd call the police," Sue stated indifferently. "Let them take care of her. She's not your problem, why make it yours?"

"But look at her, Sue, she's so beautiful. I don't consider her a problem. I'm thinking..."

"You're *not* thinking of keeping her...?"

"I want to keep her," Rebecca said simultaneously with her sister.

"What?" Sue whispered loudly. She grabbed Rebecca's arm and pulled her out of the room, quietly shutting the door. "What're you, nuts? We're not talking about a stray puppy you get to bring home, name, and keep forever."

"But why not, Sue?" Rebecca tried pleading her case. "I can take care of her. I used to have a baby, you know."

"So, let me see, you're thinking if at first you don't succeed, try, try again?"

Rebecca glared at Sue for a moment, squinted her eyes, then turned and walked away from her. "You can go now. I'm sorry I asked you to come over."

Sue grabbed her arm. "I'm sorry, Sis. That was out of line. I know Tyler's death wasn't your fault."

"I can't believe you said that, Sue. That was just plain mean," Rebecca said as she spun around and faced her sister.

"I'm sorry! What do you want me to say? You know me, it just came out."

"Okay then, why don't you want me to keep her? Why shouldn't I keep her?"

"Because she's not yours to keep. What if the mother decides to show up in a month, or a year or two, and tells you she wants the baby back? What are you going to do then?"

"I don't know." Rebecca sounded dejected and walked away from her sister.

"Think about what you're doing. What about her future? How will you get her into school? You don't even have a birth certificate; she may even be considered an illegal alien. And what are you going to tell everybody? You found her on your doorstep?" Sue's eyes widened. "What are you going to tell Mom?"

She shadowed Rebecca, walking in circles around the kitchen table, matching her step for step. "What if the baby was kidnapped? What are you going to do if her picture is plastered all over the news tonight or tomorrow? Becca, you could be the one arrested for kidnapping her."

"I don't know, I don't know, I don't know." Rebecca slowly turned to face Sue, "But I really don't think she was kidnapped." They went back to the living room.

"Oh, no!" Sue stopped and raised her hand over her mouth.

"What?" Rebecca turned all the way around, scanning the area for an emergency. Her niece looked all right on the floor and she couldn't hear anything coming from the baby's room. "What is it?"

"I bet I know where the baby came from—who dropped her off on your doorstep."

"Who?"

Sue bent down and sat on the floor next to her daughter. "Think, Becca," she said as she pulled a bottle from the diaper bag and gave it to Christina. "Who would want you to have a baby again? Who wants to snap you out of your depression? Who keeps trying to talk with you again and again?"

"Oh, come on, Sue. Craig may want all those things, but how would he get a baby? Kidnap her? Buy her on the black market and drop her off in front of my house on the steps? Just to talk with me and get back with me? You're dreaming! He may be upset, but he's not crazy."

"I wouldn't put it past him. He hasn't been a happy camper since he left you and you won't talk to him. I'll bet he's just desperate enough to do something like this."

"He may be anxious, Sue, but he's not foolish enough to steal a newborn."

"Who else did it then?"

Rebecca smiled. "I want you to see something." She went to the closet and pulled the note out of her coat pocket. "Here, read this. It was pinned to the baby blanket. It doesn't even look like his writing."

Sue read the note then looked up at Rebecca who was standing over her with her hands on her hips. "Who would leave a note like this?" she asked. "I guess I'd have to agree it doesn't sound much like him. But who was it then? It sounds to me like a person who knows you."

"I'm not sure, but I think whoever left her really wanted *me* to take care of her when they abandoned her. She didn't even have any clothes on when I found her. No clothes, no food, no name. She was butt naked, with the exception of a small blanket around her. How can I turn her over to the police or social services to be placed in fifteen different foster homes? She'd never have a chance at a decent life."

Sue was calmer now. "I have to agree with you there." She picked up her daughter, hugged her and put her on her shoulder, patting her back. "So, what's your master plan?"

"I'm getting a headache thinking about it." She put the back of her hand to her forehead. "I don't have one, except, I know I want to keep her. But what do I tell Mom and Dad? What about the neighbors? What about work? That's why I called you to help me think this through. I need a solid story—one nobody will see through."

"And that's why you asked me over? I'm your favorite liar?" Sue joked.

Rebecca didn't catch the joke. "No, no. I need help from someone I can trust."

"Ease up there, Sis. You have to tell Mom and Dad. I'm sure they'll want to help. I know they'd love to have another grandchild, and Christina can sure use a cousin her own age." Sue put her child back down on the blanket and started pacing the floor. "I'm going to have to tell Ted, too. I can't keep something like this from my husband."

"Do you have to tell him how I found her?"

"Yep, but only if he asks."

"You know I don't trust him."

"I know you don't, but I do. He's my husband, Becca; we don't keep secrets from each other."

"You mean *you* don't keep secrets. I'll bet he's got plenty."

Sue gave Rebecca a dirty look and paced the floor some more while she was thinking. "You don't know that, Becca."

"No, but that's what my gut tells me."

"Look, you can tell everyone at work that you have a young niece who had a baby. She decided she was too young to take care of it and gave the child to you, and you intend to adopt and raise her."

"No, that won't work. Just about everyone I work with knows I only have one sister and that you just had your baby. They'd ask why you couldn't take care of her."

"Oh, right. Scratch that one." She contemplated some more. "It's your cousin. She lives in Poughkeepsie, New York."

"Sounds good so far. Might work." Rebecca thought a moment. "What about the nosey neighbor?"

"Hmmm, you can tell her the same. I don't think you're going to like this, but I think you should move to a new neighborhood."

"Why?" Rebecca was bothered at the suggestion.

"For two reasons. New neighbors aren't going to ask where she came from, they'll just naturally assume she's your daughter, and two, if the mother, or whoever left her here, does come back and tries to find her later, maybe she won't be able to. That is, if you don't want her to."

Rebecca thought for a few seconds then smiled at Sue. "I knew I asked my big sister for a reason."

"Whoa! We aren't done yet. Now for the *big* question."

"What's that?"

"When or what are you going to tell Craig?"

She stared at her sister for a moment then smiled. "Tell him what?"

They both laughed. "Oh, little sister, you are bad. I wouldn't want to be in your shoes."

"Seriously, I'll tell him *if* and when he apologizes to me, and *if* we decide to get back together. It'll have to be a package deal, though, both or nothing. Besides, I don't know if he'll believe how I found her."

"That's up to you. Leave me out of that one. She's going to need a name, have you thought of one yet?"

"I was thinking about Arielle Rose, after our great grandmother."

"Mom would like that and it's a beautiful name; I've always loved it."

For the rest of the morning the two sisters discussed more of their plan for informing their parents and figuring out where Rebecca should move. Sue left her with enough liquid baby formula for lunch and went to meet her mom at the farmer's market.

Rebecca went shopping later that afternoon for everything Arielle was going to need: new clothes, shoes, and blankets. She couldn't let her little girl grow up with everything blue, sporting red trucks and footballs on them. She was going to be raised a little lady and wear pink, with lace and ruffles.

CR80

Later that evening, Rebecca bathed Arielle, put on a fresh diaper, fed her, pulled out a new pink sleeper and placed her in the crib. She stood stroking the child's soft, golden hair. As she leaned over the crib railing to kiss her goodnight, the baby opened her right hand. For the first time, Rebecca saw something very strange about this *Gift from God*. Several tiny, sparkling, gold orbs of light rotated and danced in the child's palm. Rebecca jumped back from the crib. She closed her eyes and shook her head. She had never seen anything like this and it startled her. Slowly, she approached the crib again and stared at the oddity, watching the orbs dance in the baby's hand for a while. It seemed to hypnotize—to mesmerize her. Rebecca felt strangely at peace, as Arielle seemed to look straight into her soul.

She hesitantly reached into the crib and quickly attempted to touch the orbs. Her finger seemed to pass right through them; or, did they pass through her? She tried again. They were... untouchable. Arielle's hand slowly closed and the orbs disappeared.

Soon, the baby's eyelids grew heavy and she fell fast asleep. Rebecca stood watching her little chest rise and fall with each breath; those precious baby breaths. *Who is this child, and where did she come from?*

CHAPTER 4

Tragedy

"How's the little darling doing these days?" asked Lois, the head nurse on duty in the emergency room. She and Rebecca were just leaving the nurse's break room, heading back to the ER. So far, it had been a slow night.

"She's doing great," Rebecca replied. "She's wearing me down but growing like a dandelion, and never stops eating. Half the time I think she has a tape worm."

"She's such a cutie. You have to stop in with her again sometime so we can all spoil her some more."

"Believe me, she's spoiled enough. Mom and Dad see to that. They've bought her so many toys I'm running out of space to put them. I've never seen so many things that make noise and use up batteries."

Lois chuckled. "Isn't that the truth." Her facial expression took on a more serious, concerned look. Hesitantly, she turned to Rebecca, who instantly knew Lois wanted to ask her something.

"Well, what is it?"

"Tell me if it's none of my business, Becca, but have you spoken with Craig lately?"

"Why? What makes you ask that?"

"Well, you were in a depression for such a long time, and now you seem to have come out of it, I thought, maybe…"

"Oh, I get it." She smiled. "It just so happens that he called me yesterday and asked me out to supper tomorrow night."

"Well?"

"Well, what?" Rebecca baited.

"Well, are you going?"

"I told him…" Rebecca waited a few seconds before completing the answer, stringing out Lois's anticipation, "I would meet him."

"Good for you!"

"Where're you meeting? I'll bet he's taking you someplace really special!"

Rebecca looked at her friend with a big grin. As they entered the E.R. and Rebecca was about to respond, a crackle came over the radio from an ambulance that had been dispatched to a motor vehicle accident. "We're coming in with one male, late twenties, E.T.A. ten minutes. Blood pressure—sixty over forty. Head trauma, breathing labored but steady. Multiple contusions, a compound fracture of the right leg and unconscious. Also believed to have internal injuries."

"Sounds like we're going to get busy. Make room three ready," Lois barked. "Notify orthopedics and the neurologist on call. Call Cindy in x-ray and tell her to get down here now."

Ten minutes later, two EMT's rolled the crash victim on a gurney through the emergency room entrance. An oxygen mask covered the lower half of his face. Blood and bandages covered the rest.

"Take him into three," Rebecca yelled as they passed her. "Has the family been notified yet?"

"I don't think so. He was the only one in the car," replied one of the EMT's.

A flurry of activity immediately ensued. The doctor on duty, three nurses, and several other aides were immediately at the patient's side. Lois unwrapped the gauze and bandages on his leg and started cutting his shirt and pants off. A bone was sticking out from the lower right leg.

"Here, get the wallet from his trousers so we can see who he is," Lois said to Vicki, the other nurse, as she pulled the pants out from under the man. "Give the I.D. to admissions. We need to notify the family before surgery, if we can."

"This poor guy is a mess. I don't think anyone would even recognize him right now," stated one of the aides as she washed him off.

"Don't say that in front of him," scolded Lois. "He might look unconscious, but he still may be able to hear you."

Rebecca was busy setting up the equipment and preparing the drugs the doctor ordered.

Vicki took the wallet from the pants pocket and pulled out a driver's license, staring at it for a moment. She looked at the victim then back at the license. She took it over to Lois. "I think you ought to see this."

"I'm kind of busy right now, Vicki," she responded as she continued checking his pulse and blood pressure. "Give it to admissions."

"But I think you'll *want* to see this," she said adamantly as she held the victim's license in front of Lois's eyes.

Lois stared at the license for a few seconds then grabbed it and held it close to the victim for a moment. "Oh, no. It can't be," she said quietly. She dropped the chart she was writing on into a tray, "Take over here, Vicki." She took hold of Rebecca by her arm. "Come with me."

"But I have to…"

"Come with me," she said, gently pulling Rebecca's arm.

Lois removed her mask and went past the reception area into a small office with Rebecca following. She closed the door.

"Rebecca, please sit down for a minute."

"Why, what did I do?" She sat down on the edge of one of the chairs and pulled the latex gloves off her hands.

"You didn't do anything, hon. I've got some bad news."

Haltingly, Lois gave the driver's license to her.

"Where'd you get this?"

"Rebecca, that's him—-in number three."

"It can't be. I..., I'd have recognized Craig." Rebecca started to get up, but Lois put her hand on her shoulder.

"It is him, so I need you to stay out here—out of the room for now."

"Why? Why can't I help?"

"You know the hospital policy. You can't treat, or help treat any immediate relatives."

"But, Lois..."

"I'm sorry, Becca. I can't make this an exception. I know you want to be with him, but you'll have to stay away at least until we stabilize him and find out what's wrong. Why don't you go and get some coffee or something in the cafeteria? I'll let you know as soon as we get the x-rays and tests back."

Rebecca reluctantly agreed to stay out of the room. "Okay."

"Do you want someone to go with you?"

"No. I'll be fine," she said softly.

She wandered the halls of the hospital for a while before ending up in the cafeteria. Filling a paper cup with water, she sat down in one of the orange plastic chairs at a corner table. With one swoop of her arm she wiped the accumulated crumbs from the last customers off the table onto the floor. Her mind was spinning a hundred miles an hour; even the heavy, mixed odors of spaghetti and tacos didn't impinge on her thoughts. *Why didn't she recognize her own husband?* She could feel tears welling up. She had to talk with someone. Pulling her cell phone out of her pocket, she pressed number three on her speed dial.

"Mom? Mom, there's been a terrible accident." Rebecca choked back the tears.

"What's wrong, dear? Are you okay?"

"It's Craig, Mom. He's hurt real bad."

"What happened to him?"

"I don't know everything yet. He was in an auto accident and looks horrible. He's unconscious. He has a compound fracture and probably a lot of internal injuries. He's banged up pretty good. Now they won't let me in the room to see him."

"How come? What's the problem?"

"It's policy. We can't treat relatives. I have to wait for them to tell me what's wrong, but he didn't look good. Can you do me a favor?

"Sure. What do you need?"

"Call Craig's parents. Please?"

"Of course I will. What do you want me to tell them?"

"Just tell them he has been in an accident and ask them to come to the hospital and see me. I'll be in the cafeteria. I may need them to help me make some decisions."

"It's that serious?"

"Yes, very."

She knew this was going to be hard on Craig's parents; he was their only child and the possibility of losing him could drive his mother to the edge.

Rebecca had been in the cafeteria for almost an hour when Craig's parents, May and Harry, arrived. As they crossed the floor of the cafeteria, Rebecca stood and waited for them. May, holding a white handkerchief, had obviously been crying. She came over to Rebecca and hugged her.

"Your mother told us what happened," she said between sniffles. "How bad is he? What's his status?"

Rebecca waited for Harry to join them. He was taking a little longer to cross the floor as he relied on his cane to support him. She shook his rough, leathery hand when he got to her. His wrinkled, weathered face displayed his concern as he pulled her to him, hugging her tightly.

"Hello, Rebecca," he said softly in her ear.

They sat down across the table from Rebecca, Harry removing his wife's coat and carefully placing it on the table next to them. She filled them in on what she knew—which wasn't very much.

"When will we know, Rebecca? How soon can we find out?"

"Lois promised to come down and tell me when the x-rays and tests are finished. It shouldn't be too long now."

For close to a half hour, an uncomfortable silence shrouded the table. It hung over them like a dark cloud. Only small talk from Harry about the weather and questions about Rebecca's job as a nurse broke the stillness once in a while. Rebecca could tell something was on May's mind though. The darting eyes and her inability to sit still told her something was about to break open. She had seen it before.

After she and Craig were married, May never seemed to be pleased with anything Becca did. There always seemed to be some type of criticism encased in one of her questions or comments. It was a constant problem between them, as Craig had never fully taken his wife's side and stood up to his demanding mother. Rebecca didn't have to wait long.

"I don't know what you want to do here, Rebecca—and I don't want to pry into your lives, but I know things aren't good between the two of you. If you and Craig are planning to get a divorce, I really don't think you should be making any medical judgments for him. It wouldn't look right if anything goes wrong. Why don't you let us take over and make any decisions that need to be made?"

Rebecca looked up—she knew this woman had gumption, but couldn't believe what May had just implied. She stared at her for several moments. "You mean let *you* make the decisions, don't you, May?"

"Excuse me?" May looked shocked.

Her jaw set, Rebecca went on the offensive. In a hushed voice she zeroed in on May's eyes. "Absolutely not! First of all, if it's any of your business, we're not planning on a divorce. We have some problems to work out, but Craig is still my husband and *I'll* make the choices that need to be made. Secondly, I invited you here as a matter of courtesy, to help me make those decisions, not to let you take over. So please," she held her hand up, "don't start with me."

With a huff, May rose from the table and went over to the food line. Harry winked at Rebecca.

"You hold your ground, girl. Don't let her bully you. She don't mean to be so demanding, she's just kind-a built that-a-way."

"I know, Harry," she said as she tried to calm down. "I'm sure she's upset and on edge. I guess I would be too if he were my son. Maybe I was a little rough on her."

"No, you got every right to say what you did. It's about time someone stood their ground. Lord knows, Craig don't. You watch, give her a little while; she'll back down."

A couple minutes later May came back to the table and sat down with a cup of coffee.

"I think I owe you an apology, Rebecca," May said looking into her drink. "I had no right."

"That's all right, May. No harm done. Let's forget it."

A short time later Lois came into the cafeteria. As she approached the group, everyone became silent.

"I've got good news and not-so good news," she stated putting her hand on Rebecca's shoulder. "Craig's critical but stable for now. He's in surgery to set his leg, but his brain is swollen and I'm afraid he's in a coma."

Lois pulled out the remaining chair and sat down next to Rebecca. She folded her hands together. "We need permission to operate to relieve the pressure. That means we have to drill a hole in the top of his head to release some of the fluid."

"Drill a hole in his head?" May questioned, alarm in her voice. She sat up straight in her chair, the color draining from her face. With her mouth open, she turned to Rebecca for an answer. "Rebecca?"

"Yes. It's standard procedure for this, May. Something they have to do. He could die if the pressure isn't released." She looked at Lois and stated, "I'll sign the papers."

"Good. I'll let them know," Lois said. She got up and turned to Rebecca before she left. "Don't worry, we'll take good care of him."

"I know," Rebecca said. Tears streamed down her face dropping onto her uniform. She slowly wiped her face with her hand.

May came around the table. "We'll get through this, dear," she said as she put an arm around her and hugged her tight. "Craig's a tough guy."

"I just feel so terrible, May. Craig has been trying to talk to me for months and I kept refusing. I haven't even seen him since he left. We were supposed to have supper together tomorrow. Now look at him. I always thought there would be a tomorrow."

"And there still will be," May said softly. "There's always tomorrow."

Just then, Rebecca's mother came into the cafeteria, holding little Arielle Rose. Rebecca wiped her tears with a tissue and held out her arms. Alice gave the baby to her as she exchanged greetings with May and Harry.

"And who is this cute little thing?" asked May reaching over and touching the infant's cheek. "Who does she belong to?"

Rebecca looked at her mother with a glance that told her "Help me!"

Alice smiled at Rebecca as if to say "I'll handle this."

She introduced the infant to May and Harry. "This is Arielle Rose. Rebecca's younger cousin had a baby. She has some problems right now and can't take care of her and asked Rebecca to be her guardian for a while. Becca just couldn't turn her down, and personally, after seeing her, I don't blame her. I'd take care of her myself if she hadn't."

I hope she never finds out the truth. Rebecca threw a glance and smile at her mother to say "Thanks."

"I don't blame her either. She's such a beautiful child," added May as she played with Arielle's little hand.

Rebecca held her breath when she saw Arielle open her hand. She watched the orbs dance. *God, please don't let May be the one to see the lights!*

"Does Craig know you have her?" May asked.

"Not yet. It was on my list," Rebecca said glancing between May and her mother.

Hours passed and the baby slept as they waited for word on Craig. Finally Lois came back to the cafeteria. When she saw Arielle, she broke into a huge grin.

"There she is! Can I hold her?"

Rebecca put Arielle into Lois' outstretched arms.

"Craig is finally out of surgery," she said cradling the child in her arms. "He's doing fine."

"Oh, thank God," May said, raising her hands to the heavens.

"They relieved the pressure on his brain and he's in the recovery unit. The problem is, the doctors believe he is going to be in a coma for a while. We're not real sure for how long though. You can go up and visit with him now if you would like."

"Thanks, Lois," Rebecca said as she got up and gave her a hug around the neck.

Lois carefully transferred the baby back to Rebecca. "She's such a good baby."

Rebecca guided everyone up to the recovery unit. They stalled at the entrance to the unit as she went in and talked with the attending nurse and came back out.

"Hospital policy restricts visitors in this area to two people at a time, but Theresa says as long as we're quiet, we can all go in."

Theresa was also a close friend of Rebecca's. She had always called her *Sister Theresa* because she was so calm and pleasant with every person, even when *it* was hitting the fan. And you never heard an ill word come from her mouth.

Rebecca turned to May, "I want to warn you; what you're going to see won't be a pretty sight. Craig's hooked up to many different monitors, machines, oxygen, and drips and the bruises and cuts are all bandaged, so prepare yourself."

CHAPTER 5

Kidnapped!
(Six Years Later)

"So, how does she like school?" Sue asked Rebecca as they sat on the front steps of Sue's two-story, brick townhouse, watching the young cousins play together.

"She loves it," Rebecca said. "Her teachers say she seems wise beyond her years. After she was tested, they wanted to put her into advanced classes, but I thought keeping Arielle with her peers for the first year or so would be best."

Each sister was sipping a cold glass of iced tea with a wedge of lemon clinging to the side. They watched their two little girls race each other up and down the sidewalk on their bicycles. The temperature was in the mid-nineties and the kids wore their two-piece swimsuits. The front lawn sprinkler was oscillating back and forth, spraying the girls with cool water as they rode by, causing them to squeal with laughter.

"You know, it'd be nice being a child again. Good is good, bad is bad, right is right, and wrong is wrong."

"Yeah, it's not until you get older and get confused with all those gray areas that life starts to get complicated."

☙❧

Rebecca had taken Sue's advice years ago and moved to the other side of the city, closer to her parents, but to a neighborhood where no one knew her. Of course, her parents and Sue knew Rebecca's secret of Arielle; to just about everyone else who asked, Rebecca had adopted her. Most people believed Rebecca was just naturally Arielle's mother and never asked anything, and that was the way she wanted it.

"Have you told Arielle yet?" Sue asked.

"Told her what?"

"That she's adopted—and about Tyler."

Rebecca was slow to respond.

"Sorry, I didn't mean to hit a nerve," Sue said.

"No, it's not that. I want to tell her she's adopted and how she came to me, but I haven't quite figured out how to do it yet. How do I tell her I found her on my front steps? That I've lied to many people about who she is, but it's not right to lie."

"And Tyler?"

"When her turtle died, I took the opportunity and told her she had a brother who died when he was a baby. We talked about dying for a while and I told her all about him. She cried with me and hugged me. She told me Tyler was with God in heaven. You could have knocked me over with a feather."

Rebecca took several deep breaths shaking her head and stretching. "It's hard to believe it's been six years."

Sue nodded. "I know."

"How's it going with Ted?" Rebecca asked. "Has he decided to give up the fight and give you custody of Christina yet?"

"You know how to ruin a perfectly good day, don't you?"

Rebecca laughed.

"Are you kidding? He's going to fight to the last breath for her. It's really gotten nasty, Becca. My lawyer promises he won't be able to get custody though. There's no way he can show I'm a bad mother, and that's what he'd have to do. The absolute worst that could happen is I'd have to share joint custody; that would be tragedy enough in itself. He's too harsh with her. I think he'd want her to start wearing a burka now if he could force her to. Of course, then he'd have to deal with me."

"Your lawyer promised you? You know how to tell if a lawyer is lying, don't you?"

"No, how?"

"When his lips move." Rebecca smiled. "Be careful, Sue. Don't give in an inch. I've never heard of a lawyer promising anything."

"I'm doing the best I can with what I've got to work with, Becca. Lawyers aren't cheap, you know."

"What does Christina say about her father? Is she scared of him or want to see him?"

"She won't talk about Ted. I don't know what he's told her, and I don't know what she's thinking. It makes me nervous sometimes."

"When is he leaving for Saudi?"

"Tomorrow. I think his flight is supposed to leave at six in the morning. I hope he stays there and never comes back. He wanted to take her for a visit tonight before he left, but she has a dance recital and doesn't want to miss it."

"That's too bad. He's had all this time to see her and never did."

"Let's talk about something else. My blood pressure is high enough."

"Okay, what?"

Sue looked at Rebecca with a smirk. "You have to tell me," she said, "how in the world did you get a birth certificate to get Arielle into school? I've always wondered."

Sue scooted over closer to Becca as if this was going to be the secret of all secrets. Rebecca smiled as she looked over at Sue. "You *don't* really want to know."

"Ahh, but I do little sister, and you're going to tell me."

"Or what?" Rebecca chuckled and pushed her sister away.

"Or...I'll figure out something. Besides, you owe me. I helped you with all this when you needed me. *Remember?* Now it's your turn to spill your guts."

"Are you sure you want to know? You may be complicit in a serious crime." She stopped, looking around as if to see if anyone was lurking in the bushes, listening. She looked her sister right in the eye and summoned the best poker face she could muster. "A crime that could put both of us away for a very long time," Rebecca warned, daring her sister to call her bluff and inquire more.

Sue dropped her smile. "Is it that serious? Now I don't know if I want to know. I can't go to jail. I've got Christina to worry about and Ted would love that."

Rebecca looked at her sister. A slow smile emerged on her face and she burst into laughter pointing at her sister. "Gotcha! You're so easy!"

Sue hit her sister on the leg. "You're such a liar! That's not right!"

"I had a really great teacher!" Rebecca had a good laugh for several minutes. She could see Sue was steaming. "Okay, okay. But this is absolutely serious. You can't ever breathe a word of it or I could be in big trouble and Arielle could be taken away. Promise?"

"Of course I promise. I've never told anyone except Ted how you got her, have I?"

"Well then, you've been a good girl. I just hope he keeps his mouth shut." Rebecca patted her sister on the shoulder then sipped her tea for a moment as she watched the girls go by. "You know all those overtime shifts I used to work after Craig left?"

"Yeah, what about them?"

"Well, on one of them they needed me to work in obstetrics. I learned the paperwork process for the new babies. I stole one of the certificates the doctor completes.

I brought it home and forged Doctor Beasley's name, put Arielle's name on it and brought it back in the next day. I slipped it in with the other newborn forms that were to be forwarded to the city registrar-recorder that day."

"You are scheming, aren't you?"

"Yeah, but I was scared to death someone was going to catch me. I waited for a week on pins and needles. Sue, I was so nervous I threw up almost every day. I could hardly eat or sleep and when I did, I'd wake up sweating like crazy. I kept having nightmares they had caught me, I got fired, they took Arielle away, put me in jail, and Craig was standing outside my cell laughing and pointing at me."

"Wow, I wish I knew. I would have been laughing at you too."

"Thanks a lot."

Sue took a long drink of her tea. Casually she asked, "Who'd you put down as the parents on the birth certificate?"

Rebecca didn't respond.

"Come on, who's our promiscuous cousin?"

Rebecca glanced sideways at Sue. "I put myself down as the mother."

"*You what*? What about everybody at the hospital who knows you're not the mother?"

"I'm just praying no one ever catches that. That's why I was so nervous."

"And the father? Did you make up a name as your secret lover? I know Craig wouldn't have given you permission to use his name. If you got divorced, he'd have to pay child support for the next eighteen years for a child he didn't even have the pleasure of creating."

"Su-ue... You're terrible. I haven't seen anyone or dated anybody. I'm still married."

"Still married! Ha!"

"Well, we *were* still married when I found her, we were just separated. He hadn't had the accident yet. Remember?"

"Yeah, I remember." Sue took another drink from her iced tea. "Becca, he's been in a coma now for what, five, six years? How long are you going to wait for him to wake up? You're going to be an old maid by that time, if he ever does. You need to find someone and enjoy life."

"Stop it, Sue." She paused. "I named Craig as the father."

Sue looked at Rebecca and rolled her eyes. "You what? You put Craig down as the father without even asking him? He's a father and doesn't even know it?"

Rebecca gazed up at the sky. "Doesn't seem to make much of a difference right now, does it?" She finished her drink.

"Guess not. Funny how things work out."

"Besides, think about it," Rebecca said. "If and when he wakes up, he probably won't remember too much, if anything. I could tell him she's his daughter and I'll bet he wouldn't know the difference. He may not even remember we were separated, if he remembers me at all."

"Those are pretty big ifs. I have to admit though, that's pretty good, Sis. I don't think I could have thought all that through. I don't think I would've had the guts to do what you did, either."

"Well, I'm not proud of what I did, but it had to be done and everything kind of fell into place. I was going to tell Craig all about it if we got back together, 'cause I know he'd love Arielle, but now I guess it doesn't matter. If I had told him while we were separated, he would've had a cow and then the you-know-what would've hit the fan. As it stands now, he doesn't even know Arielle exists."

Sue laughed. "Well, let's hope he gets better. I just want to be there when you tell him he has a daughter. I want to see his eyes! Probably put him back in a coma."

Rebecca grimaced. "You would."

Sue went inside and refilled their iced teas. When she came back out and sat down, Rebecca turned to her, "Speaking of Craig, something weird happened the other morning."

"What's that?"

"Arielle told me when she got up that she had met her father."

"Met her father? Did she mean Craig? In a dream?"

"I think that's what she meant. I've never taken her with me to see him, maybe I should. She's old enough now. I asked her what he looked like and she kind of generally described Craig."

"That's strange. You think she was describing a picture she saw of him?"

"I don't know. She told me she knew he was still in the hospital, but not to worry, he's going to be okay."

"Spooky."

"Yeah. I know."

∞

Rebecca watched as an older, large, white van drove slowly down the street past the townhomes. The front bumper was missing and light blue smoke spewed out the tailpipe, hanging in the still air. The front windows were down and as it neared them and drove past, she noticed two men in the front seats. It stopped at the corner and turned right, accelerating out of sight.

"That was weird," Sue said. "I wonder what they're looking for."

"Probably just lost, looking for an address. These townhomes all look the same," Rebecca said.

After a couple of minutes, the van reappeared at the opposite end of the street where it had last been observed.

It had apparently gone around the block and was still moving slowly.

"They don't appear to be looking for house numbers, Becca. I don't like the looks of this."

From what Rebecca could see of the two men seated in the front, they did not seem to notice her and Sue, but were concentrating on something ahead of them. As the van passed the townhome, Rebecca stood up on the top step to see where the girls were. She could barely see them over the shrubbery at the corner where the van was headed. They were off their bikes, turning around.

"Sue, look at this." She climbed to the top step with Rebecca.

As the van edged slowly to the stop sign, the man in the passenger seat hopped out, leaving the door open. He was dressed in blue jeans and a dirty white t-shirt. He quickly scanned the neighborhood, ran up behind the girls, grabbing Christina in one arm and Arielle in the other. Sue watched in horror as she heard both of the girls scream, kicking and crying for their mothers. The bikes fell to the ground.

"Arielle!" Rebecca screamed.

"Christina!" Sue screamed.

Both ran towards the corner.

∞

"Ouch! You little... Stop that!" yelled the scruffy looking man.

Arielle bit him on the arm again.

"Ooww!" he yelled.

"Let me go!" she yelled.

She kicked, bit, and punched the captor until he lost his grip on her. She finally pushed free, falling to the pavement. The man had a better grip on Christina. He carried her over and tossed her into the van through the open door as she continued to scream and kick. The driver grabbed her, pushed her down on the floor of the van and held onto her.

"Arielle!" she yelled. "Help me!"

The kidnapper turned and headed back towards Arielle, but she was already up and running away from him. He then saw two women running towards him, yelling and screaming at the top of their lungs. He turned around and rushed back to the van, jumped in and slammed the door. It sped off down the street, streaming a trail of blue smoke from the tailpipe.

❦

Arielle stopped running and looked back toward the van, holding her knee. It was skinned up and bleeding from the fall.

Tears running down her cheeks, she ran toward her mother and Aunt Sue as fast as her little legs could carry her.

Rebecca and Sue were still running toward the corner. Sue still screamed for help to anyone who could hear her. When they met up with Arielle, Rebecca scooped her up, hugging and kissing her.

Rebecca pulled out her cell phone and dialed 9-1-1. Immediately, she reached a recording indicating there were a heavy number of calls and if it were an emergency to standby, the calls would be answered in the order they were received. She was then placed on hold with soft music playing in the background.

"I can't believe this!" Rebecca yelled into the phone as she held it in front of her face. She turned toward Sue. "They put me on ignore!" As she listened and waited for a warm body to answer, Arielle held onto her tightly. Her whole body was shaking.

"He took her, Mommy. The man. He took her," Arielle cried and pointed down the street as Rebecca set her down. "She wanted me to help her, but I couldn't. I was scared." She looked at her knee. "I'm bleeding."

"I know, honey." Rebecca said, holding her daughter's head to her. She bent down and wiped Arielle's tears from her cheek. "Don't worry. It's not your fault. We'll find Christina. We'll get her back." She pulled a tissue from her pocket and gently dabbed at her daughter's wound.

"Go get your car," Rebecca yelled to Sue who was distraught, practically running around in circles, crying, screaming for her daughter. "Who knows how long I'll be on hold."

Sue ran back to her house.

While she was waiting on hold, Rebecca glanced over at Arielle who had walked a couple feet away from her. She watched her look up towards the sky and nod her head several times, appearing to have a conversation, as though someone stood right in front of her. The look on her daughter's face seemed to turn from distress to peacefulness as she wiped the tears from her eyes with the back of her hand.

"9-1-1. What's your emergency?" the voice finally came over the phone.

"My niece... she's been kidnapped!" Rebecca blurted out fast. "Two men in a white van... they just grabbed her and sped off!

"Ma'am, calm down and tell me what happened."

"Two men in a white van. They just cruised by and one of them jumped out and grabbed my daughter and niece off their bicycles."

"What is your location?"

"5702 Blue Feather Way."

There was a pause. She could hear the dispatcher repeating the emergency.

"The officers are on their way. Do you have a description of the vehicle?"

"I told you, it's an older white van, one of the large kind, I think it's called a cargo van. The front bumper is missing. There are two men in it. The one in the passenger seat has a white t-shirt and blue jeans on. He's got long black hair and a moustache. I didn't get a look at the driver."

"Okay. The police should be there shortly. Stay where you are and wait for them. Can I have your name, please?"

"It's Rebecca Price and I can't sit around and wait for the police. We're going after them."

"No, don't do that. Stay where..."

She hung up. "Come on Arielle, let's go. We have to find Christina." Rebecca grabbed Arielle's hand and started pulling her towards Sue's house. They left the bikes where they lay at the corner.

"Mom, wait. I have to do something." She pulled away from her mother.

"No! Come on, we have to go now."

"I have to help Christina."

Arielle turned toward where the van was last seen, lifted her right arm and gently blew across her palm. Rebecca's eyes widened as she watched, stunned. A small gold orb left Arielle's hand and shot off in the direction the van had disappeared. Arielle turned and walked over to her mother.

"Okay, we can go now."

"What just happened? What'd you just do?" Rebecca asked, still not believing what she had just seen.

"I helped Christina," Arielle said still wiping the tears from her eyes with the back of her hand. "She'll be okay now, but we have to go get her."

"Where?"

"Down the street. I'll show you."

Just then, Sue came speeding down the block in her light green minivan, honking her horn and skidding to a stop in the sandy gutter of the street. Rebecca unlatched the sliding door and shoved her daughter in ahead of herself. She slammed the door and Sue took off.

"What took so long?" Rebecca asked. "The police are on the way."

"I couldn't find my keys. I forgot where I put them. Then I almost hit a pedestrian as I backed out into the alley. That guy must think I'm a fruitcake the way I was waving and yelling at him."

"Arielle says to go straight," Rebecca yelled.

"How does she know where they went?" Sue yelled back as she accelerated. Rebecca put Arielle's seatbelt on.

"She's the only one who saw them, so unless you have a better idea...just follow the smoke!"

They drove almost a half-mile down the street, Sue barely yielding at four different stop signs. Both were looking up and down every side street and driveway for the van.

"Becca. Look. Up ahead. There's the van—and a police car. They sure got here fast." She looked at the cars a few more seconds. "What's going on?"

"It's the van all right, but, look! It ran into the police car!"

"Oh, please, I hope they haven't hurt Christina," Sue pleaded.

"She's all right," Arielle said, but neither paid attention to her.

As they pulled up to the accident, Sue threw the van into park before it had stopped, causing the gears to grind the vehicle to a halt. She jumped out of the minivan screaming like a madwoman as she approached the accident. The officers appeared to be taking information from the driver.

"My baby! Where's my baby?" Sue screamed. The police officers, surprised by a screaming woman coming at them, braced themselves as though ready to take down a psycho.

"Stay back, lady," one of the officers ordered, his arm outstretched to halt her.

Instead, Sue kept coming, "Christina!" A few feet from the accident, Sue was wrestled to the ground where she was handcuffed, still screaming, "Where's my daughter?"

"Lady, I told you to stay back. What's wrong with you?" the officer asked as he stood her up and leaned her over the cruiser's hood.

"Please. My daughter. Those two kidnapped my daughter. Where is she? Christina!" Sue was so distraught she was hard to understand.

"What in the world are you yelling about?" the officer asked.

Sue couldn't see Christina anywhere, but she could see the two men who had been in the van. They were now standing in front of it, and were not in handcuffs. In fact, they were still smiling.

"What've you done with her?" Sue screamed at the men, still struggling to get at them. She turned toward the officers. "Why haven't you arrested them?" she yelled, still trying to twist out of the officer's control.

The officer leaned Sue against the cruiser again. "Those two, arrest those two!" Sue screamed. "Not me!"

The two men eyed each other and took off running down the street. One of the officers gave chase. As a backup cruiser arrived, it followed the pursuing officer with lights and siren blaring.

Rebecca jumped out of Sue's minivan and approached the officer who held his arm out and told her to stop, which she obeyed.

"Officer, those two men just kidnapped her daughter down the street," Rebecca said pointing to Sue. "I called 9-1-1. Where's her child?"

The officer looked at Sue. "Is that true?"

"That's what I've been trying to tell you," Sue slowly said, gritting her teeth. She struggled to turn around and face the officer. "Where is she? Christina!"

Christina came running around from the passenger side of the van and ran up to her mother. She was crying, and threw her arms around her. The officer turned Sue around and uncuffed her as he apologized. Sue picked up Christina and hugged her.

"Mommy!"

"Where were you? Didn't you hear me calling you?"

"I was scared, Mommy. Those two men, they were still here. I thought they were going to hurt me."

The officer listened to a transmission on his radio. "Ma'am, I'm very sorry. I just got the information about the kidnapping from dispatch. Wait for me here. I'll have to talk with all of you."

He called on his radio for more help, and ran down the street in the direction of the two kidnappers and the other officers. Several minutes later the officers returned with the men in handcuffs. They placed one in the rear seat of the damaged cruiser and the other in the backup cruiser.

"We'll need to take a statement from you and your daughter and ask some questions. Can both of you meet us at the station?" one of the officers asked Sue.

"Of course. They tried to take my niece too. Do you want to talk with her also?"

"Yes, have her come too."

"We'll be there as soon as we can."

Rebecca and Arielle stood next to the minivan waiting for Sue and Christina. Arielle had a big grin on her face as she watched Christina walk back to her, accompanied by her mother.

"Thanks for helping," Sue said to Rebecca. She looked at Arielle who was hugging Christina. "How did she know?"

"They tried to take her, too," Rebecca said. "Beyond that, I don't know." There was no way Rebecca was going to try to tell her sister about the orbs in Arielle's hand or what she saw her daughter do with one of them. This wasn't the time or the place, and she didn't know if there ever would be.

"I can't believe those idiots ran into a police car. What a couple of losers," Sue said. She was laughing, but to Rebecca, it was a nervous laugh.

"Well, it's a good thing they did. We may never have found them."

"I can't even think about that."

They all piled back into the minivan and Sue drove to the police station. A female officer at the front desk escorted them upstairs to a small room with a table and four hard, steel chairs. The drab green walls were barren, with the exception of a few names and dates etched into the paint. A single, black, metal light fixture hung from the ceiling by a black cord. Grey tile covered the floor that had numerous scrape marks from the chairs. It was a depressing space.

"Is this an interrogation room?" Rebecca asked the officer.

"Yes, it is. I apologize for the accommodations, but we're short of room. Can I get anything for you? I've heard you've been through quite a lot."

"No, but we need a restroom," Sue said. "I want to wash her up." She grabbed her daughter's hand.

"Before you wash her, I need some photos of her injuries. I'll be right back," the officer said as she left the room.

Christina had a bump on her forehead that was starting to turn black and blue. Her arm had bruises where she was initially grabbed, and she had a cut on her ankle. The officer returned within a minute with a camera and photographed Christina and Arielle's injuries.

"Now we can get you washed up, young lady. Please come with me," the officer said. Christina and Sue followed the officer.

∞

After everyone left the room Rebecca turned to Arielle. She was sitting in a chair with her elbows on the table swinging her feet, as though she didn't have a care in the world.

"Arielle, what happened back at Sue's house? Who were you talking to?"

She looked up at her mother. "I helped Christina."

"Helped her? How?"

"The angels told me what to do. They said Christina would be okay if I helped her, so I did what they said. They showed me what to do and I did it."

"Angels?"

"Yes."

"What angels?"

"The ones that came to help."

Rebecca shook her head as though she was trying to shake out the cobwebs. "Where did your light go?" That is what Rebecca called the gold orbs. They never spoke of the orbs, as Rebecca was sure only she and Arielle could see them.

"It went to Christina. It helped her."

What was going on? Rebecca had practically forgotten about the orbs, and now, she had seen Arielle use one. "Did it make those men crash into the police car?"

Arielle didn't answer.

"Arielle. Did you hear me?"

"Mommm…" she whined. "I told you. I did what I was told to do."

"By the angels?"

"Yesss."

One of the officers walked into the room. "A detective will be here in a few minutes to take your statements. Is there anything you need?"

Rebecca stroked Arielle's hair. "Could I get a band-aid and something to clean her knee?"

"Of course." The officer left for a minute and came back with a band-aid and cleansing tissue. Sue returned with Christina while Rebecca wiped Arielle's wound and applied the band-aid.

A few minutes later, a gentleman in a tweed sports jacket holding a pad of paper entered the room and introduced himself to everyone as Detective Ritter. He took a statement from Christina. She told her story in bits and pieces of being kidnapped off her bicycle, ending with the accident. He then turned to Arielle, who answered an additional barrage of questions about being grabbed by the kidnapper. She was more than enthusiastic in answering his questions, especially when she told him about biting the man.

"I saw the bite mark on his arm. Good job, young lady!" the detective said patting her on the back. "You did exactly what you should do."

Arielle was beaming.

When they all returned to Sue's house, Rebecca and Arielle said their goodbyes and started home. On the way home Rebecca wanted to question Arielle more about the orbs. That's all she could think about. She had asked her about them several times before when she was younger, but Arielle always replied she didn't know what they were.

CRSO

Rebecca thought back to her own unease of dealing with the lights. When the decision was made to keep and raise Arielle, she needed a babysitter so she could go back to work. Her mother volunteered until she could find a trustworthy person. After the first few days had passed and her mother hadn't brought up the orbs, Rebecca asked her indirectly if she had observed anything strange about Arielle's hand. When her mother denied seeing anything, Rebecca knew. She was puzzled, but she knew. No one else could see them. This was confirmed again a short time later when her sister babysat one night and Sue didn't say a word about seeing them either. To Rebecca, they were there, plain as a snowstorm in July. It remained a mystery to her, but how could she talk to anyone or say anything about something no one else could see?

"Arielle, I want to talk again about the light you sent to Christina. What did the angel tell you to do?"

"He told me to send one to Christina, and then he showed me how to do it."

"You actually *saw* him show you?"

"Yes."

"Why did they want you to send it to Christina? Why her?"

"Mom, Christina is special."

"Who told you she was special?"

"The angel did," Arielle said matter-of-factly.

"I wonder what he meant by that?" Rebecca asked herself out loud. Then she realized what she was thinking and shook her head. *Wait a minute, what am I saying? There's no way she's talking to angels.* She thought back to the whole scenario. *But she did talk to something—or someone. But who or what was she talking to?*

"He said someday she would help a lot of people."

"Christina?" Rebecca asked.

Arielle didn't respond. She just looked out the window as if nothing out of the ordinary had occurred.

Rebecca thought about telling Sue what Arielle had just told her. She was sure she'd want to know that Christina was considered special by someone or something, but angels? How would she tell her sister this without her thinking she was totally insane? Then she would have to tell her about the orbs and the conversations Arielle supposedly had with angels. And she would have to tell her how Arielle's orb might have made the van crash into the police cruiser. It would have to wait. She wasn't quite ready to be institutionalized.

Over the next twenty-four hours, the radio, television, and newspapers were full of stories of how lucky two little six-year-old girls were after an attempted kidnapping; how the van in which the clumsy kidnappers drove off in had a front tire blowout, and then ran straight into a police car right after the abduction. Rebecca finally unplugged the phone after answering questions from a dozen or so reporters.

⋘⋙

The next day after breakfast, Sue received a call from Detective Ritter.

"Yes, what can I do for you, Detective?"

"Yesterday you said you and your husband were separated and in the process of a divorce. Do you know where your husband is, Mrs. Habib?"

"Yes, he left for Saudi Arabia this morning."

"When is he returning?"

"I would suspect in a about a week, that's how long his trips usually last. Why?"

"Do you have a recent photo of him?"

"I believe so. Why do you want it? Why are you asking me all these questions about my husband?"

"The two men who tried to kidnap your daughter and her cousin have confessed and we're trying to confirm their story. According to them, they were paid by your husband to take your daughter. We want to corroborate their story with a photo line-up that they know who he is."

"That son-of-a... We're going through a divorce and he told me he wanted custody, but I never thought he would stoop to something like this."

"I'm afraid he had planned to take her to Saudi with him, Mrs. Habib. We checked with the Feds and there was a passport issued for your daughter about a month ago. So, all the pieces seem to fit. All he needed was a notarized letter from you stating it was all right to take her out of the country, and I'm sure he could have forged that."

Sue was speechless. She had never considered or suspected Ted might try to take Christina to Saudi. She could only imagine what kind of future she might have over there. Still, she had doubts.

"If that's true, why did they also try to take Arielle? Was he going to take her with them?"

"No. They said they weren't expecting two little girls and they couldn't tell which one was Christina at the time, so they decided to grab both and turn one loose later."

"Turn one loose? Where? Just dump her on the street?"

"These two aren't the brightest light bulbs in the store, Ma'am."

Sue was seething. "I'll have the photos ready for you when you care to pick them up. Thank you, Detective."

"If the two suspects pick him out of the line-up, we'll have a warrant issued for his arrest. If you hear from him or see him, please let us know."

"You can count on that, Detective."

CHAPTER 6

The Picnic
(Four Years Later)

At ten years old, Arielle was growing into a beautiful, charming young girl. That spring she was promoted from the third to the fourth grade and enjoyed the summer months playing with her cousin and her friends.

Each year on the 4th of July, Rebecca's employer held a company picnic at Turkey Run, a local state park. The annual event was so popular that just about every employee of the hospital who wasn't on duty at the time attended the festivities with his or her family. There were literally hundreds of kids running around, swimming in the lake, playing baseball, soccer, or one of the other various games provided. All gorged themselves on hot dogs, hamburgers, cookies, popsicles, and ice cream. It was a perfect holiday, and this year, since it fell on a weekend and the temperature was a balmy eighty-five degrees with crystal-clear skies and a slight breeze, it seemed there was a smile on everyone's face.

CRSO

Rebecca and Arielle shared a picnic table by the lake with Betsy and her seven-year-old freckle-faced son, Mark. Betsy and Rebecca worked together in the emergency room at the hospital and had become close friends. Her husband, Charlie, a police officer, had to work on this holiday and couldn't be with them.

"Too bad Charlie couldn't join us today," Rebecca said. "I'll miss his humor."

"And he's going to be upset he missed all this food!" Betsy replied. "Don't be surprised if he happens to show up to 'check things out.' That'll be codeword for 'have a couple burgers and hotdogs ready!'"

Rebecca laughed. "I'd be surprised if he didn't."

Betsy and Mark had just brought a plateful of hamburgers and hotdogs from the grill, while Rebecca and Arielle retrieved the buns, drinks, a bowl of potato salad and baked beans for everyone. The kids dug right in.

"Arielle, you're eating like there's no tomorrow. What's with you?" Rebecca smiled and winked at Betsy as she watched her daughter devour another hamburger.

"I'm hungry, Mom. We've been playing kickball all morning. We even won two games." Arielle had a hamburger oozing with ketchup in one hand, a soft drink in the other and was alternating between the two and a plate of potato chips as her pigtails swung in her face.

Mark, apparently not one to pass up an opportunity to tease, snuck up behind Arielle and pulled on one of her pigtails just as she was taking a drink of soda from her can. Her head jerked to the side. She choked on the cola, coughing, and spilling some down the front of her shirt and shorts. Mark took off running, laughing heartily and pointing back at Arielle.

"Mark!" Arielle squealed as she caught her breath. She dropped her burger on the plate, set her drink down and leapt from the table, wiping the remnants of her cola from her clothes. She ran after Mark, chasing him along the beach until she caught up with him. She grabbed hold of him and pushed him down in the sand. He was laughing so hard he couldn't get up. Arielle straddled him as she sat on top of his back, and repeatedly pushed his face down in the wet sand.

"Say you're sorry," Arielle demanded as she held him down.

"No way!" Mark said, still laughing, turning his head from side to side. "Get—off—me!" he said, now half sputtering, half laughing.

"Not until you say you're sorry. Look what you did to me. I've got sticky cola all over me, and it's all your fault." She grabbed the collar of his shirt and kept pushing his face down in the sand while he continued laughing.

A group of kids gathered around the two. The girls were chanting, "Go, Arielle, go! Go, Arielle, go!"

"Okay, okay. I'm sorry," Mark said in between fits of laughter.

"I don't think you really mean it. Say it like you mean it," Arielle demanded as she scooped up and dropped handfuls of sand on his head.

"I mean it," Mark sputtered. "I give up. I give up." He was spitting sand. Several of the girls who had been watching the incident started cheering and clapping again.

Arielle got up off Mark, took a bow, and marched like a soldier back across the beach to the table. She was proud of herself. She sat down and continued eating.

"Well, what happened?" asked Rebecca. "Do we need to go rescue Mark?"

"No. He said he was sorry."

Rebecca and Betsy looked at each other with knowing broad grins, and affirming Rebecca's belief that Arielle was definitely a tomboy.

CRSO

"Help! Help me!" came a woman's cry from out in the lake. The shriek for help was just barely audible above the noise of a hundred kids splashing and playing in the water.

A lifeguard bounded down from his perch, running across the sand and into the water with an orange and white flotation device. With broad, quick strokes he headed out past the roped-in area where the woman was splashing, struggling to keep a child's head above the water. She was trying to swim in to shore, scream for help, and hold on to him at the same time.

Another lifeguard blew his whistle and motioned the children out of the water. "Everyone out. Out of the water," he ordered.

A crowd gathered on the beach, watching as the lifeguard and the woman brought the child back into the cordoned-off area of the water.

"Call 9-1-1," the lifeguard yelled out to his partner.

"Everyone, get back," yelled the woman who was helping the lifeguard bring in the limp body. Exhausted, they carried the child onto the beach where the other lifeguard joined them and began assisting with CPR. One was breathing into the child's mouth while the other applied chest compressions.

A young woman in a two-piece bathing suit cried out as she tried to push through the crowd. "My God! That's my son! Tommy!" An older, gray-haired man blocked her path, and while trying to comfort her, convinced her to let the lifeguards do their jobs. He led her to a table away from the life-saving efforts.

"Will everyone please stand back," the guard doing the compressions again pleaded with the crowd. The throng of onlookers grew larger and pushed in closer to the guards. At that point several men intervened and, while pushing back the crowd, told the children to go back to their parents, waving them off. Most of them ignored the order and hung around, watching the drama unfold. Others started to walk away, but came back once they saw other kids had stayed.

Arielle was with her mother at the picnic table when the commotion began.

"Mom, let's go see what's going on."

"No. You stay here for a few minutes. I'm going to see if I can help."

"I'll come, too," Betsy said.

They approached the lifeguards and identified themselves as registered nurses, "Can we takeover the CPR for you?" Rebecca asked.

"That'd be great," the lifeguard doing the chest compressions answered. The lifeguards thanked them, got up and the two nurses immediately took over. Rebecca did the breathing while Betsy did the compressions on the limp boy. Several minutes later, two sirens could be heard in the distance. One of the lifeguards went to direct the ambulance and police car to the beach.

After the emergency vehicles arrived, the paramedics immediately took over life support from the nurses. One paramedic placed a mask over the child's nose and mouth and pumped oxygen into his lungs from an oxygen tank; another continued the chest compressions while sticking several adhesive tabs to his chest. He connected wires from the tabs to a small machine next to him to detect a heartbeat.

"I'm not getting a pulse," one of the paramedics told the other, who nodded.

The paramedic looked up and told everyone to stay back. He looked at the machine, then the boy and yelled, "Clear." He pushed a button on the defibrillator. The child's body convulsed and jumped as a shock was delivered. Some children, who had stayed around and watched, started crying.

"Clear!" the paramedic repeated. Another shock was delivered and again the boy's body jumped. Soon, many adults were also sobbing as several more shocks were delivered to the small body. After numerous attempts at resuscitation, a blanket was pulled over the child and the paramedics started packing up their equipment. A mother's wailing was heard all over the grounds. No other sounds could be detected with the exception of a few birds circling overhead. A perfect day was coming to a tragic end.

೧೩๛

When Rebecca returned to the picnic table, she put her arm around her daughter and hugged her. "A little boy, Tommy, drowned. I'm sorry. They couldn't revive him."

"I know, Mom. I have to go see him," Arielle said as she looked up at her mother.

"No. You stay here. They have enough problems and don't need any more children over there. They've already told all the kids to go back to their parents."

Arielle clasped her mother's face in her hands. "Mom, I'm not going to be a problem. I have to go over and see the boy and his mother."

Rebecca stared at her daughter. There were tears streaming down her cheeks. She hadn't heard this tone in Arielle's voice before. She took hold of Arielle's hand. "Okay," she finally said, "but I'm going with you."

They walked slowly to the beach where they were loading the small boy's body on a gurney. A police officer was speaking to the woman who found Tommy in the lake.

"Charlie, what are you…?" Rebecca asked.

"I was on my way here to join everyone for a sandwich, so they gave me the call. It's too sad."

"It is. Betsy's over there," she said pointing to their table. "We helped work on the boy—gave him CPR. I wish we could have saved him."

"Who gave the mouth-to-mouth?" he asked.

"I did. Why?"

"The last time Betsy did it, she had this terrible taste in her mouth for several days. It was on an older gentleman who'd had a heart attack and ended up dying. She said it tasted like death."

"I've heard of that occurring before, but Betsy never told me it happened to her. So far, I'm okay."

"They say it's psychological, but Betsy would argue it."

Arielle let go of her mother's hand and walked a couple steps toward the boy's body as they started to load him into the ambulance. She raised her right arm and blew softly across her palm. Rebecca and Arielle watched as a gold orb floated over to the boy and disappeared into his chest. Rebecca walked over to Arielle.

"What...?" Rebecca asked.

"Please wait here, Mom."

"Where are you going?"

"To see his mother and the paramedic."

Arielle walked over to Tommy's mother and hugged her around the waist. She was crying on the shoulder of another woman. The mother turned to see who had their arms wrapped around her and looked down at Arielle. She wiped her eyes, bent down and gave her a hug.

"God wants you to know he heard you," Arielle whispered to her while looking into her eyes.

With more tears flowing down her cheeks, the woman looked at the little girl; she didn't seem to know what to say. Her child had just died.

"What do you mean, 'God heard me?' Why would he do this?" she shot back at Arielle, crying and confused.

Arielle kissed the woman on the cheek. "He didn't do this. Your son will be fine. He's going to grow up to be someone you'll be proud of."

Arielle let go of Tommy's mom who stood with her mouth agape. She watched as Arielle walked over to one of the paramedics standing next to the ambulance. He was writing feverishly on a form held on a brown clipboard. Standing in front of him, she looked up at the extremely tall man and tugged on his pant leg.

"Hello there, young lady. What can I do for you?" the paramedic asked as he kept writing.

"The little boy is okay," Arielle said to him.

The paramedic stopped writing and looked down at her. "What?"

"The little boy is still alive."

The paramedic bent down and put his hand on her shoulder. "I'm so sorry, honey, but the little boy is with God now."

Exasperated, Arielle put both hands on her hips and looked the paramedic in the eye. In a hushed, but confident voice she said, "No, he's not with God yet. He's still here. Please check him again."

The paramedic appeared stunned at this admonishment from the little girl. For several seconds he stayed bent down, looking into her eyes. He slowly stood up and without saying a word, climbed into the ambulance. As Arielle turned and started walking back to her mother, the paramedic yelled out the back door, "I have a pulse! Get me some help in here!"

Immediately, his partner, who was speaking to the lifeguards ran back to the ambulance and jumped in the rear. The crowd, which had been dissipating, started coming back, gathering around.

Arielle grabbed her mother's hand and together they walked back to the picnic table. On the way, Rebecca turned and looked back at the ambulance as a head poked out from the rear looking towards them.

"What did you say to the mother and the paramedic?" Rebecca asked.

"I told the mother that God heard her."

"And the paramedic?"

"I told him the boy was still alive, to check him again." She looked up at her mother. "He tried to tell me the boy was with God. I told me 'not yet'."

CRSO

Rebecca was stunned. She had never heard Arielle say anything like that—but she was also very curious about seeing the orb float into the boy's chest. "Did you help that little boy? Did you bring him back?"

"I helped him. I didn't bring him back."

"Well, who or what did?"

"God did," Arielle replied as she seated herself at the picnic table. Her mom sat down on the opposite side. Betsy and Mark were by the ambulance.

"Well, what did you do?"

"I just did what I was told to do."

"What do you mean? God told you to do that?" Rebecca, frustrated, appeared to want all the answers at once.

"The angels. They told me what to do and say." Arielle laid her head down on the table. "I'm tired, Mom, can we go home now?"

"The angels again, huh? I thought you'd grown out of that."

"Grown out of what?"

"Saying the angels told you to do this or that. I know you used to say you talked to angels when you were younger, but you're ten years old now. It's time to stop using that explanation for anything strange that happens."

"I'm telling you the truth, Mom. You have to believe me."

"We'll talk about it later. Get your things together and let's go home."

CHAPTER 7

Questions

As a small child, Arielle started collecting figurines of angels. In her bedroom, hundreds of small collectibles lined her many shelves and the tops of the bureaus. The headboard of her bed displayed young angels, older angels, black, white, yellow, brown, male and female. Her grandparents always brought another home to her after a day of shopping, her birthdays and holidays adding to the collection.

ॐ

The orbs floating in Arielle's hand constantly hung in the back of Rebecca's mind. She never said a word to anyone about them, as she knew only she and Arielle could see them. By the time Arielle was ten and a half years old, Rebecca had witnessed two of the orbs leaving her hand, but she never received what she considered a straight answer from her daughter as to what they did or what they were for, if anything. Yes, the situations had happily resolved themselves when she sent an orb, but were they connected? And how? Or had everything simply been a coincidence?

One morning on the way to school, Rebecca again asked Arielle directly about the orbs.

"Arielle, how come only you and I can see the lights in your hand?"

"I don't know, Mom. Isn't that the way it's supposed to be?"

"Supposed to be? Who told you that?"

She thought for a moment. "Nobody. I just thought that's the way it is."

"What are the lights? Why do you have them?"

"They're gifts."

"Gifts? What kind?"

"They are gifts from God."

"From God? How do you know that?"

"The angels told me."

"There you go again with the angels. Who are they for?"

"I don't know. They let me know when the time comes to use one."

Arielle looked over at her mother. "They also told me once that you should know about gifts from God—-that you've received one."

Rebecca kept glancing at her daughter in the rear-view mirror while driving. She stopped for a stoplight. "They who? What kind of gift?"

"The angels. They wouldn't tell me what yours was, but they did say that one day you'd know, that you'd figure it out."

She turned around to look at her daughter. As far as she was concerned, God had only caused her grief—a son who was taken from her and the inability to conceive again.

The blare of a horn impatiently sounded from behind her; the light had turned green. Frustration set in again as she tried to understand what Arielle was telling her. It seemed she was always talking in circles.

They arrived at school and Rebecca still didn't know how to respond. "Arielle, I just don't know what to think about all this. Maybe we should go see someone."

"Who?"

"Maybe a doctor or... We'll talk more about it at home tonight, okay?"

"Sure, Mom."

"Have a great day, honey." Rebecca kissed her daughter on the forehead. Arielle looked at her mom for a moment then got out of the car without saying anymore, and went in to school.

As she drove to work, Rebecca was perplexed and concerned about what her daughter had told her and what she had seen at the picnic. The memory of her daughter sending the light to the young boy haunted her. Could Arielle really be talking with angels, or was it just the vivid imagination of an ten-year-old? If she really was talking to angels, how could she tell? Could it be she has one of those *invisible* playmates kids often have when they are young? Should she take her to see a psychiatrist? But then again, what were the lights she always carried with her?

She thought about others who claimed to speak with God or angels. They all appeared to want power, money and sometimes sex. Greed seemed to follow these smooth talkers like ducks to water. She had read about many of the cult leaders when she was in college taking a comparative religion class. They had all claimed they conversed with God. History was littered with them, along with the deaths and ruined lives of their followers. They were mostly psychopaths, delusional, just plain nuts most of the time she thought: Jim Jones in Jonestown, Guyana, and David Koresh with the Branch Davidians in Waco, Texas. Some have established religions that even exist today with followers in the millions.

There was no way her daughter was like them. Her thoughts returned to the *gift* that the angel said was given to her. What could that be?

An hour into her shift, Rebecca couldn't concentrate on her work. She knew she needed to talk with someone about all the questions that were plaguing her. But whom could she talk to? Who would possibly believe her about the lights no one else could see? Her sister? No way. Her mother? Nope, she would just patronize her. Everyone else would think she was nuts and ready for the rubber room.

CRXSO

Rebecca considered herself to be a Christian and had raised her daughter the same way, going to church every Sunday and religious holiday. She always prayed for the healing of her husband and those less fortunate than herself. She not only enjoyed the closeness she felt to God on those days, but also was fond of the fellowship of the other worshipers. In addition, they both went to Bible study classes each Wednesday night. Arielle seemed to especially like those classes, and often challenged the teacher over different aspects of what was taught. She didn't intend to sharp-shoot them, but often asked very pointed questions that made them think hard about the answers they gave.

Rebecca smiled when she thought back to one of those classes when Arielle was younger. She had come early to pick up her daughter and thought she would sit in and listen to the class for a while. There was a substitute teacher that day and he was teaching the children about angels. It looked as if Arielle took over the class, answering every question that arose on the subject. The teacher had become upset, trying to prove he knew more than a child, but Arielle just kept smiling as she answered all the questions directed at her.

Rebecca didn't want to be at work today; her thoughts were in a different place. Too many things pulled at her, begging for answers and resolution. She spoke with her supervisor, told her she had personal things to take care of and asked about taking a vacation day. It was a slower than normal day, so her day off was granted.

CRBO

"Hello, Pastor, this is Rebecca Price. I have some personal problems that are really bothering me. I took the day off work. If you're available, I'd like to stop in and talk with you for a while. Would that be possible?"

"I can see you in about an hour, Mrs. Price. Is that soon enough?"

"Yes, thank you. I'll see you then."

"Come to the church. I'll be in my office."

Rebecca had been going to Pastor James Sherman's New Trinity Bible Church for about five years. It was a relatively new, independent house of worship, with a younger congregation than most. She had tested the waters of several different religious denominations, but she never felt comfortable or at home in any of them, preferring to worship through prayer and Bible study instead of song and ritual. She had met the pastor on several occasions, but never had cause to meet with him privately to discuss her personal life. She enjoyed his sermons, his sometimes-irreverent humor, and his interpretations and insight of the Bible.

She used the extra hour to stop by the nursing home and talk to Craig. He was being well looked after, but ten years later, his features had changed. He looked frail and his hands were atrophied as though he were catching a baseball, despite the physical therapy efforts. He didn't look like the husband she knew long ago. Still, she loved him and kept faith that some day he would wake up and be with her again. And Arielle, too.

CRBO

Rebecca arrived at the church as agreed and was met by Pastor Sherman. After greetings were exchanged, the pastor took a seat behind his desk. His demeanor was very formal. He offered Rebecca a seat on a leather couch across the room from his light oak desk. The door was left open to the hallway. As she looked around, Rebecca could hear the murmur of other voices in the building. The office was very simply furnished; pale yellow walls made a soothing backdrop against white and black Berber carpeting. Three walls of very plain white painted bookshelves containing hundreds of books enveloped the small room. Three gold-framed documents hung on the wall above and behind him—his ordination certificate, his seminary diploma, and his degree in Liberal Arts from a university.

"Could we close the door, please?" she inquired.

"I'm sorry, Mrs. Price, but I can't. It's my policy not to be in a closed room with a woman by myself—for obvious reasons. We can leave the door open, or I can ask my wife or Margaret in the accounting office to come sit in with us. Then we can shut the door. I know this may seem odd, but it's to protect both of us. I hate to admit it, but some of my staff do gossip, and it wouldn't take long...."

"I understand, Pastor. It'll be fine. I'm just very uncomfortable with anyone hearing what I am going to tell you."

"Well, I can appreciate that. Tell you what; I'll turn the radio on. That'll give us some background noise," he said getting up from his desk. "Most of us don't want others to know about our private lives or the complications that arise from our, uh, associations or indiscretions."

The pastor walked across the room and tuned the radio to one of the local *Oldies* stations he liked.

Rebecca stood up, intending to follow him across the room, but stayed where she was. *He already has the wrong idea about me!* "Pastor, this is not about me," she said adamantly. "It's nothing like that. And if that's what you think of me, I might as well leave right now."

The pastor turned around, waving his hands back and forth. "I apologize, Mrs. Price. I didn't mean to insinuate anything."

"But you did. I came to you looking for help, and you immediately categorized me as doing something morally wrong. We all need a little help once in awhile, and not necessarily because of immoral behavior. I'm here about my young daughter."

"Again, I'm sorry, Mrs. Price. Please tell me about her," he said returning to his desk.

Rebecca slowly sat back down on the couch. She was now leery about revealing everything since the pastor was so quick to jump to conclusions. She started out slowly. "She's saying things, and doing some things I don't quite comprehend. I don't know if you will either, but I thought maybe you might have run into it before, or know someone who has. Maybe it's just a phase she's going through. Either way, I need help understanding what she's doing and telling me."

"Let me pull a chair up next to my desk so we can speak discreetly."

He went across the room to a closet, retrieved a metal folding chair and placed it next to his desk, motioning for Rebecca to come and sit there, which she did.

"Better?"

"Yes, thank you."

"All right, why don't you start at the beginning. Tell me everything."

"It's hard to know where the beginning is. But first, I'm going to reveal some things that no one else besides my sister and parents are aware of—family secrets I suppose. It's very important—I need to know it will remain here; that no one else will ever know."

"Rebecca, anything you tell me here is strictly confidential."

Rebecca didn't know how to start. She had gone over and over in her mind how and what she would tell the pastor about Arielle, but now, everything she had planned to say seemed to be blocked from her memory. No matter what she would say, she was afraid he wouldn't believe her. She alternated fidgeting with her purse and twisting her wedding ring. *A Bridge Over Troubled Waters* played in the background. How apropos she thought.

"For reasons you will understand later, I'm very hesitant to talk about this."

"Would you like me to get you some coffee while you think about what you would like to say?"

"That would be nice. Two sugars, please."

The pastor left the room, looking back at her as he exited.

Panic took over her thoughts. *What am I doing here? He's not going to believe me. Nobody is. Arielle is going to be mad at me for telling about her lights. Should I tell him? What's he going to think of me? A fruitcake?*

He returned with two cups of coffee and gave one to Rebecca. Her hands shook as she took it.

"Are you okay, Mrs. Price?"

"Yes, I'm just nervous." After a few seconds, Rebecca took a deep breath, then blurted out, "Pastor, do you believe in angels?"

He smiled. "Why yes, of course I do," he said as he sat back in his chair, sipping his coffee. "The Bible is full of references to angels."

"Do you believe people can speak to angels?"

"Well, I'm sure some people pray to certain ones at times—like Michael the Archangel, for strength in difficult situations."

Rebecca put her coffee down and repositioned herself to look directly into the eyes of the pastor. "But do you believe angels talk directly to people?"

His eyes narrowed. "Talk, you mean, as in conversations? Like we are?"

"Yes."

"Well, uh, I don't know. I suppose they could, but I've never heard of it. Most people I've encountered who tell me God or angels have spoken to them, it was in their mind, their subconscious—not something they could hear with their normal human senses. Why do you ask?"

Rebecca leaned forward and looked around the room, scanning for anyone who might be eavesdropping. Hesitantly, almost whispering, she started telling the pastor about her daughter. "Arielle… is not really my daughter, not my natural daughter anyway. She was left on my doorstep in a basket when she was about three months old, with a note addressed to me to take care of her. I don't know where she came from or who her biological parents are."

"She was left on your doorstep?"

"Yes," she said, nodding her head.

"And you kept her? Didn't you call the police?"

"No, I didn't."

"Why not?"

"I just couldn't let her be tossed around to different foster families. I see too much tragedy with these kids in the emergency room, I guess. I thought I could give her just as good or a better home than anyone else. As you remember, I'd recently lost my son and I think I needed her as much as she needed me."

"Weren't you worried about who she belonged to?"

"Not really. I believed if they were that concerned, they wouldn't have left her on my steps."

The pastor scribbled something in a notebook.

"Are you writing this down?"

"These are just my notes, Rebecca. They are strictly for me and confidential. No one will ever see them."

"Are you sure? I can't have any of this get out. They could take Arielle away from me. I can't take any chances."

"Positive."

After a brief moment, Rebecca, still twisting her ring, continued. "Anyway, the first evening I was with her, I noticed these small lights, like gold colored orbs, circulating in the palm of her hand—like they were dancing. I couldn't believe what I was seeing and at times I thought I was losing my mind. I tried to touch them, but it was like passing your hand through a beam of sunlight."

"Lights in her hand? Orbs? What're you talking about?" The pastor shook his head as he sat back in his chair.

"You don't believe me, do you?"

"Rebecca, are you sure?"

"Yes."

"Okay." He hesitated. "How many were there?"

"There were lots of them, but I can't tell you how many. The easiest way for me to describe them is they looked like an atom with a cluster of neutrons circling about."

"Strange."

"If that doesn't sound crazy enough," she hesitated again, looking at the pastor out of the corner of her eye, "no one can see them except for me and Arielle."

The pastor again sat back in his chair. "No one can see them, huh?"

"So far, no one else has been able to. I know it sounds bizarre, but they are always there."

"Is that it?"

"Oh, no!" she said, shaking her head. "That's just the beginning. I hadn't ever really questioned Arielle directly about the lights until this morning."

"Never questioned her about them? How come? Weren't you curious this whole time as to what they were?"

"I assumed she would tell me when she was ready. She acts like they don't exist, but I know better."

"What do you know?"

Rebecca paused momentarily. "I've seen her use the lights."

"Use them? How?"

"I'll explain that in a minute. This morning, like I said, I asked her about the lights. It seemed she didn't really want to talk about them, but when I asked what they were, she told me they were 'gifts from God'."

"Did she say how she knew where they came from?"

"Yes." Rebecca looked the pastor in the eye. "She says the angels told her."

Rebecca stopped. She wanted to see if the pastor was ready to write her off as a lunatic or if he believed what she told him. He was shaking his head again.

"This is quite a story, Rebecca. Are you sure this isn't just a little girl's imaginary friend or a dream she's telling you about?"

"I don't know, that's why I'm here talking to you." She then told him all the details about the picnic with the little boy drowning and how Arielle said she had to see him. After that, she summed up the story of the two girls' abduction when she was younger, and how Arielle sent off an orb of light at each event.

"So, you believe that Arielle's orbs, the ones only you and she can see, somehow affected the outcome of each of those incidents?"

She shrugged. "I don't know what to believe anymore. I do know they had stopped all resuscitation efforts after the little boy drowned; they said they were unable to revive him. The paramedics had pulled a blanket over him, loaded him in the ambulance and told his mother there was nothing they could do. After Arielle sent the light to him and told the paramedic to check again, there was pandemonium—the boy was alive."

"Did she do anything else?"

"She told the little boy's mother that God had heard her prayers."

The pastor pushed back from his desk, crossed his legs and folded his hands in his lap. "I have to say, Rebecca, this is fascinating. I've never encountered anything like this. Are you sure these weren't illusions, something you *think* you saw?"

"Talk to her, you'll see."

"You know, I've counseled people who say they talk to God or hear voices, some of them obviously psychotic. But never have I had one who has conversations with angels, especially a child, and certainly no one who has orbs of light in their hand. I'd really love to have a session with Arielle. Can you bring her in to see me?"

"That shouldn't be a problem, but please, I do have one request. Go easy with her. She seems to believe, and acts as if all of this is perfectly normal. I don't want her to feel like she's different from any other child her age, and I certainly don't want her to know I'm not her real mother."

"Of course, I understand."

"When would you like to see her?"

"Tonight, if possible. How about after dinner, around seven? I can meet you here in the office."

"We'll be here, Pastor. And thank you for your discretion. I wouldn't want any of this to get out."

CHAPTER 8

Insight

The cold, driving rain came down in sheets as Rebecca and Arielle arrived at the church. Since it was not one of their regular service nights, Rebecca informed her daughter that the pastor wanted to chat with her.

"Why, Mom? Why does he want to talk with me?"

"I thought it might be a good idea to have a conversation with him about the angels you are talking to. I'd like to know more myself."

"Mom, all you had to do was ask."

"Well, honey, lets have a discussion with Pastor Sherman and we'll see what he says."

"Okay."

As she got out of the car, Rebecca popped open an umbrella and held it over both of their heads. They circumvented the puddles of water and went into the dimly lit church. As they entered the office, the pastor welcomed them, motioning them over to two chairs that he had set up next to his desk.

"Good evening, Arielle. Rebecca. How are you tonight?"

"Good, Pastor Sherman," Arielle replied. "But wet."

He chuckled. "It is a little damp out there. Can I get you two anything? How about some hot chocolate?"

"Yes, please," Arielle said.

"Rebecca?"

"No, thank you."

He went out and returned quickly with Arielle's cocoa, setting it in front of her, then crossed the room and clicked on the radio. Returning to his seat, he turned his attention to Arielle. "Did your mother tell you why we are here tonight?"

"She said you wanted to know more about the angels that I talk to."

"Yes, I do. I also hear you have some very special gifts. Would you like to tell me about them?"

"Gifts? What are you talking about?" Arielle squinted her eyes and looked toward her mother.

"The lights—the ones in your hand," he said.

"You know about them?" Arielle looked over at her mom again with a quizzical expression.

"Yes, your mother told me. Was it all right for her to tell me? You're not upset at her, are you?"

"Of course not, Pastor. She can tell whomever she wants."

The pastor held out his arm. "May I see your hand?" Arielle opened her hand and showed it to him. He couldn't see anything but the soft, delicate palm of an ten-year-old.

"Are they there?" he asked.

"Yes," Arielle replied.

"Why can't I see them?"

"They're only for my mom and I to see."

The pastor looked over at Rebecca and raised his eyebrows. Rebecca nodded her head affirmatively.

"Why do you think that is, Arielle? Why can't I see them, too?"

"I don't know."

"What are they for?"

"They're gifts for those who need them. I think they're for people who get into trouble."

"And what makes you say that? Did the angels tell you that?"

Arielle leaned back in her chair as if contemplating her answer. "No, not exactly. It's more a feeling I have."

"I see. And who are they from?"

"The angels told me they are gifts from God. They also tell me when to use them."

"What do they do?"

"That's up to God."

The pastor nodded his head. "Okay, let's move on to something else." He poured himself a glass of water and took a drink.

"From what you just told me, and from the conversation I had with your mother earlier, I understand you have discussions with angels, is that right?"

"Yes."

"When do you have these exchanges?"

"I think they talk to me when they need to—or when they think I need help."

"Need help? When would that be?"

"Sometimes I'm asked questions I don't know the answers to. They give me what I need to know, and sometimes they sing their songs and I just listen."

"Is that how they converse with you? They sing?

"At times they teach me with their songs. Other times we just talk."

"Do you ask them anything or do you just listen?"

"I ask questions and they answer what they can."

"Can't they answer all your questions?"

"No, sir. I've asked some questions they aren't allowed to answer."

"What's keeping them from telling you what you want to know?"

"I don't know, but they said I would know all the answers some day."

"Give me an example of a question you asked they wouldn't answer."

Arielle thought a moment. "They told me Mom was given a gift from God. I asked what Mom's gift was. They wouldn't tell me. They said she would figure it out some day on her own."

The pastor looked over at Rebecca. "You've received a gift?"

"That's what I was told."

Arielle looked over at her mother, "Mom, can we go home now?"

"Soon, honey. Try and answer a few more of the pastor's questions."

"But I already did."

"Arielle," interrupted the pastor, "Are you uncomfortable with my questions?"

"No Sir. I'm just tired."

"If I ask a question, will the angels help you answer it?"

"If I need help, they usually come and give it to me, if they're allowed."

"If they're allowed, huh?" The pastor stroked his chin. "Can you tell me why bad things happen? Why does God allow bad things to occur?"

Arielle waited a few moments. "God doesn't *allow* or *cause* bad things to happen. There are many disasters that occur which are the natural course of the universe. Man-made disasters, such as wars, must be resolved by man. God doesn't usually intervene, unless it's for special circumstances."

"What kind of special circumstances?"

Again, Arielle hesitated, and then nodded. "Such as when demons or Satan have influence over or in a particular situation."

The pastor sat back in his chair. "Satan?"

"Yes."

"Did the angels help you with that answer?"

"Yes, sir."

He tapped his hand on the desk, leaned over closer to Arielle and spoke softly. "Are you telling me the truth?"

"Yes, sir."

"Do you know what a lie is?"

"Yes, of course I do."

"Tell me, what is it? Can you define it for me?"

"It's not the truth."

"Tell me, how would I know if you weren't telling me the truth when you say you talk to angels."

"I don't know what you mean."

"Well..."

Arielle's attention was suddenly diverted. She cocked her head, looked above the pastor and nodded. "Pastor, you have an angel above you right now." A broad grin lit up her face. "She wants me to ask you something."

He jumped from his seat and looked all around at the ceiling above him. "She did? The angel's a she? She's here now?"

"Yes, this one is. She just told me to ask you a question."

He eyed Arielle suspiciously as he slowly sat back down at his desk. "And what would that be?"

"She wants to know if you read the Bible."

"Of course I read the Bible. I'm a pastor. I teach the Bible. If she's an angel, why would she ask that?"

"She says she knows you do—but she wants to know how you know you are reading the truth."

The pastor rubbed his chin again as he studied Arielle. "It's faith, I suppose."

Arielle smiled. She looked towards the ceiling and nodded. "She said she wants you to explain."

"I have to have faith that whoever wrote the different passages of the Bible was telling the truth and knew what they were talking about."

There was an uncomfortable silence. The ticking clock on the wall made each second feel like minutes. The pastor looked back and forth between Arielle and her mother, then walked around to the front of his desk.

"This is the strangest thing that has ever happened to me."

Arielle smiled. "She says you have your answer."

"Answer to what?"

"To the question you asked me." Arielle looked over at her mother. "She's gone now."

Rebecca nodded.

The pastor stared at Arielle for several moments, shaking his head.

"That's my answer? Faith?" The pastor sighed. "That's quite a show you put on here."

Arielle sat cold-faced, looking at the floor. "Mom?"

"It's okay, hon. It's time to go anyway. Would you go into the church foyer and wait for me for a few minutes while I speak with the pastor?"

"Okay." She got up from her chair and waved. "Goodnight, Pastor."

"Goodnight, Arielle. I hope we can talk again sometime."

"So do I, Sir."

Rebecca waited until her daughter was well out of the office and hearing range. "Pastor, I don't think she was putting on a show. What you saw was almost an exact repeat of what happened when her cousin was abducted. I believe she was talking to something or someone. To whom or what, I'm not sure."

"So you think she is talking to an angel?"

"I don't know, but I don't think a ten-year-old child could come up with the question about the Bible and then tell you that you have your answer. She also gave you a fairly complete answer to your question about God. I don't think I could have come up with an answer like that."

"Granted, that was strange. But tell me, did you see the orbs of light in her palm tonight?"

She nodded. "Of course. They're always there."

"Rebecca, I'm really trying to be gentle with her, like you requested, but I'm also having a hard time believing she actually converses with angels. At some point I have to ask her some hard questions."

"But what if she is?"

"I have to assume at this point that she's not. I have to assume that she believes she can talk to angels, that she is having some kind of illusions. Have you taken her to see a psychologist or psychiatrist?"

"No. Up to this point I've always thought she may just have an imaginary childhood friend, but if it is that, it doesn't usually last to this age."

"I think you may want to consider having her see someone. Of course we can continue our discussions here also."

Arielle appeared at the entrance to the office with a large grin on her face and knocked lightly on the doorframe.

"Excuse me," she said.

"Yes?" the pastor asked.

"Can I tell you something, Mom?"

"Of course."

She walked over to her mother and whispered in her ear.

Rebecca looked up at her daughter and then over to the pastor.

"She has something to tell you."

"What is it, Arielle?"

Still beaming, Arielle said "The angel came back and told me to tell you that after we leave, you will know."

"What does that mean?"

Arielle hunched her shoulders. "I don't know exactly. But she says you will."

"Well, your mother and I are done here for tonight and I have another appointment in ten minutes. Maybe we'll see what your angel means, maybe not."

The pastor rose from behind his desk.

"Rebecca, I'll be in contact with you. I hope we can have another session soon. I'm very interested in what's going on here. Please consider what I asked you to do."

"Very well, Pastor, we'll talk later." Rebecca and the pastor shook hands then she and Arielle left the office.

"He thinks I'm making everything up, doesn't he, Mom?"

"Let's just say he's not completely convinced yet."

As they were leaving the church, an alarm went off in the Pastor's office, followed by loud music. They could hear the lyrics of the song, *I Believe In Angels*.

Rebecca looked at her daughter and smiled. "I think that ought to give him something to think about, huh?"

Arielle grasped her mother's hand and nodded.

CHAPTER 9

Betrayals and Prophecy

It was a week before Thanksgiving break. Arielle walked to the corner bus stop to wait with the other kids. The excitement of the coming vacation could be seen on all their faces.

Today was the annual fourth grade school play and Arielle was dressed as an Indian princess for the show. The older kids at the bus stop teased her, pulling on the beads of her costume and tugging on her pigtails. Two of the boys danced around her in a circle, hooting, acting like Indians. Arielle just smiled and went along, pretending it didn't bother her. She knew she looked great in her costume and was proud of it. She and her mother spent many hours creating it; sewing on the different colorful beads and buttons by hand.

When the school bus arrived, the kids lined up and piled in. They went to their assigned seats and sat down. Peter, the pastor's son, sat down behind her. He was the same age and in the same class as Arielle. He was short and pudgy, with reddish-brown hair and a freckled face. Just looking at him, anyone could see there was mischievousness written all over his face. She'd known him since kindergarten, and as he got older he had become an aggressive bully. He loved to tease and harass Arielle and her friends whenever he got the chance. He was big for his age, so no one in their class ever challenged him.

"I know something you don't know," Peter chanted to Arielle as he sat in the seat behind her. He pulled on her pigtail one more time as he taunted her.

"What, that you're a troublemaker?" Arielle asked without looking back at him. "And stop pulling on my hair. The last boy who did that ate sand."

"Just ignore him," Sally said, as she sat down next to Arielle. "He's such a pain in the butt sometimes." She was one of Arielle's closest friends. In school, they were inseparable.

Arielle giggled. "He doesn't even know what he's supposed to know. How could he know something we don't?"

Peter leaned forward and put his head between Arielle and Sally. "It's about you, Missy Arielle. I know something about you and your *mother* you don't."

Arielle turned around to face Peter. "I could care less, Peter. If it's something you know, then it's probably not something I want to know. Now leave us alone." She turned back around.

"Give me a quarter and I'll tell you what it is."

"I'll give you a quarter just to be quiet." She reached into her pocket and turned around again. "Here. Now shut up." She threw the quarter at him.

"Okay, now that you paid for it, I'm going to tell you."

"I don't want you to tell me anything, Peter," Arielle yelled.

Peter put his hands up to Arielle's ear and whispered loudly, "You're adopted. Your mom isn't your real mother." He sat back down, a smug smile stamped on his face. "Ha! Score one for the boys," he mocked as he slapped the back of Arielle's seat. He high-five'd the boy next to him.

Sally turned to Arielle, her eyes wide with surprise. "You're adopted?" she asked. "Who's your real Mom?"

There were several seconds of silence as Arielle thought about what to say. She couldn't lie.

"It's not like that," she explained to Sally. "Don't believe a word he says." She turned around to confront Peter. "You don't know what you're talking about. You've been watching too many cartoons again, Peter. Now keep your mouth shut and leave me alone."

"No. I swear. I read it on my dad's computer last night. It had to be you. I don't know of any other Arielle around with a mother whose name is Rebecca. You had a meeting with my father, didn't you?"

Sally turned around. "Peter, you're nothing but a pest. Why don't you mind your own business?"

"Really. I peeked at my dad's computer last night when he left for an appointment. He wrote things about talking to her mother. She's adopted." He jerked on Arielle's pigtail. "You didn't even know, did you?" He had a large grin on his face.

Arielle turned around, but turned back without replying. She wasn't going to give Peter the time of day if she didn't have to, but Peter wouldn't quit.

"You didn't, did you?" he questioned again.

"You don't know anything," she said, "so quit spreading rumors."

"Yeah, right. That's why you don't really look like your mother. Why do you think you have all that blond hair and she has dark hair? You don't look like her at all."

"Peter, does your mother fix your meals and wash your clothes?"

"Yeah, why?"

"Does she do a lot of things for you because she loves you?"

"I guess so."

"So does mine. So what makes your mother a mother and not mine? I know, Peter. I know a lot more than you think."

"You think so, you brat? I know much more." Peter whispered again, "You think you talk to angels, huh? Let me see your right hand."

Her eyes narrowed, her voice was like sharpened steel. "Oh, you think you know something about that?" Arielle asked as she turned around, kneeling on her seat.

"Here, see?"

For a flash, Arielle let Peter see the gold, rotating orbs. She laughed at him as he recoiled from the sight. His eyes were as large as half-dollars. As fast as the orbs appeared, they were gone.

"Hey! Where'd they go? Do that again."

Arielle wasn't about to let him see them again.

"Do what? See what again? Peter, what are you talking about?"

"You know what I mean. The lights."

"What lights?"

"In your hand. I saw them. I know I saw them!"

Arielle turned to Sally. "Peter thinks he sees lights in my hand. Do you see any?" she asked as she held her hands out for Sally to see.

"Of course not. What are you talking about?"

She turned back to Peter with a smile. "I think you're seeing things, Peter. Be careful. You know what they do to people who see things that aren't really there."

Arielle could tell Peter was getting frustrated. She had turned the tables on him.

"No, what?"

She put her hand up to her mouth while motioning for him to come closer to her. She spoke in a low voice,

"They take them away and give them all kinds of drugs until they don't see them anymore."

She let it sink in for a moment. She then motioned for him to come close again. She continued, "The same as they do for people that snoop around and don't mind their own business."

Peter stared at Arielle for a moment, then sat back in his seat and looked out the window without saying another word. They arrived at school several minutes later. Peter had not even looked at her again. As they were getting off the bus, Arielle got in line directly behind him.

"Score one for the girls," she whispered to him.

CR&SO

That night, Arielle and her mother were sitting in the dining room having supper together.

Arielle sat back in her chair. "Mom, can we talk?"

"Sure, honey. What's on your mind?"

"I had a argument with Peter, the pastor's son, on the bus today. I think I lost my temper and did something I probably shouldn't have."

Rebecca stopped eating and paid closer attention. She had never heard this from her daughter before. "Okay, what happened? What did you do?"

"Well, Peter told me he knew some things about me I didn't know."

"And?"

"I kept telling him to leave me alone, but he kept pulling on my hair. Then he told me I was adopted. I told him he didn't know what he was talking about. He told me he read about it."

All at once, fear and anger gripped Rebecca's insides. She felt her face flush, her left hand, resting in her lap, clenched into a fist. *The pastor—he didn't keep his word! He let out some of the most intimate, private details of my family. How could he do that? After he promised!*

She didn't know what to say, but now the truth had to come out. She had intended to tell Arielle someday about how she appeared on her doorstep, but now it looked as though it was going to be forced on her. She dropped her fork on the table and pushed her plate away. Lowering her head, she folded her hands and held them to her forehead. *How could he do this? What do I say now?*

"There are some things I have to tell you, Arielle. I've been meaning to for years, but I wanted to wait for the appropriate time. It just never seemed to be right."

Arielle smiled. "That's all right, Mom. I already knew. It doesn't matter one bit to me. You're my mother. I just didn't want Peter to think he knew anything special."

Rebecca was puzzled. "You already know? How?"

"The angels told me—a long time ago. They said you loved me so much that you took me in as a baby and raised me as your own. How could you not be my mom? You brought me up, and you're the only mother I know and love."

Rebecca reached over and pulled Arielle to her, hugging her tightly. "You are my daughter, adopted or not, and I love you very, very much." She wiped a tear from her eye. "I've kept this a secret from everyone for so long. I was always scared someone might find out and tell you before I got the chance."

"I know you love me, Mom. I've never doubted that."

"So tell me," Rebecca asked as she let go of her daughter, "how did Peter know about your adoption?"

"He told me he saw it on his father's computer. That's all he said."

Rebecca smiled. "Oh, *he did*, huh. Now tell me how *you* really knew about being adopted."

"I just told you. The angels told me. They woke me up one night when I was younger and talked to me for a long time. They said not to say anything to you then about what they told me, but to wait until it was revealed."

"Arielle, are you sure it wasn't just a dream you had?"

"I'm sure, Mom. But during the talk, they also told me something I still don't understand."

"What's that?"

"Someday I would understand why I was adopted. What did they mean by that?"

"I don't know, honey." Rebecca then described to Arielle how someone selected her to be her mother. "So, what else did the angels tell you?"

Arielle looked down at her food and was quiet.

"What's the matter?"

"I can't repeat it."

"Why?"

"They told me I couldn't repeat it. I promised."

"Who told you not to say anything?"

"The angels." Arielle looked up at her mother. "I'm sorry, Mom."

Rebecca didn't know what to say, but she figured it was either a dream Arielle had which seemed very real to her, or it was that invisible friend she had been talking to again.

"That's okay."

"There's one more thing, Mom."

"What's that?"

"I don't know who, but I was told someone we know is going to die before the end of the year. We're not supposed to worry though, they'll be with God in heaven."

Arielle continued eating her supper, downing the rest of her milk, acting as if nothing special had occurred.

"And the angels told you this?"

"Yes."

"When?"

"A couple days ago."

Rebecca was confounded for a moment. Hoping she wasn't talking about Craig, she sat back in her chair and tried to think of someone else she knew who was sick or dying. Her thoughts turned to her husband. But then, there was her great aunt, Louise, who was very old, about ninety-two, and lived in Hawaii. Could it be her? They weren't very close though. As a matter of fact, she had never met her.

"What you're saying is very serious, Arielle. I hope you're not fooling around." Rebecca really hoped Arielle was wrong—otherwise, that would mean someone she knew, possibly close to her, is going to die and she didn't want that either.

Arielle was quiet for a minute. She sat on her chair with her head down. "Mom, you don't believe me either, do you?"

"Believe what?"

"Anything I told you. You think I'm making it all up."

"Honey," her mom put her arm around her after thinking about what to say, "it's not that I don't believe you. You're telling me things I've never heard before. I think that you believe what you told me, but beyond that...."

Arielle looked up towards the ceiling and nodded her head.

"What is it?"

"The angel told me to understand it's very hard for you to accept everything I tell you and for me not to be upset."

"You just heard an angel?"

"Yes."

"What else did it tell you?"

"She said for me to be patient, someday you'll believe me."

"Be patient with me?" She laughed. "Tell her to let me in on something. Show me something. I'd love to listen to them with you."

"They're gone, Mom. They're not always here. They come and tell me something and then leave."

"Can you call them? Will they show up?"

"Only if it's real important. They seem to know when I need help and they just appear—like at the pastor's office."

"Can they talk to me also?"

"I suppose so. I've never asked them."

Rebecca smiled. "Next time you talk with them, ask for me, will you?"

"Okay, I will."

"Was that the only time you talked with them recently?" Rebecca wanted to know all she could—in case she had to talk to a psychologist or the pastor about it again.

Arielle put her head down once more. Her chin was almost touching her chest. "No."

"When did you talk with them again?"

She was slow to respond. "Today. After Peter told me I was adopted and I got off the bus."

"What did they tell you?"

"They scolded me. I told them I was sorry." Her eyes were brimming with tears.

Rebecca cracked a smile, and put her hand over her mouth to hide it. She put her arm around Arielle and softly asked her, "The angels scolded you? For what?"

"I showed Peter the lights in my hand for a second. When he asked what they were, I told him he was seeing things. He kept telling me he wanted to see them again. I laughed at him."

Rebecca turned away to hide her smirk. "That's not like you, honey. Why'd you do that?"

"Mom, he wouldn't leave me alone. I got so mad. I knew I shouldn't have done it." She hung her head. "The angels told me not to do it again."

CHAPTER 10

Peter's Lesson

After supper, Rebecca went to her room and called the pastor while Arielle did her homework. She wanted an explanation of how his son knew the confidential information she had been so hesitant to divulge to him. He had promised her that their conversation would remain private. It was eating at her and she was furious. Her stomach was still churning.

"Pastor, you have a lot of explaining to do," Rebecca spoke bluntly over the phone. "Some things have happened that shouldn't have, and I am very..." she held her breath, "upset at you."

"What happened, Rebecca? Do you want to come over now? I have about an hour."

"No, I can't. I'd have to get someone to watch Arielle. Can we make it tomorrow around three-thirty when I get off work? The kids are on vacation, so I'll have to pick up Arielle from her friend's house and drop her at her grandmother's."

"Why not just bring her with you? I'd love to continue my conversation with her after we finish."

"No, we can't do any more meetings until we get this resolved. I'll talk to you about it tomorrow."

"Okay, I'll see you at three-thirty."

❦

The next day, Rebecca arrived at the pastor's office at the appointed time. She was glad she had to wait a day; she had been able to gather her thoughts. She sat down next to his desk and ignored the coffee he placed in front of her.

"Pastor, my daughter told me yesterday your son has been harassing her on the school bus."

"He has? I had no idea." He seemed truly surprised. "Is that what is troubling you?"

"Absolutely not. That's a problem, but not the one I came to see you about."

"Oh, what is it then? I can't imagine why you would be so upset at me."

Rebecca took a deep breath. "Yesterday, Peter told Arielle she was adopted. I want to know how in the world he found out. I thought I had your word what we discussed here was absolutely confidential."

The pastor's face turned red and he shook his head. "It is private, Rebecca. I assure you he didn't find out from me."

"I believe he did Pastor, though maybe without your knowledge. Peter told Arielle he read it on your computer."

Pastor Sherman sat silent for a moment, looking at the top of his desk. "Oh, no!" He reached for the phone and quickly dialed a number.

"Dear, what's Peter doing right now?" he asked. After a short pause, "Have him come over to the office immediately. Thank you."

As soon as he hung up, he moved toward Rebecca and spoke. "Do you remember the notes I wrote from our meeting?"

"Yes, I do."

"After each of my sessions with anyone, I sit down and transfer the written notes to my computer at home, for future reference. Peter knows he is not allowed to touch that computer, so I don't see how he could have read the notes—but I'm going to find out."

Rebecca raised her eyebrows. "I hope so."

"I'll get to the bottom of this right now."

The parsonage was right next door to the church. Peter arrived within a couple minutes of his dad making the call. He stopped at the entrance to the office. "What's up, Dad? You want to see me?"

Rebecca turned around to see Peter.

"Oh, hi, Mrs. Price," he said in a quieter voice. He shifted in the doorway, looking at his feet.

"Come over here, Peter," his father ordered.

Peter slowly walked over to his father's desk.

"I understand that Arielle has been having some problems with you on the bus."

Peter just looked at his father.

"What did you say to her? I want a *complete* answer."

Peter's head dropped. "I told her... she was adopted, and..."

"And what?"

"And I know she says she talks to angels."

The pastor shook his head. He hesitated for a moment.

"How did you find out Arielle was adopted?"

"I..., I read it on your computer."

Again, the pastor's face flushed red. "Son, you know you're not allowed to touch my computer."

"I didn't, Dad."

"Then just how did you read it?" he demanded.

Peter perked up. "I went in the office to get a pen from your desk drawer. You left the computer on when you went to that meeting last night. I read it on the screen, but I didn't touch it."

The pastor nodded his head. "We'll talk more about this later. For now, you go to your room and stay there until I come home."

"Yes, Sir."

Peter hung his head, turned, and left the office.

The pastor raised his hand to his forehead, shaking his head from side to side. "I'm so sorry, Rebecca. I don't know what to say. It was my fault; I didn't shut the computer off before I left. Peter knows that everything in my home office is confidential, and he's not to touch any of it. He hardly ever goes in there. This shouldn't have happened."

"But it did—and from your own carelessness, Pastor."

"I know, and I'm asking for your forgiveness."

Rebecca was taken back for a moment. The pastor was asking *her* for forgiveness! She definitely wasn't used to this!

In a more conciliatory tone she said, "Look, Pastor, I know things happen with children. I just want you to guarantee me that you'll talk to your son and that he won't harass Arielle anymore at school or on the bus. Plus, I really would like him to keep quiet about the adoption. This isn't something I want spread around."

"I'll talk to Peter tonight. Please tell Arielle I'm very, very sorry and I want to know if he bothers her anymore."

She got up to leave.

The pastor rose from his chair with her. "By the way, how did Arielle take the news she was adopted? How did you handle it?"

Rebecca was slow to answer. "Can we talk about it another time?"

"Certainly."

The pastor walked her to the door. "May I still have another session with Arielle? I do want to talk to her more about her conversations with angels."

"That's up to her, Pastor. I'll ask her and give you a call."

"Thank you."

CRISO

The pastor went straight home and directly to his son's room. Peter was lying on his bed looking at the ceiling, his hands folded on his stomach, waiting for his father. He sat down on the bed next to his son.

"Why did you tell Arielle she was adopted?"

"Well, she is. I didn't lie. I read it on your computer."

"That's no reason for you to tell her. You know that information is confidential. And if you read the whole note, you would have seen that Mrs. Price didn't want Arielle to know. What were you thinking? You have almost ruined the relationship I have with two members of my congregation. I'm deeply ashamed of what you did, Peter. I've had to apologize to Mrs. Price for my actions, and for yours."

"I'm sorry, Dad."

"Did you tell her anything else?"

After a few moments, through wet eyes, Peter replied, "I told her I also knew about the lights in her hand."

"What?"

"You know, the lights her mother said she sees." Peter turned and looked up at his father, his eyes widened. *"I saw them too, Dad."*

"What do you mean, 'you saw them, too'?"

"I did. They were in her right hand. I only saw them for like, real fast; but I saw them. One second they were there, and then they were gone. I think I was the only one who saw them."

The pastor tilted his head slightly, wondering what his son had seen.

"Why did you tell Arielle all this?"

"Dad, she's such a teacher's pet. I was just having fun. Besides, she said she already knew she was adopted."

"She already knew?" *That's strange. Her mother said she never told her. What was she so upset about if Arielle already knew?*

After thinking for a few moments, the pastor told his son, "For your punishment, you're going to write a letter."

"Write a letter? To who?"

"To Arielle."

"Aww, no, Dad. Do I have to?"

"Yes. You might have just been having fun, but it was at someone else's expense. Your letter will be an apology. You will tell her you are very sorry for what you did and you will never read your father's computer again or violate a person's trust or privacy."

"Please Dad, don't make me give it to her."

"Yes, you will. And while you're at it, you will also tell her you won't harass her on the bus anymore or tell anyone else she is adopted. You will give it to her the next time she is here with her mother. What you did is terribly wrong, Peter, and I want you to realize that. Now get going, I want it done by bedtime and I want to read it."

CHAPTER 11

The Bridge

"Angie, how long has it been since we left Indianapolis?" Paul asked his wife as they drove west on Interstate 70 through Illinois. She could see that the continuous drone of the engine and the monotonous hum of the tires on the road was making her husband sleepy and in need of a break. His eyelids looked droopy and he was blinking more than usual.

Angie looked at her watch; she was also feeling the strain, although she had dozed off several times. "About five and a half, six hours," she said. Her neck muscles were sore from the *head bob* while she dozed; time for a real rest.

A few minutes later, a loud buzzing noise broke the boredom—a rumble strip—the van was veering onto the shoulder of the road! A large orange and black sign with blinking lights, mounted on a trailer warning vehicles of road construction ahead, loomed less than a hundred feet in front of them.

"Paul! Look out!" Angie yelled as she slapped her husband on the arm. Two of the kids in the rear seat screamed. Cars in adjacent lanes of traffic were sounding their horns.

Braking hard, Paul swerved the van back onto the pavement, just barely missing the sign.

"You almost killed us!" Angie cried. She held her hand over her mouth, shaking, trying to contain her fear.

"Oh, my God, I'm so sorry!" Paul rubbed his hand over his face and shook his head. "I must have drifted off." After a couple moments, the realization of the real danger he had put his family in with the near miss, hit him. "We'd better stop somewhere. I'll get some coffee."

"That's a good idea," Angie said. "I'm sure everyone's hungry. Let's find a decent place to eat."

Paul followed the next exit ramp off the highway onto a four-lane road boasting multiple restaurants. After obtaining a consensus from his family, he pulled into a popular family eatery where they ordered lunch and he downed several cups of coffee with his meal.

CREO

Paul apologized to his wife and kids again before returning to the road. He promised them he would pull over the minute he started feeling the least bit sleepy.

Angie knew it was going to be a long ride to Colorado Springs. She turned and looked at their five kids, three of whom were watching a DVD and two playing video games.

She laughed. "We used to make this trip in what, fifteen, sixteen hours before we were married? Now it's two days minimum. Those were the good ole days!"

Paul smiled and gave his wife's hand a squeeze. "Mom and Dad were sure surprised we're really coming out this year for Thanksgiving. I didn't realize we had been promising them a visit for so many years. I hope you didn't mind pulling the kids out of school early."

"No, they are all doing well. Rounding up five kids for a week, canceling all their activities and getting them ready is like herding cats on an ice skating rink. But at least we made it this time. I'm thankful it worked out."

"I'm really glad the new van came in last week. I wouldn't have wanted to make this trip in the old clunker." He rubbed the soft brown leather of his seat.

Angie just smiled at her husband. All the lighted gauges and dials made the view from the driver's seat look more like the instrument panel of a small airplane. She knew he would have rented a vehicle if he had to. He wasn't going to let anything mess up this trip, especially since they had been planning it for so long. The kids and Paul's parents would have been very disappointed, and she would've, too.

"It does ride nice. I've always loved the smell of a new car," she added, inhaling deeply.

"It's been so long since we've had one, I forgot what they smelled like."

Hours later as they were approaching the Illinois-Missouri state line, Paul turned to Angie, "Tell the kids to put their movies and games on hold for a few minutes. We're going to cross the Mississippi River soon and I want them to see it."

Angie turned around and tapped her son, Todd, on his knee, motioning for him to take his headphones off. "Tell your brothers and sisters to pause their games and movies, the Mississippi River's coming up."

All of them looked out the windows, but the only thing they could see was heavy traffic lining up to cross the massive bridge.

"That garbage truck in front of us stinks worse than an overflowing cesspool," Paul said. "I'm going to try to get around him."

"And here I thought that was you," Angie teased with a smirk on her face.

Paul smiled and put his turn signal on, trying to get over into the passing lane. Traffic had all but stopped and no one would let him in.

"Well, I guess we're stuck behind him for the next couple of miles," he said.

"Oh, no!" Angie said with a nasal sounding voice. He looked over at her; she was holding her nose.

Just then, traffic started moving again and the driver of a silver Cadillac in the next lane honked his horn. He was waving, indicating Paul could come over in front of him. He promptly moved over and was able to pass the garbage truck—leaving its accompanying aromas behind them.

"I don't see a thing yet, Mom. Let me know when we're closer," Todd said. He put his headphones back on.

Angie sighed and looked at Paul with a smile. "It's not like when we were kids anymore."

"It sure isn't," he replied. "Never has been."

CRSO

It was noon recess and Arielle was on the playground talking to her friend, Sally.

"Here he comes, Arielle," she said.

"Who?" Arielle asked.

"The troublemaker, Peter."

"Hi, Arielle."

"Hi, Peter."

"Can I talk with you a minute?" They walked a short distance away from Sally. "I heard you're coming over to see my dad again."

"Yes, Mom says he wants to talk to me."

"I have to give you a letter I wrote. It's an apology. I wanted to tell you before. I am sorry about what I did and said on the bus."

"That's all right. I guess I got a little carried away myself."

At that moment, a strange look came over Arielle. She looked above Peter and cocked her head as if she was listening to something.

"I'm sorry Peter. I have to go."

He shook his head and waved her off. "Whatever."

Arielle left Peter and Sally and walked to the other side of the playground where she sat down on some bleachers. She watched from the corner of her eye as Sally walked toward her. Arielle's attention was diverted as she looked up at the sky and spoke to an invisible presence. She started crying as she blew across the palm of her hand and watched an orb disappear into the distance.

"What's wrong, Arielle? What are you doing?" Sally asked, seeing Arielle blow on the palm of her hand. "Why are you crying?"

"Many people are going to drown today, Sally. I had to help some of them."

"*What* are you talking about?"

"At the river. I saw it..." Arielle suddenly looked at Sally and realized what she had just said and that it wouldn't make any sense to her at all. She probably sounded silly.

"Forget it," she said and walked away, wiping tears from her eyes.

Sally just stood there and watched Arielle walk away, then yelled, "Arielle, wait for me!"

CRWD

A sudden flash of light in front of the van startled Paul and Angie. Both looked around for the source.

"What was that?" Paul asked.

"I don't know," Angie replied as she turned around and looked toward the rear of the van. The kids were still looking out the windows or playing their video games. It was apparent they hadn't seen the flash. They continued inching along in the snarled traffic.

"I'm sure glad we left a couple of days early. I'd hate to see this traffic the day before Thanksgiving," Paul said.

The engine light suddenly came on and the new van began sputtering, lurching them forward.

"What's wrong, Daddy?" asked Jenny, the five year old. "What'd you do?"

"I didn't do anything, honey."

Paul signaled and was able to pull off the road just as the engine started knocking and then died.

"Aww, what now?" He smacked the steering wheel. "This isn't supposed to happen to a new car."

Shaking his head, he tried turning the key to restart the van, but nothing happened. The engine wouldn't even turn over. Paul held his head. This same thing occurred on his sixty-seven Mustang fastback. That engine repair cost him over two thousand dollars. But this was a new vehicle; nothing should be wrong with it, and even though it was under warranty, they didn't have the time to stop for repairs. A nightmare scenario he thought.

"We might as well have driven the old clunker," Angie complained.

Grabbing his jacket, Paul glared at his wife and quietly said, "I don't need this right now."

She turned her head and looked out her window. He went outside, put his jacket on and unlatched the hood. Although he had no idea what might be wrong, his family was depending on him and he had to make it at least look like he knew what he was doing. He pounded on the battery, hit the air filter a couple times and checked the fan belt. The new vehicle wasn't like the cars he used to work on when he was young; this was completely computerized. Back then he could fix any car. Now he just took it to the local garage for repairs.

He couldn't find anything. Out of frustration he kicked the front fender and hoped no one in his family saw him do it. He went to the side window. "Try and start it now," he said.

Angie leaned over and turned the key. The engine turned over slowly several times and then suddenly came to life. Paul looked at the engine, scratching his head. It showed no sign of trouble and he closed the hood. As he took off his jacket and was about to get back into the van, he saw the garbage truck pass them and caught the perfume of its load once more. Not again, he thought to himself.

"What was wrong?" asked Angie as he climbed back in.

"Oh, something was just loose," Paul said, hoping the same problem wasn't going to happen a second time. "It's really hard to explain."

∞

Angie looked at Paul out of the corner of her eye and smiled. She knew better than to ask for details.

"Did you see that garbage truck pass us again?" he asked.

"I saw it," she said. "At least it's going to be several cars ahead of us."

Paul turned his signal on and cautiously pulled back onto the highway amid the heavy traffic. About a half-mile down the highway they approached the I-70 bridge, which spanned the Mississippi River, and were soon crossing on it. The traffic they had been inching along in suddenly came to an abrupt halt. Moments later, horns began blaring from all around them. After sitting in the same place for almost ten minutes they watched other drivers and passengers exiting their vehicles, walking toward the center of the bridge. They heard shouting and a woman scream for help. Some people ran past them, going the opposite way.

"What's happened?" Angie asked.

"I haven't the faintest..." Paul said as he put the van in park.

She turned the radio on and hit the seek button, searching for a local news station to get a traffic update while Paul grabbed his jacket.

"I'm going out there to see what's holding up traffic. It's probably an accident, but keep the doors locked. I'll be right back," Paul ordered.

CR&SO

Angie kept advancing the tuner until she found an AM news station. Country music was playing, but she hoped they had news updates on the half hour, and it was almost one-thirty. After the song finished, a special news flash was aired.

"We bring you this important news bulletin from our eye-in-the-sky chopper that is just arriving over the Mississippi River."

Sounds of a helicopter could be heard in the background of the broadcast. Angie looked out the windshield and saw a bright yellow helicopter in the sky, hovering over the bridge just ahead of them. It had large letters painted on the side, matching the call sign of the radio station.

"Several spans of the westbound bridge of Interstate 70 have collapsed into the Mississippi River. Many vehicles have plunged into the swiftly running water. The authorities we have spoken to say all available boats and crafts in the area have been notified and are speeding to the scene of the disaster to look for survivors. Rescue crews from the police and fire departments are enroute. Stay tuned to this station for updates as we get them."

Angie turned the radio off. "Kids, you stay in the van. Don't move," Angie said as she slipped into her coat. "I'll be right back with Dad." Without waiting for a response, she slammed the door shut and ran towards the center of the bridge to find her husband.

She found him a few feet from a jagged edge of the bridge, the balance being swallowed by the river below. He was standing there, staring at a truck hanging halfway over the edge, teetering on the precipice, the front wheels and cab suspended over the raging river below. The truck's driver was screaming out the window for help, terror in his eyes.

Angie didn't want to venture so close to the edge.

"Paul," she called to her husband.

Paul didn't respond; he just stood there, staring. Cautiously, she walked over and took hold of his hand, clasping it tightly. Looking into his eyes, a blank gaze greeted her; a thousand-yard stare she had never seen on him before.

"Do you recognize that truck?" Paul finally asked her, pointing to the garbage truck.

"Yeah." Angie then realized what Paul was saying.

CR&O

A man appeared with a tow strap. The operator of the truck, a young man who looked to be in his early twenties, cautiously opened his door. Holding tight to the steering wheel, he caught the strap as it was thrown to him. Three men, including Paul, joined in holding the other end. The driver tied his end around himself and slowly started working his way out of the cab. Each time he slightly shifted position, the truck started rocking, teetering precariously.

"We'll pull you up if you don't make it," Paul yelled to the operator, "but you're going to have to take the jump." He could tell the driver was scared. Cautiously, the young man poised himself for the six-foot, life-saving jump he was going to have to make.

"C'mon, you can do it," one of the other men yelled.

After several false starts, the driver leapt, barely catching the edge of the bridge with his fingers. The bridge shook as the truck edged over and careened into the river. The three men held the rope taut as two others rushed over and helped pull the driver up. Visibly shaken, the young man fell to his knees, kissed the ground and thanked everyone profusely.

A few minutes later Paul and Angie returned to their van, horror-struck expressions still on their ashen-white faces. Sirens blared from every direction. As they looked at each other, they slowly opened the van doors and got in. They sat in stunned silence for several seconds.

"What's going on?" asked Mary, their oldest daughter, breaking the silence. "What did you see?"

"Daddy, I'm scared," the five-year-old cried. "The car keeps shaking."

"We have to get the kids off this bridge," Paul said. He turned around. "Everyone out. Let's go. Right now."

"Why, Daddy?" Jenny asked.

"I'll tell you later, sweetheart. Go with Mommy for now."

After locking the car, they walked quickly past the backed-up traffic towards safety. "Dad, what happened?" Mary asked again.

"The bridge collapsed. A lot of cars and people fell into the river."

"Oh, my God!"

Paul looked at his wife and grabbed her hand as they walked. "You do know where we'd be if the engine hadn't died?" he whispered.

She looked at her children and nodded her head. "Thank God."

CHAPTER 12

Father Joe

Rebecca and Arielle were on their way to church to see their pastor for another round of questions and answers. He had asked Rebecca for another meeting after she read him the riot act a few weeks before.

"Are you sure you don't mind seeing the pastor again, Arielle?" Rebecca asked as she stopped for a red light.

"I don't mind, Mom. He's basically a good person, he just has some of his priorities mixed up like many church leaders."

"Arielle, please don't start an argument with the pastor tonight. Just answer his questions the best you can then we can go home."

"Mom, I never like arguing with him, but it just seems he never believes me, especially when I tell him about the angels." Arielle made a face, cocked her head and tried to sound like the pastor. "She's a kid. What's she know?"

Rebecca laughed. "You sound just like him!"

"Seriously, Mom, he thinks because of my age I don't know what I'm talking about. How many times do I have to tell him the same thing over and over before he stops asking me the same questions?" Arielle looked over at her mother and gave a big smile. "Besides, he thinks he has a surprise for me when we get there."

"What kind of surprise?"

"You'll see. He won't be by himself tonight. He's invited another person to the meeting who won't believe me either."

"How do you know he's not going to believe you? Have you spoken to him already?"

"No. I've never met him."

"Then you really don't know yet."

"Okay, Mom. I don't know."

"Well, have some patience, dear. There are many things going on we don't understand. I'm hoping you'll be able to enlighten me about your angels tonight, too."

Arielle sighed. "Mom, you know I've always told you, if you want to know something, all you have to do is ask."

"I know, sweetheart, but I don't totally understand your answers. Even if I believe you are talking to angels, it's like I don't have the same insight you possess and it frustrates me. I don't know if I'm asking the right questions."

"Like what?"

"Like the lights in your hand, why are you and I the only ones who can see them? When you were younger, I thought I was going crazy. I'm sure the pastor still thinks I'm totally insane."

"I've told you, Mom, they're gifts from God. If everyone could see them, I'd be forever answering questions. And if everyone knew what they were, there'd be too many people begging me to use them, and I can't do that. They can only be used for very special purposes."

"What are those?"

"I never know until I'm told by the angels."

"See, there you go again about the angels. I wish I could see them or talk to them as you do. Then I'd know for sure."

"What would you do or say if you could talk to them?"

"Why,—I would ask a lot of questions."

"Like what?"

"Maybe... what heaven is like? What is God like? Questions about the Bible. I don't know, just questions."

Arielle giggled. "No angel questions, huh?"

Rebecca smiled and looked at her daughter. "You're such a smarty-pants sometimes."

"I did ask them about it, Mom, like you told me to. They said that one day you *will* see them and they *will* speak to you, but for now you must have faith."

Rebecca was silent. *How in the world can I argue with that?*

Faith. That was always the *big word*. The *big word* spelled with a capital 'F'. Where did faith come from? What exactly was it? She did have it though, she thought. She was not overly religious, didn't proselytize or stand on the street corner with a sign, but she did try to live a good life, tried to keep Sundays and the religious holidays holy by going to church and conversing with God. Several times she thought she felt Him answer her, actually speaking to her in a subtle, subconscious voice. Was her daughter confused? Was that actually the way she heard the angels speak to her?

Her faith had wavered only once, when Tyler died. She prayed to God that night to bring him back, to make it all a bad dream. When her baby was buried, she cursed the heavens and all who resided there for taking her child. How could a loving God take her son, destroy her life, and at the same time take her ability to have another child? She couldn't understand what she did to make Him so mad at her, to so destroy her life. Later, she repented and desperately asked for God's help and forgiveness. She knew she did not know His ways or what He had in store for her.

Arielle looked up at her mom. "Did you hear me?"

"Yes, I did, honey. Thank you for asking. I guess I'll have to wait for that day. I just hope it comes before I go completely crazy!"

Arielle laughed.

CRSO

They arrived at the church and went directly to the pastor's office. Another man, dressed in black with a white collar, was sitting on the couch across from the pastor's desk holding a notepad. He stood up as Arielle and her mother entered the room.

"Good evening, ladies," greeted the pastor.

"Good evening." Rebecca glanced over at the visitor. Her eyes darted between the priest and her daughter, who wore an expression that spoke to her, "I told you so!"

"Rebecca, I have invited an old friend of mine, Father Joe from Saint Catherine's, to sit in on our conversation tonight. I hope you don't mind."

Father Joe was a heavy-set man with a balding head. His blue eyes were set back in his head making his nose look much longer than it was. His ruddy cheeks seemed to give away his penchant for maybe more than an occasional sip of communion wine.

"I don't mind, Pastor, but I think it's Arielle you should be asking."

"You're so right." He turned to Arielle with a smile. "I'm sorry, I hope you don't mind."

"It's fine with me," she quickly stated, and went over to shake the priest's hand.

The pastor turned to Rebecca. "He's written a book on angels and spirituality and I thought he might be able to help us gain some insight on what Arielle has been telling us."

She nodded.

"I knew you would be here," Arielle whispered to Father Joe as she shook his hand and gave him a private wink.

"And how did you know?" Father Joe bellowed so everyone could hear.

"Know what?" asked the pastor, his broad smile disappearing.

Arielle turned around and walked over to the chair next to her mother, which placed them right in between the pastor and the priest.

"I knew Father Joe would be here," Arielle said.

"You knew?" asked the pastor.

"The angels told me. They said they would be with me tonight, and that a priest who writes about angels would also be at this meeting."

"When did you supposedly get this information?" Father Joe asked.

"This afternoon. After lunch," she said confidently.

"How can that be?" the pastor quizzed. "Father Joe didn't even know he would be here until a few minutes before he came. So how could you or anyone else have known?"

Arielle smiled as she waited a moment before answering, nodding her head. "You asked him to come here yesterday, right after breakfast. Father Joe told you he would be here, except a couple of hours ago he called and said he had to give the last rites to a dying friend. He still made the meeting, although he arrived just before we did."

The priest's eyes were the size of half dollars. The pastor was speechless.

"That's amazing. How did you know all this?" the priest asked in a weak voice. He was visibly shaken. He dropped his pen on the floor as he looked up at the pastor, "Did you tell her any of this?"

"No, I didn't," was the only answer he could muster as he slowly sat down behind his desk, still shaking his head moments later.

Arielle was sitting in the chair with her hands clasped in her lap. Her feet were swinging back and forth inches off the floor. "You're not a bad person, Father, maybe a little misguided. What did you think you would find out here tonight?"

"What?" he asked.

Arielle looked up above him. She put her hand over her mouth, looked over at her mother and giggled.

"What is it, Arielle?" Rebecca asked.

"I'm sorry, Father," she said. "I'm not supposed to repeat everything I hear. I thought they wanted me to say that." She giggled some more.

The priest rubbed his chin as he picked up his pen. He turned and eyed the area where Arielle had been gazing. "I understand you have made some pretty amazing claims, Arielle. What exactly did you hear?"

She turned toward the priest. "The angels also told me you were going to ask me questions about angels and God, and then most likely declare I don't know what I'm talking about." She stopped for a few seconds and cocked her head. "Is that really what you were going to do?"

"The angels told you that, huh?"

"Yes, Sir."

The priest hurriedly scribbled some notes. The room was quiet. Without looking up he said, "I definitely would like to ask you some specific questions." He raised his head and looked into Arielle's eyes. "I'll determine whether I consider your claims valid or not after we've had a chance to talk."

Arielle perked up. "How are you going to do that? I talk to angels, but how are you going to tell if I am telling the truth or not? Do you want me to take a lie detector test? Pastor Sherman has asked me if I knew what a lie is, so I already know he doesn't believe me."

The priest looked over at the pastor, who nodded, then looked back at Arielle. "And what did you tell him?"

"Of course I do. May I ask you the same question?"

"Why would you want to do that?"

"Haven't you ever told someone, or preached to members of your congregation things you really don't believe? Haven't you ever stretched the truth a bit?"

Silence ensued for several seconds. Father Joe started writing again. "We aren't here to discuss my beliefs or what I've preached. We've all made mistakes in our lives. We're here to discuss your claims."

"Then would you like to question me on church doctrine? You are free to ask me anything you like."

"I thought I might first ask you a few questions on the Bible, Arielle. If you truly talk to angels, then the answers shouldn't be a problem."

"They won't be," she giggled. Arielle looked above the priest again and nodded her head.

"Okay, then let's begin. There's a book in the Bible that in the original translation is written in two different languages within the first ten chapters."

"Yes," Arielle said, "there is."

"Well, what book is it?" The priest seemed annoyed. He impatiently snapped his fingers and stared directly at her, wanting an answer right away.

Arielle glanced at him. "Just a minute. I'll have your answer." She hesitated a moment longer, then began. "The book of Daniel. It starts out in Hebrew, and then transitions to Aramaic in chapter two. It reverts back to Hebrew in chapter eight."

"Very good. And why does it do that?"

"Chapters two through eight focus on Jewish concerns, while the rest are Gentile concerns."

His eyebrows shot up. "Fascinating. I'm impressed, Arielle. I see you know your Bible. Your pastor told me you seem to know more about the Bible than any person he knows."

Arielle beamed. "Thank you. Do you have more?"

He thought for a moment. "The Bible speaks of one particular sin that is unforgivable. Do you know what it is?"

Again, Arielle hesitated. "The sin against the Spirit, blasphemy of the Holy Spirit. Next!"

This time the priest paused. "The Trinity is a concept that most people find very hard to understand. Where in the Bible is the Trinity stated or discussed?"

"That's an easy one, Father. The word *Trinity* is never used in the Bible, only the concept. Matthew 28:19 and 2 Corinthians 13:14 are examples. Any more?"

"I think that will do."

She sighed. "Can we get to what I am really here to discuss, Father? Can we talk about church policies and practices?"

"What?" He put his paper and pen down and folded his arms.

"I came here tonight to give you and Pastor Sherman guidance, to deepen your spirituality, your beliefs."

"And how do you intend to do this?" he asked.

"The angels want me to tell you that God loves us all, without reservation. He doesn't love just those who choose to love Him; He loves everything and every person He has created. He doesn't want us to be frightened by strict rules created by man and which tend more to scare His flock into submission, much like you're trying to do to me; and much like many of the rules and laws you have and promote. He wants us to come to Him out of love, not fear."

"Arielle, you do speak eloquently, but it may be on the subject of things you do not know that much about." He wrote feverishly as he spoke. "Why do you persist in telling everyone that you speak to angels, when you know and *I* know you don't?"

Arielle felt herself becoming angry with Father Joe for seemingly trying to change the subject. How could he be so sure of himself that she didn't speak to angels after she had answered all of his questions and had given him so much information no one else knew? She couldn't tell whether the priest was trying to bait her, test her, or was stating a true belief. "First, Father, I haven't told *every-*

one—just my mother, a couple of classmates and the pastor. I always tell the truth, and I've told these people only because they asked me. Angels *do* speak to me Father, and I speak to them. How do you think I knew you would be here?"

The priest answered quickly. "I would guess that you really didn't. You're just saying you did. As far as this other stuff—you had a lucky guess or you found out in some different way. Maybe you're a psychic. The world is full of heretics, conjurers, magicians and sleight-of-hand fools. I've seen it before and they almost had me convinced when I discovered the truth."

Rebecca stood up and spoke, her words direct, her hands clenched together. "Father, you may not believe me either, but as we were driving over here, Arielle told me there would be a surprise for her when we got here, that another person besides the pastor would be here."

Before he could respond, Arielle continued. "Father, you may think I am using tricks or deceit, but I am telling you the truth. I was told by angels. I don't know of any other way to tell you."

The priest repositioned himself on the couch and hesitated.

"Arielle, do you know what Hebrews 13 through 17 says?"

After a moment, she smiled broadly. "Yes. It basically says to submit ourselves to those who rule over us and watch our souls." She smiled. "That's a good one, Father."

He slammed his pad of paper down next to him. "Maybe you should heed the verse."

Arielle shot right back. "Father, do you know what Acts 4, verse 19 says?"

Annoyed, he said, "No, I can't say off the top of my head I do, although I'm sure I've read it. Are you going to tell me?"

"Yes, it speaks of false shepherds and self-seeking leaders. Maybe you ought to re-read it sometime."

Silence gripped the room as Father Joe picked up his pad and wrote feverishly. Rebecca placed her hand over her mouth to hide a smirk and turned away. Arielle's legs were still swinging; her mood light. She didn't seem to have a care or the understanding of how infuriated she was probably making the priest. On the other hand, Father Joe seemed to be steaming.

"Why do you think we can't see or hear the angels when, as you say, they are here with us?" he asked pointedly.

"I don't know, but I do know they speak to others too."

"Why don't we know about them? It would kind of help your case if you could tell us who they are, wouldn't it? Make your story more believable?"

"I don't have a *case* or a *story*, Father. They probably don't tell anyone as they have learned, as I have, that no one believes them. After a while, I'm sure they've learned to just keep quiet, as most just mock them and tell them to see a psychiatrist."

"Do you know any of these other people?"

"No, I don't"

Father Joe took several deep breaths, his frustration showing. He didn't seem to be getting anywhere trying to poke holes in Arielle's story or obtaining an admission she was making it all up.

"Why do you think angels speak to you and not to anyone else here?" This time the priest's voice was harsh; he was tapping his pen on the notebook, his eyes fixed on Arielle.

"Until I was told differently, I always thought they did speak to everyone."

Rebecca stood up, looking between the priest and the pastor. "I think that's enough, Father. For Pete's sake, she's only a ten-year-old child and this isn't the Inquisition. I think it's time for us to leave now."

"Ten-year-old! She speaks like a twenty-year-old," Father Joe stated sarcastically.

Arielle's voice was calm. She reached over and placed her hand into her mother's. "It's all right, Mom. We're just getting started. I'm supposed to be here today to teach, and that is what I am going to do."

"To teach whom?" asked the pastor with a smirk. He seemed amused by Arielle's statement.

Rebecca slowly sat back down, looking puzzled.

"Everyone here," Arielle replied as she turned to the priest and then her mother. "Father, the angels *are* in the room with us. They told me they will answer any questions you or the pastor may have, so ask anything and the angels said they will respond through me."

"How many are here?" asked the priest.

Arielle smiled, she knew the priest still didn't believe a word she was saying. She counted the angels, pointing to each, so Father Joe could see where they were. "Six."

The priest was temporarily at a loss for words. He studied Arielle for a moment, finally asking, "Pastor, do you have a recorder to tape this conversation—so I can study it later?"

"Yes, I certainly do." He pulled a recorder from his desk drawer, placed a tape in it and turned it on.

"Do you mind, Arielle?"

"Of course not."

"Arielle, please ask the angels why they are here tonight," Father Joe said.

Arielle smiled. "You may ask them directly yourself, Father. Don't be shy. I'll give you their answers." She paused for a moment. "They say they are here doing God's will."

"What kind of angels are they?"

"They don't understand the question."

"There is a hierarchy of angels. Where are they in the hierarchy?"

Arielle laughed. "They had a good laugh and said there is no hierarchy. The hierarchy you are referring to is man-made; they are just angels."

"Why have they chosen you to speak through?"

Arielle paused. "The angels said they did not choose me."

"Who did?"

"God did."

"Why you?"

Arielle hesitated, cocking her head slightly, as though she was listening.

"They said God chooses children many times to work through because they are still pure and are not yet corrupted with any power or authority. Children have nothing to gain and won't use it for power, self-advancement or self-enrichment. When the angels speak, they listen. Grown-ups may listen, but then many times they aren't sure what the messages are or they interpret them incorrectly."

"Interesting. You speak about power, authority, and corruption. Is having power or authority bad? Is it in itself corrupt?"

Arielle waited. "The angels say yes and no. It depends on how it's used. When Jesus made Peter the head of his church, He did so as He knew Peter had come from very poor roots and would head the church with the love and understanding that He had modeled. Jesus did not intend for religion to be employed the way it is today. It was supposed to be used to nourish everyone with the love of God and bring His children closer to Him."

Arielle paused again. "Instead, in many ways it has turned into strict laws and rituals which bear no resemblance to what God wanted or what Jesus taught. Too many practice religion like you would practice a piano—an hour a week, which keeps them in tune with their church."

The pastor and Father Joe kept looking at each other, a silent conversation, seemingly not knowing what to think or say.

"Isn't that the truth!" the priest said.

The Pastor finally spoke up. "Arielle, are you... I mean, are the angels saying we demand too much of our congregation?"

Arielle's attention focused on the angel above the pastor. She nodded, then stated, "Yes. You both ask more of people than Jesus did or ever would. God wants everyone to come to Him for His love and out of love, not out of fear. This is a concept neither of you teach or really understand. If your people don't abide by your rules and laws, you try to scare them into submission by telling them they won't be saved; they won't have eternal salvation. That isn't what Jesus wanted and it couldn't be further from the truth. It's like you enjoy holding the power of their salvation over them."

Arielle then stood up, imitating a male voice, she pointed to her pastor, 'Follow what I say, or else.'" She giggled and shrugged her shoulders. "That's the way they told me," she said softly in her own voice as she sat back down.

Father Joe was disconcerted. "What kind of rules are you talking about?" he asked. "I don't think the church asks anything that is unreasonable or unwarranted. I don't know about Pastor Sherman, but most certainly, I don't."

Arielle paused again and then turned to the priest. "They don't know where to begin. Father, you embarrass and shame many in your congregation by asking them to personally confess their sins to you. Why is that? Isn't a person confessing to God enough? You also make your parishioners get married by a priest. You tell them that marriage outside of your church isn't valid in the eyes of God if they don't. That's not true either. People were getting married long before the church, and without a priest. Did God not recognize those marriages? You make them take marriage-counseling classes taught by a person who has never been married. Would you take driving lessons from a person who has never driven a car?"

She then turned to the pastor. "You both require members of your church to tithe part of their earnings, even when some families are so poor they have trouble paying their rent and putting food on the table for their children. Yet, you both live in very nice homes, drive mostly new, expensive cars, go on long vacations, and have never experienced the hunger or desperation some of your congregation feel every day. Jesus never demanded nor required that. He only asked that his followers give with pure motives to support His church."

"I'm confused. Are you saying we shouldn't ask our members to tithe?" the pastor asked. "The Old Testament requires tithing."

"No, that's not what I'm saying. Asking is fine; people will feel good when they respond. Demanding is another; you're not a government, don't try to act like one. The Old Testament actually required more than ten percent, but it was used to help the needy and support the church. Today, politicians rob the individual of giving, and the good feelings that come along with it. They tax heavily, just so the bureaucrats can pat themselves on the back and feel good about themselves when they create charitable organizations and give away other people's money."

Arielle stopped for a few moments and then turned back to the priest. "God doesn't mean for tithing to provide a life of luxury for his shepherds. And then you take this money, which you have literally taken out of some of their mouths, and purchase useless material objects for your church. Items which mean nothing to God. What a waste. The angels say a good example is the velvet, satin-lined curtain behind the altar in your church, which you just paid over ten thousand dollars for." Arielle lowered her head. "They also say you should be ashamed. The money should have been used to help the poor and hungry."

Father Joe's face was beet red, but he forced a smile and a composed voice. "You may be assuming way too much, Arielle. I don't have any poor or hungry in my parish that I am aware of, and I would know if there were. I'm afraid you're making accusations that you and your supposed angel friends can't substantiate."

Arielle's eyes grew wide, her face scrunched up and she put her hands over her ears as she faced the floor and shook her head. "Please," she whispered, "one at a time."

"What's the matter, Arielle?" her mother whispered, her concern showing.

Arielle finally looked up at her mother. "The angels were really upset. They were all talking to me at once and I couldn't understand what any of them were saying. I had to remind them I could only understand one at a time."

Father Joe's eyes widened and he squirmed a bit in his seat.

She turned to the priest. "You seemed to hit a nerve with the angels, Father," Arielle finally answered. "I've never seen them this way."

"What do you mean?" he asked.

"Once they calmed down, I was able to understand what they were saying. The angels want me to ask you about the parish next to yours. They asked if you believe the people in your parish are the only ones in God's flock? Are they the only ones you are responsible for? There are many very poor and hungry in the parish right next to yours, which the money used to purchase the drapes would have tremendously helped. All you have to do is open your eyes and look, but you stay locked up in your own world of luxury."

Father Joe didn't answer any of the questions, he just wrote. He didn't even look up.

"They want to ask about the homeless and the destitute downtown. Are they not to be helped also? Are they not all God's children? They said too many churches build altars of gold and silver believing they are a tribute to God, when in reality their hearts are as cold as the stones that the church is built from. Many churches are more concerned with enforcing their rules and regulations than they are with finding the lost sheep."

After another hesitation, Arielle nodded and turned facing the priest. "The angels say the Bishop brought in a new pastor at Saint Gabriel's parish two months ago. They want to know if you know why?"

"I don't know for sure, but I would suspect the Bishop had his own good reasons," he replied.

Arielle suspected he wasn't being exactly truthful. She got up from her seat and walked around the room, looking over at the priest once in awhile and nodding her head.

"They say it was because the last pastor, Father Christopher Albright, was not collecting enough money from the parishioners. The people treasured Pastor Albright and he loved them, but now, every Sunday, all they hear from the sermons of the new pastor during Mass is they need to give more money, the church needs more money, and the Bishop needs more money. Some Sundays, three collections are taken. The poor folks are made to feel terrible if they don't actually give more and more. Many of them have to choose between how much to keep towards taking care of their families, versus giving more to their church. Some have quit coming to church, it's easier than feeling belittled from the pulpit, especially in front of their children. The new pastor doesn't see or feel the misery he is causing. He is more concerned about pleasing the hierarchy than providing for those in his care. This is a poor parish, Father, not one that should be milked to provide extravagant items for the clergy or for their altars of gold."

"You may think you know why the Bishop replaced Father Christopher, Arielle, and there may have been rumors but, I'm fairly sure there were other reasons." His words were clipped and abrupt.

"It's not what I think or know, Father, it's what the angels told me." Arielle walked over to the priest and looked directly at him. "Which is it, Father, are God's children supposed to be slaves to the church, or is the church supposed to be servants and spiritual guides to the poor, the sick, and the needy? Are children to be nourished, protected, and taught the ways of our Lord, or are they play things of the clergy, only to be taught to serve the needs of the church?"

"What?" he demanded angrily. "What you're saying is slanderous!"

Arielle's face took on a glow that Rebecca had seen only once before. She took the priest's hand in hers. "Father, if you please, I am only the messenger. You are being graced with a very rare gift that few are given; yet you still maintain an air of arrogance and refuse to recognize it, accept it, and learn from it. Use your gift wisely, Father, you may never get another one."

The room was silent as Arielle walked back to her seat. Everyone suddenly became fixated as they watched a moth beating its wings against a light bulb on the chandelier.

The priest suddenly sprung from his chair. "Well, this has been an interesting evening. I definitely believe we will need future discussions. Do you suppose we can meet again sometime, Arielle?" Father Joe asked. "I will have to consult with the Archbishop before we have any further chats."

"Of course. I'll be happy to meet with you, Father, anytime; even the Archbishop."

"I don't expect that will be necessary."

Arielle smiled as she stood up again and went over to the priest. He extended his hand to her, seemingly expecting her to reciprocate as she approached. Instead, Arielle walked right up to the priest and hugged him around the waist. She looked up at him and wiggled her index finger, indicating for him to bend down to her. As Father Joe bent down, Arielle cupped her hand and whispered into his ear and then gently kissed him on the cheek. He stood up, his head tilted to the side, a quizzical look on his face. Arielle was beaming, with a huge smile on her face, nodding up and down. He walked over to the pastor who stood up from behind his desk and shook his hand, thanking him for the invitation.

"I'll call you later. May I have the tape in the recorder?" he asked, pointing to the machine.

The pastor nodded, turned off the recorder, and promptly gave him the tape. Father Joe said goodbye to Rebecca and abruptly left the room.

Rebecca, watching everything unfold, bent down and quietly spoke to Arielle who had a huge grin on her face.

"Wow. What did you say to him?"

She whispered into her mother's ear. "I told him the angels wanted him to know that God loves him and knows his intentions are good, but also wants him to know he is too authoritative and strict with the people of his parish. He needs to run his church with love and teach what he knows to be the truth. Help those who are in need and relinquish any extravagant ways."

Rebecca chuckled. "I bet he'll think about that for awhile."

The pastor, also curious, asked Rebecca what Arielle had told the priest. She asked Arielle if it was okay to tell him. She nodded and Rebecca told him.

"I'll talk to Father Joe tomorrow and see what he has to say. I bet it'll be a mouthful!"

"Arielle, it's time for us to go too," Rebecca said.

"Can't you stay a while longer? I have so many questions I want to ask."

"I'm sorry, Pastor, but we have to get over to the nursing home and see my husband before visiting hours are over."

"I understand. How is Craig? Any change?" asked the pastor.

"No, no changes. We stop and talk to him as often as we can. The doctors all say that talking to him is the best thing we can do for him."

The pastor told Rebecca he would pray for him.

CHAPTER 13

A Prophecy Fulfilled

A week later on a Sunday night, Rebecca folded a load of warm clothes fresh from the dryer while Arielle was sound asleep. After church, they had spent a long day at the zoo and aquarium, stopping again at the nursing home at the end of the day to see Craig, to read and talk to him for a while. Arielle fell asleep on the ride home.

Rebecca wanted to finish all of her chores this night as they had big plans for the next evening. It was her father's sixtieth birthday and she and her mom were throwing him a surprise party. Even though it would be a bit chilly, they had planned a big cookout for him, inviting many of his friends.

Arielle had picked out a thousand-piece puzzle as a gift. She even selected the green-striped wrapping paper and added a huge, shiny, green bow. They loved working on puzzles together, spending many evenings side-by-side piecing them together when Grandma and Grandpa watched her while her mother worked.

Rebecca finished her chores near midnight. Exhausted, she fell into bed and turned off the light. Hitting the pillow a couple times until it fluffed just right, she got comfortable and was looking forward to a good night's sleep when the phone rang. For a few moments she didn't move a muscle, debating the pros and cons of answering it. Con—it was late, she was warm, comfortable, and ready to fall asleep; pro—it must be important to call this time of night. She sat up, thinking it had *better* be important as she answered the phone.

"Hello?" she said none-too enthusiastically while making a mental note to get *caller identity* installed on the line.

"Becca," the caller said between sniffles. She recognized her mother's voice.

"What is it, Mom? What's wrong?" Rebecca asked. She turned the light on next to the bed.

"It's your father. The ambulance. It just took him to the hospital." The message was pieced together through broken words.

"Why? What happened? Did he fall?"

"No, no. I think he had a heart attack, a cardiac arrest they called it. They said his heart stopped. I have to go down to the hospital." She could hear her mother sobbing. "Oh, Becca... it was terrible! They kept shocking and shocking him. His whole body jumped like a ragdoll every time they did it. I keep hearing that terrible noise over and over in my head. It won't go away."

"Oh, Mom! I'm so sorry. Did they get his heart started again?"

"They said they got it going, but it's very weak. He could have another arrest at any time."

"Wait there, Mom. I'll come and get you." Holding the phone to her ear, Rebecca tore the covers off and jumped out of bed as she started putting on her house robe and slippers.

"No, Becca. It's too late. You've got Arielle to worry about. I'm sure she's sound asleep. I don't want to disturb her. I'll get a taxi."

"No you won't. I'll get Arielle up and we'll be there in about fifteen minutes. Just hold on till I get there."

There was a pause. "Okay. Can you call Sue for me?"

"Sure, Mom. I'll take care of it."

Rebecca called her sister and arranged to meet her at the emergency room, then went to Arielle's room and tried to wake her. She was in a deep sleep and didn't seem to understand what her mother was telling her, but she let her mother dress her while she sat on the edge of the bed.

"Go lay down on the couch while I get ready," Rebecca told Arielle after she finished dressing her.

"Okay" she murmured, her eyes half-open.

In five minutes Rebecca was dressed and ready to go. She shook Arielle and tried to wake her again, but couldn't. She ended up carrying her out to the car and belted her in the rear seat.

Traffic was light this time of night and Rebecca made it to her mother's house in record time. As she pulled up in front, the sudden stop woke Arielle.

"Where are we, Mom?" she asked rubbing her eyes and yawning.

"We're at Grandpa and Grandma's house. We have to pick up your grandma and take her to the hospital. Grandpa's heart stopped and they took him there in an ambulance."

"Is he going to be okay?"

"I don't know yet, honey. Here's Grandma, we'll see if she knows any more."

Alice, came out to the car and got in the front passenger seat. Holding a tissue in one hand and her purse in the other, she wept quietly while her daughter drove to the hospital.

"Grandma, what's wrong with Grandpa?"

"He's very sick, Arielle. He's very sick," she repeated, dabbing her eyes with the tissue. "You must pray for your grandpa."

"Have you heard anything from the hospital yet?" Rebecca asked.

"No. Not yet. I called while I was waiting for you, but was put on terminal hold, *ignore* I think you call it. I finally hung up."

Ten minutes later they arrived at the hospital. After identifying themselves in the Emergency Room, they were directed to a visitor's room where Sue was sitting, waiting and watching for them.

"Have you heard anything yet?" Rebecca asked Sue.

"Nothing. They only asked if Mom was here yet."

"Where's Christina?"

"She's still asleep. I called a neighbor. She's staying with her until I get back."

"I wish you worked here," Alice said to Rebecca.

"Why is that?"

"Because you could find out what's going on and get your father the best doctors. We don't know who is working on him or how good he or she is."

"I'm sure he's being well taken care of, Mom. Emergency room doctors are usually very versed in heart attacks and cardiac arrests. They get a lot of practice with those kinds of emergencies."

"That's what I worry about the most, dear, they're just practicing."

Rebecca smiled at her mom and gave her hand a squeeze. Even in times like these, she still had a sense of humor. Within a few minutes a doctor came into the room holding a clipboard. He asked for Alice and pulled up a chair across from her. He spoke directly to her.

"I'm very sorry, Mrs. Colburn, but there was nothing we could do. Your husband passed away enroute to the hospital and even with repeated defibrillations, we weren't able to restart his heart when he arrived in the emergency room."

Alice was crying before the doctor finished, holding her tissue to her nose. Rebecca put her arm around her.

"I'm very sorry," he repeated. He waited a moment before getting up to leave, asking if he could do anything for them.

"I do need someone from the family to sign some papers. Take your time, when you get a chance."

The doctor left the room.

"I'll go take care of things," Sue whispered. She followed the doctor out, wiping her tears as she left.

Rebecca tried not to cry as she consoled her mother and Arielle, but the tears fell from all three of them. As she stroked her mother's hair, Rebecca recalled the prediction that Arielle had given her weeks before—someone they knew would die before the end of the year. The angels had told her.

She turned to Arielle. "You told me this was going to happen. You predicted it," she whispered. Rebecca pulled her in tightly to her.

"But I didn't know it was going to be Grandpa," she replied between sobs. "They didn't tell me."

"Can't you ask them to do something?" Rebecca asked, still whispering.

"Ask who?" Arielle replied, quizzically looking up at her mother.

Quietly Rebecca leaned over. "The angels," she again whispered.

"Mom, I can't," she whispered back. "They aren't here right now."

"Can't you call them?"

"I can try... but they may not come. I never know..."

"Well, can't you use one of your lights, like you did for the little boy? Bring Grandpa back?" Rebecca wasn't whispering anymore.

Arielle pulled back from her mother. "No, Mom, I can't use them unless I'm told to. It won't do any good. It doesn't work that way."

Rebecca broke down. She was crying. "Well, I'm telling you to. Save my father, your grandfather. Do it. Please." She covered her eyes with her hand.

Arielle hugged her mother around her neck and stayed there for several minutes.

Alice wiped her nose and stopped crying. "Becca, what in the world are you trying to get that child to do?"

Rebecca knew she had a lot of explaining to do. Between sobs she said, "Mom, I could tell you..., but you wouldn't believe me."

"Well, tell me anyway."

"Arielle has... angels... she says she talks to. Not all the time, but once in a while. I asked her if she could speak to them now and ask them to bring Dad back."

Alice scrunched up her face. "What? That's ridiculous. What's wrong with you?"

"Mom, I'm telling you..."

"You leave that child alone," Alice said shaking her finger at her daughter. She wiped her nose again. "Don't you think she's mourning her grandfather, too? It was his time to go. The Lord knows what he's doing, even if we don't. We can be sad and cry for our loss—and we will miss George a lot, but don't put this on your child or blame God. Pray for him, and hope he is with the Lord. He had a great life, a son and two beautiful daughters and granddaughters who loved him dearly; so don't be sad for him. Rejoice for the great life the Lord blessed him with."

Rebecca reached over and hugged her mother. "I know, Mom, but I'm going to miss him. He was my rock, my solace, and I could always depend on him." She turned to Arielle. "I'm sorry, honey."

"He was mine also," Alice said, "but remember, we aren't here forever. George loved all of you and wouldn't want you to anguish over him."

Both Rebecca, and Alice's attention was suddenly drawn to Arielle as they watched her cross the room and look toward the ceiling.

"Look, Mom," Rebecca whispered. "That's what I was telling you about. She's talking to her angels now."

Arielle nodded her head. Her face was beaming as she turned to her mother and grandmother. She was excited.

"Grandma! Mom! Grandpa is in heaven with God! The angels say not to cry for him or worry, he is very happy and doesn't hurt anymore; his headaches and the pain in his legs are gone."

Alice and Rebecca looked at each other.

"I told you," Rebecca finally said.

"How did she know that? I never told anyone about all the pain your father was in, and neither did he. He was on quite a bit of medication to combat those problems."

Arielle walked over to her grandmother and took her hand. "They also said to look in the closet for a brown steel lock box. The key is in his gray socks in his sock drawer. What you find in there will take care of your needs."

"What kind of things?" Alice asked.

"I don't know," Arielle said. "Just things. I thought you would know."

Alice stared inquisitively at Arielle for a moment, then at Rebecca.

"I told you." She said again. "She says she talks with angels," Rebecca said as she recalled the encounter with the priest, "and I'm beginning to believe her."

"I do, Grandma, I really do," Arielle said nodding her head.

"What's with the steel box?" Rebecca asked her mom. "What's in it?"

"I haven't the faintest idea. I've no clue what she is talking about. George kept many things secret from me. Well—not really secret, just things I didn't care about and he handled. We'll just have to look for it." After a brief moment she continued. "Wouldn't it be strange if we find the box in the closet and a key in his gray socks!"

"Don't be surprised if you do, Mom. She's done this before."

Rebecca reached over and placed her hand on her mother's arm. "We should go now."

"What are we going to do with George? I don't know who to call; he always took care of everything. I don't even know how much it's going to cost to bury him. I think he said he had a life insurance policy for the both of us, but I wouldn't have any idea where it would be or how much it will cover."

"Let's go home, Mom, and look around. Maybe we can find something. The hospital will take good care of him until we can make arrangements."

"It's three o'clock, Rebecca. You drop me off and take Arielle home. Both of you get some sleep. We can look around in the morning."

"Do you want us to stay with you tonight?"

"No, no. I'm fine. You go home."

"Do me one favor, Mom."

"What's that?"

"Don't mention any of Arielle's predictions or her talking to angels to Sue. I don't think she would understand and I don't want to explain it to her."

"All right, but I think you ought to tell her sometime."

"I'll try."

They met up with Sue at the registration and admissions office where Alice had to sign some paperwork. The sisters agreed to meet at their mom's the next day. Rebecca drove her mother home and then returned to her own house. Arielle was again sound asleep by the time they arrived. Rebecca carried her in and placed her in bed. She then called her hospital and told them about her father, requesting bereavement days off. After being approved, she flopped down on her bed without changing into her nightgown or turning out the lights. She was totally exhausted and out in moments.

CHAPTER 14

Secrets

Rebecca didn't wake up until noon the next day. At first she thought she'd had a bad dream that her father had died. She looked at the clock and soon realized she was still in her clothes, the room lights were still on and her bad dream was, in fact, reality. After two large cups of black coffee, she called her mother and told her she and Arielle would be over after they had something to eat. She then called Arielle's school to explain her absence.

When they arrived, Alice was busy washing dishes, baking chocolate-chip cookies and cleaning the kitchen. They all hugged each other and Alice returned to her chores. Eyeing her grandmother mischievously, Arielle grabbed a handful of warm cookies off the counter and quickly headed out of the kitchen, thinking she wasn't noticed.

"Hey, hey," Alice yelled. "Just where do you think you're going with my cookies, young lady?" Her grandmother smiled at her as she watched Arielle sheepishly take a huge bite out of one and retreat towards the living room.

"I'm going to watch television, Grandma," she yelled back with a mouthful.

Rebecca laughed. "Have you checked Dad's socks yet, Mom?"

"No, dear. I had several things I wanted to get done today and I've been busy with those. I got a late start as it is."

Maybe she is better off staying busy right now. But is she in denial? Grief can cause people to act strangely.

"Where's Sue? Have you heard from her yet?"

"She called. She had to take Christina to the doctor's office, then they're coming over." Alice pulled more cookies out of the oven. "I did call George's retirement board this morning," she said.

"What did you do that for?"

"Well, I had to notify them of his death."

"What did they say, anything important I need to know?"

"No, they said they would do the paperwork, but...," Alice hesitated, her voice broke, "they also told me his benefits would be reduced now. I have to send them a death certificate. I'll only be getting a little less than half of what we were receiving. Even with Social Security I don't know if it'll be enough." Her voice broke. She turned away from her daughter.

Rebecca went over to her mother and put her arm around her. "Don't worry about that now, Mom. You can always move in with us. We'll take care of each other."

Alice sat down at the kitchen table. "I just don't know what to do, Rebecca. I feel so exhausted and confused."

"Why don't you go lie down for awhile. You probably just need a little more rest. It was a long night. Did you get any sleep at all?"

"A couple hours."

"C'mon, let's go." Rebecca guided her mother upstairs to her room to rest. She slipped her shoes off and helped her into bed. "Where is Dad's sock drawer, Mom?"

Her mother pointed to an old oak bureau; cologne, a brush, and a picture of his two daughters and granddaughters neatly arranged on top of it. "That one, third drawer down."

Rebecca opened the drawer and pulled out three pairs of gray socks rolled together in pairs. "You get some sleep, I'll wake you in an hour."

She took the socks with her downstairs and unrolled them one at a time. A small silver key dropped to the floor from the final pair.

"I'm not going to ask you how you knew this was there," Rebecca said looking at her daughter and holding the key up for her to see. "We'll wait until Mom wakes up before we look for the steel box."

Arielle smiled.

CRSO

Two hours later Alice came downstairs. Arielle and Rebecca were watching a movie on television and eating a bowl of popcorn.

"I hope you don't mind us eating your snacks, Mom. Did the television wake you up?"

"No. No. I slept enough. Why didn't you wake me? You said an hour."

"You needed the sleep," she said with a mouthful, not even looking at her mother.

"I need to get things done more than I needed the sleep," Alice mumbled. She went to the kitchen to make some coffee.

Rebecca followed her mother. "I found the key in the gray socks."

"You did?" Alice seemed surprised. "Your daughter must be psychic or something. How does she know all this?"

"I told you, Mom. I'm going upstairs to look for that steel box. We need to find out if there's an insurance policy so we can give Dad a proper burial."

"Okay. Go ahead," she said as she waved Rebecca off. After the coffee was ready and she'd poured herself a cup, she went in the living room and sat down next to her granddaughter.

"Arielle, can I ask you a question?" she asked softly.

"Sure, Grandma."

"How do you know all these things about your grandfather?"

Arielle pushed the mute button on the television remote control and looked at her grandmother. "Angels tell me, Grandma. You probably don't believe me, cause I know Mom and all the others don't, but it's true."

Alice sipped her coffee and thought a minute. "I think I do believe you."

Arielle gave her grandmother a big hug around her neck.

"What was that for?" Alice asked.

"It's for believing me. You're the only one who does. Even our pastor doesn't believe me."

"You've told him?"

Arielle nodded. "Mom told him too." She looked up at her grandmother, "Can I tell you a secret?"

"Of course you can, dear."

"When we go to visit Dad, I talk with him also."

Alice scrunched her face, she didn't understand. "You talk with him like I'm talking to you?"

"Kind-a, but only if I hold his hand. He says he knows he has to stay there a while longer, but he knows he'll get better someday."

"Have you told your mother this?"

"Oh, no. Dad said not to tell her; it would upset her. It's our secret." After a moment she continued, "She wouldn't believe me anyway."

Rebecca came back down the stairs carrying a brown steel lockbox. Arielle looked at her with a big smile on her face.

"What are you two talking about?" Rebecca asked.

"Girl talk." Alice quickly changed the subject. "You found it?"

"Yep. What'd I do with that key, Arielle?"

"You put it in your pocket, Mom," she said as she turned the mute off.

Rebecca sat down at the dining room table and unlocked the box. On the bottom were three envelopes, one old and thick, yellowed with age, one larger manila, and one thinner, business envelope that looked almost new. She pulled them out.

"There's just these three envelopes, Mom."

"I've never seen them," Alice said as she came over and sat down next to Rebecca.

"Let's check out the large manila one first." Rebecca unfastened the metal clasp and pulled out official looking documents.

"Looks like the life insurance policies you told me about."

"Is it enough to pay for his funeral?"

"I'll say," Rebecca said as she folded over the top page and thumbed through the rest. "Twenty-five-thousand ought to be enough!"

"Oh, Lord, thank you!" Alice said as she folded her hands and looked toward heaven. "I was so worried I was going to have to sell the house, Becca."

"You should be all right now."

"What's in the other envelopes?"

"Let's see," Rebecca said as she tore the end off the newer business envelope. Inside was another sealed envelope, smaller, with her mother's name handwritten on the outside.

"It's addressed to you, Mom. Here, you open it."

Alice took the envelope, tore it open on the end, pulled out two folded sheets of paper, and started reading the letter out loud.

"My dear Alice, if you are reading this, I am probably not with you here on earth..."

She stopped reading aloud, but continued reading to herself. Rebecca watched her. A minute later, with hands shaking, tears streamed down Alice's face. She put the letter down, closing her eyes, crying silently. Rebecca pulled her mother to her, hugging her tightly.

"What is it, Mom? What'd it say?"

Rebecca went over and pulled several tissues from a box on the coffee table and gave them to her mother, who wiped her face and eyes.

"Your father was telling me how much he loved me and how much he enjoyed our life together."

Alice folded the letter and put it back in the envelope, holding it tightly to her breast. "George was such a good man."

After several minutes she blew her nose and turned to Rebecca. "What's in the last one?" she asked softly.

Rebecca opened the yellowed envelope. Stuffed tightly in it were several documents. She slowly unfolded them and gasped. Stock certificates, ten of them. Microsoft, Google, Ford; some certificates for a thousand shares, some for five hundred. Another life insurance policy for fifty thousand dollars was included in the small stack of papers.

"Mom, these stock certificates have to be worth a small fortune. They're all very old and probably date back to the company's start-up. I'm sure they've all split, maybe many times!"

She handed the insurance policy to her mother. "This alone will take care of you for a long while."

Her mother smiled as she read the policy. "He always said I'd be taken of if anything happened to him."

"I'd say he kept his word," Rebecca said.

Later, as Rebecca and Arielle were getting ready to leave, Alice hugged Arielle, cupped her hand to her ear and whispered, "It's our secret."

Arielle smiled and returned her grandmother's hug.

CRWD

George's funeral was held three days later. Many people in the community showed up to pay their respects and offer their support to Alice.

"Dad sure had a lot of friends," Rebecca whispered to her mother.

"Yes, he was loved by many. So many. He helped a lot of people you will never know about."

Later that day George was laid to rest at Mount Evens Cemetery near his home.

CRWD

Over the next several days, Rebecca kept busy and helped her mother in her spare moments. She took some vacation time in addition to several days of bereavement leave, and tried to keep herself active so she wouldn't be consumed with thoughts of her father.

To everyone but her daughter, Rebecca seemed completely absorbed with things to do. But Arielle knew her mother wasn't acting normal. She slept for long periods of time during the day, even after a full night of sleep. She didn't eat much and kept to herself more. She skipped making meals for her daughter. Whenever Arielle tried to have a conversation with her, it was cut short. Everything was *later*.

The next Sunday she took Arielle to church and dropped her off, but did not accompany her. She had never done that before. When her mother picked her up, Arielle knew she needed to talk with her.

"Mom, what's wrong with you lately? You're sleeping all the time and hardly eating. Now you won't even go to church with me."

"I'm just going through a rough time right now, honey. I'll be all right."

"Why won't you talk to God about it? He knows what you're going through. He'll help you if you ask Him to."

Rebecca looked over at Arielle. "You know, your grandfather was a really great person. I miss him terribly. He was always there for us when we needed him and it seemed he always had the right answers. Now I can't see him and talk with him and ask for advice. I miss him and so does your grandmother." She paused. "And... I never got to say goodbye or tell him how much I loved him. I guess I always thought he'd be around."

Arielle could see her mother trying to wipe silent tears from her face with her fingertips. "But your other Father is still with you. He misses your conversations with Him just as you miss them with Grandpa. He still has answers for you if you ask Him."

Rebecca pulled her car off the road and stopped. She pulled a tissue from her purse and blew her nose. She pulled another and wiped the tears from her face. Arielle was in the backseat; Rebecca turned around to face her. "Where do you get all this from?"

"I've told you a hundred times, Mom." Arielle looked out the window, "Someday you'll understand and believe me. I don't really expect you to now."

"Well, wherever you're getting it from..."

"He hasn't abandoned you, Mom. I know you feel like He has, but Grandpa says to have faith."

After several minutes and several deep breaths, Rebecca regained her composure and pulled the car back into traffic. She gazed at her daughter in the rearview mirror.

"You know, I think I do believe you."

CHAPTER 15

The Archbishop

Over the next two years Arielle continued to live pretty much a normal child's life, with the exception of the meetings she was asked to attend at the pastor's office. She always read and studied her Bible every chance she had. The pastor told her she could recite more verses than anyone he knew, probably even more than he could. But what really amazed him was the understanding and perception she possessed.

Rebecca was not surprised at Arielle's astuteness. She was proud that Arielle was well ahead of kids her own age, and had also taken on some advanced classes.

Every once in awhile, Rebecca would receive a request to bring her daughter in to the pastor's office for another interview. It seemed there was always one more minister, priest, deacon, or rabbi who had heard of Arielle and her messages from the angels. They each wanted to meet her and discuss different theological and biblical questions, or interrogate her.

At first, Rebecca tried to put an end to the meetings after some turned very heated, but Arielle convinced her they were supposed to take place and were needed. Besides, Rebecca realized Arielle always held her ground during the examinations with messages from her angels. She usually silenced any party who just wanted to argue faith or a different version of the Bible.

One evening Rebecca's phone rang as she was preparing for supper.

"Hello," Rebecca answered.

"Good Evening. Is this Mrs. Price?"

"Yes, it is."

"I hope I haven't interrupted anything. This is Father Don McMillan, and I'm calling on behalf of Archbishop Scanlon. Would you have a minute?"

"Yes, but Arielle isn't available at the moment, she's doing her homework."

"No, no, Mrs. Price. I wanted to speak with you."

"Oh, that's unusual. What can I do for you, Father?"

"The Archbishop has heard many things about your daughter, and her declarations of speaking to angels. He would like to meet with her and investigate the claims himself. It seems Father Joe is also a believer of her messages. He's been talking about her for years."

"I'll have to ask her, though she's never turned down a request. Where and when would he like to meet if she were to agree?"

"If you would be available this Saturday, I'll send a car for both of you, around one o'clock. It'll bring you to the Archbishop's residence. A light lunch will be served."

"Can you hold a moment?"

"Certainly."

Rebecca went to Arielle's room and asked about the appointment, to which she heartily agreed."

"That will be fine, Father."

"Very well, one o'clock on Saturday it is."

CR80

Saturday morning, Rebecca took Arielle shopping for a new outfit for her meeting with the Archbishop. After two hours of shopping, they settled on a white cotton dress trimmed with light pink and yellow flowers.

"Mom, this really isn't necessary," Arielle stated, looking at her mother out of the corner of her eye.

"I know, dear, but being invited to the Archbishop's residence is a real privilege. I just want you to look nice. Besides, you haven't had a new dress in a long time."

"It may be a privilege, but he's going to be very upset by the time we leave. I don't think he'll be looking at my dress or care what I am wearing."

"That may be, but in any case, I want you to feel good about yourself when you go to see him. He's an important man in the religious community, even our pastor respects him, so be on your best behavior."

"Oh, Mom, don't be so enamored with status. Remember, he's supposed to be a servant of God for us, we're not his."

⌘

At one o'clock sharp, a black limousine pulled up to the house. The driver, a pleasant looking man about thirty-five years old, came to the door and introduced himself as Ralph. He was impeccably dressed in a black suit and tie with a white shirt.

Rebecca called Arielle, who was wearing her new dress, and they were escorted out to the limo. The driver opened the door for them, waited as they climbed in and closed the door.

"I've never been in a limousine before, Arielle. This is really nice."

"Yes, Mom."

The limo had white leather seats with plush black carpeting and gold trim throughout. Two seats spread across the vehicle and faced each other. A privacy window separated them from the driver and a stocked bar with ice and glasses sat off to the side.

Ralph lowered the dividing window as he started the drive to the Archbishop's house. "If there is anything I can do for you, please let me know. There's a button right next to the door lock that will buzz me. If you would like something to drink, there are soft drinks in the bar. Help yourself."

"Thank you, we're fine," Rebecca stated. The window rolled back up.

Twenty minutes later they were at the Archbishop's residence. A high, spiked, iron fence surrounded the estate and a gate opened as the limo approached. Arielle turned and watched the large gate swing closed after their car passed through. Ralph drove up to the building's entrance and stopped at the front doors. He came around, opened their door and escorted them into the residence, a three-story brick Victorian building with large white-trimmed windows and doors.

As they entered, the dark, solid walnut paneled walls trimmed with wainscoting awed Rebecca. Marble floors topped with oriental rugs ran down the hallway. Crystal chandeliers hung suspended from a two-story cathedral ceiling in the foyer. Paintings and photographs of men dressed in religious attire hung on the walls. She was struck with how quiet it seemed in the massive building. She smiled, wanting to yell out, "Is anyone home?"

Footsteps echoed from somewhere down a hallway. A priest appeared, smiling as he welcomed the two.

"Good afternoon. Welcome to Archbishop Scanlon's residence." He shook Rebecca's hand and then turned to Arielle. "I'm Father McMillan, I spoke with your mother earlier this week."

"Hello," Arielle replied.

"This way, please," he said, leading them down a dimly lit hallway.

Moments later he opened one of two large, glass-paned, double doors and motioned for them to enter. The room appeared cavernous, with vast shelves of books that loomed over them.

"Your Eminence, Miss Arielle and her mother, Mrs. Rebecca Price," Father McMillan announced as they walked through the massive doorway. The fresh scent of lemon welcomed Rebecca. Probably furniture polish, she thought.

An enormous picture of the Last Supper hung on the wall behind a massive mahogany desk, situated towards the center of the room. A tall, muscular man with bright green eyes and graying hair rose from the desk and greeted them with a broad smile. He wore a black shirt with a white collar and black pants.

"Please, please have a seat," Archbishop Scanlon said as he motioned to the left side of the room where a large brown leather couch and two overstuffed matching chairs sat. They settled together on the couch. On a glass coffee table in front of the couch were plates of finger sandwiches, snack cakes, and chips. A variety of canned sodas and Styrofoam cups were grouped next to an ice bucket with crushed ice. He plopped down in another chair across from the table.

"May I offer you something to eat and drink?" asked the Archbishop.

Rebecca marveled at the magnificence of the office, or was it extravagance? The archbishop's desk was huge. Every item on it was gold or brass; pens, penholders, lights, nameplate. The carpeting was so plush she felt as if she could drown in it. The long drapes covering the tall windows appeared to be a fine silk. Everything in its place, not a speck of dust on anything, she thought.

"Yes, that would be nice," Rebecca said.

After a quick prayer, the three selected finger sandwiches and chips. Rebecca nibbled daintily while Arielle took large bites of her sandwich.

The room felt so large and so quiet to Rebecca, she felt as if she were in church and wasn't supposed to make a sound. Even the slight noise of chewing her sandwich seemed out of place. She chewed slower trying to be quieter.

⟡

Arielle, it seemed, could care less. She finished one sandwich and politely snatched up another, finishing both before her mother or the archbishop were done with their first. Eyeing the snack cakes, she was eager to finish.

After they ate, the archbishop turned to Arielle. "Now, young lady, I've heard some pretty remarkable things about you from Father Joe and others." He held up a cassette tape. "I have listened to this—many times. I'm intrigued. It seems you may have some very interesting gifts. Can you tell me about them?"

"What would you like to know, Sir?"

"Well, I've heard that you say you can talk with angels. Is that true?"

"Yes. I guess you heard me on the tape."

"Yes, I did. When do you do this?"

"They come to me when they need to. Sometimes they just sing their songs and I listen. Sometimes we talk."

"How often does this occur?"

"It varies. Sometimes everyday and then maybe I won't see them for a couple of weeks."

"Do they talk to you like we are talking? Do you hear them like you hear me?"

"Yes and no." Arielle smiled. "I hear them just as I hear you, but they hear me whether I speak or not. It does seem no one else can hear them—at least no one I know of."

"So when you talk to them, is it like you pray to them?"

"Oh no. When I pray, I pray to God. I don't hear Him answer me. I know He's listening to me, but when I talk with the angels they hear me and I hear them."

"You always say 'them.' Is it always more than one that you converse with?"

"Sometimes there is one, more often there are several."

The archbishop poured himself another soft drink, then sat back in his chair.

"Arielle, how do you know they're angels?"

Arielle smiled. "They told me. What else would they be?"

He hesitated a few seconds, then ignored her question. "Do you see them clearly or are they just cloudy, hazy type visions?"

"I see them clearly, just like I see you."

"What do they look like?"

"Kind of like anyone you would meet on the street, except…" She stopped for a moment, thinking. "They kinda' look wise and gentle. They have a soft glow to them."

"Why are you the only one who can see them? Why do you think no one else can?"

"I don't know." She smiled, hunching her shoulders. "'Cause they don't want anyone to? I asked them once if Mom could see them and talk to them. They told me that someday that would happen and then she would understand. That's all they would tell me."

The Archbishop stroked his chin, turning to Rebecca. "Interesting. I hope you'll let me know if and when this ever happens."

"I know everything she predicts eventually comes true, but for this one, I'm not holding my breath," she responded.

He turned back to Arielle. "You supposedly have little lights in your right hand."

"Yes."

"May I see it?" he asked.

Arielle opened her right hand and showed him. "I don't think you'll see anything," she said.

Rebecca broke out in a broad grin. The archbishop looked over at her with raised eyebrows, as if to ask a question.

"I understand you can see the lights, too, Mrs. Price. Is that correct?"

"Yes, I do."

"Do you see them now?"

Arielle held her hand up so her mother could see.

"Yes, they're there."

He turned his attention back to Arielle. Taking a sip of his soft drink he asked, "Arielle, can you call upon the angels right now to speak to you?"

"I don't have to, Sir."

"Why not?"

"They're already here."

The Archbishop sat poker-faced, his expression never changing from one question to the next. "They are? Where?"

She didn't think he believed her. "They're in back of you." She turned around and scanned the room. "There's also one in back of me."

"They don't mind you telling me they're here?"

"No. Most people don't believe me anyway."

"What are they telling you?"

"Jacob said to tell you that you should have some faith; he knows what you are thinking, but they *are* indeed angels." She hesitated a moment. "He says things will come to pass that you will begin to believe." She then squinted her eyes. "What?" she whispered.

"What is it?" asked Rebecca.

"He called me his little sister. Then he laughed and said someday I would understand."

"You don't know what he means?" the archbishop questioned.

"No. But they tell me a lot of things I don't understand."

"Did he tell you anything else?"

"He also said you should cancel your meeting tonight with the bishops and go see Father Martin in the hospital. He needs you more than the others."

"He did, huh?" asked the archbishop. "He knows about my meeting and Father Martin?"

"Sounds like it," Arielle said with a soft giggle. "Jacob has a sense of humor."

"They have names? Who is this Jacob?"

"I know some of their names, not all. Jacob is my friend. He talks to me a lot."

"What did he tell you about my meeting tonight?"

"I don't know anything about your meeting. I just passed on the information as I heard it."

"So, did they tell you to tell me anything else?"

Arielle sat for a couple minutes just looking up above the Archbishop. She nodded her head in the affirmative and then looked back at him.

"You aren't going to like it," she said, nervously rubbing her hands on her dress over her legs.

"Tell me anyway," he said with a cock-eyed smile. He leaned back and crossed his legs.

Arielle looked over at her mother, who nodded her approval to her. "He said Jesus wants his apostles to serve his people, not be their masters. Many of the arbitrary rules that have been made by the church will not do anything to bring His children to Him. He said many of His shepherds are not collecting their stray sheep, but are milking them for their own benefit."

Arielle spoke without arrogance or cynicism. She stopped for a few seconds. "Jacob says for you to be more like a shepherd who loves and guards his flock and less like the wolf that cares only for what the flock provides him."

The archbishop's face turned a soft red; he sat up in his seat and uncrossed his legs. His poker-face fell.

Leaning forward, his voice almost a growl, he said, "There's no way that angels told you to tell me that!"

"But he did," Arielle replied.

His voice rose. "You tell your invisible friends the church is the church. It is the rock of Peter. I carry on the traditions and rules that have been handed down from Jesus Christ, Himself! That is what we are supposed to do. That is what I am directed to do. That is what I do and I won't be told differently!" He made the sign of the cross.

He looked at Rebecca and then back to Arielle. "You must have misunderstood him, or you're speaking to demons! That can be the only answer that makes any sense."

Arielle just sat and looked at the archbishop without saying a word.

"Well?" he asked.

Arielle looked over at her mother with a quizzical glance. She nodded approval for her to continue.

"I told you that you weren't going to like what they said. Mother told me to be respectful to you, Sir. What do you want me to say? Do you want me to lie and deny the angels' existence? I can't deny them anymore than I can deny the existence of God. You've asked what they said; I told you. I haven't misquoted them, and they aren't demons."

"How do you know, young lady? You're what, twelve years old? Would you know a demon if you met one?"

Arielle sat silent for a moment as if listening for instructions.

"Jacob was laughing. He answers you by asking if you would know an angel if you met one?" Arielle got out of her chair and walked over to the archbishop. She took his large, strong hand into her small, soft one.

"Please close your eyes for a minute," she said softly.

He reluctantly closed his eyes after a brief moment as if fearful of what would happen next. Arielle then strode over to his desk, opened the top drawer and pulled out a large, long-stemmed red rose. She went back to the archbishop and placed the flower under his nose.

"Can you identify what I have?"

"It smells nice. A flower?" he asked in a monotone.

"Yes—but what kind?"

"That, I can't say. What is it?"

"Open your eyes, please," she said.

Arielle placed the rose in the archbishop's hands. "They said you need to stop and smell the flowers and appreciate what God has given you. Stop treating your flock as an accumulation of flowers in a garden that brings you pleasure, but appreciate each individual rose and the pleasure it can give others."

"Where did the rose come from?" he asked, his eyes squinting, the furrows on his forehead deepening. "I didn't see you bring it in with you. I certainly didn't have any in here."

"I didn't bring it with me. I was told to retrieve it from in your desk. That is where it came from." She hesitated, looking deep into the archbishop's eyes. "Every good or beautiful thing in this world can also be used for ugliness or evil. When I held the rose under your nose, you smelled something good, something pleasant and beautiful. But if I had asked you to grasp it tightly first, the thorns would have pierced your skin and caused pain; you would have missed the beauty of the flower." She walked back to her seat.

The archbishop sat still at first, nodding his head. His voice softened and he sounded a little less confrontational when he continued. "I've also heard you've performed miracles, Arielle, even bringing the dead back to life. I don't believe these stories myself, but what have you to say about those rumors? Have you performed miracles?"

Arielle smiled. "Miracles happen everyday, Archbishop, but they don't usually take place with hundreds of onlookers present who can say, 'Yes, I witnessed that!', like Moses parting the sea. They occur in ordinary, natural ways, and most people don't recognize or believe they have been gifted. Maybe you would call the rose a miracle; does it really matter? Isn't the message, what God is trying to tell you, more important?"

Arielle continued after a moment of silence. "To directly answer your question, no, I don't perform miracles. Only God can do that. If an event happens that you may perceive as a miracle, it may be through me but not by me."

"So you don't deny, how should I say, being the instrument of a miracle?"

"I am not denying anything, but at the same time I won't confirm anything. It is up to you to pray for guidance and determine what you believe. Open your eyes and heart and see past the commonplace. Become a true instrument of our Lord. Only then will you become a catalyst for what the Lord intended you for."

"Arielle, the world abounds with false prophets and preachers who claim to heal the sick, cure cancer, and make the lame walk again. How do I separate you from them?"

"Why separate me? I don't claim to be a prophet, a preacher or a priest. I'm an instrument of God, just as you are, just as any mortal can be if that is what the Lord wants, and you are open to it."

"So the Lord wants you to be his instrument?"

"Sometimes he uses me. The angels tell me what I need to know and do. I don't feel as though I am anyone special."

"You don't? You don't think talking to angels is special?"

"No. The ones who are helped are the special ones. They will have much to do in the future and sometimes they will need help. I am told you are also chosen, but you don't know it yet. You will also need help someday."

"Chosen?"

"Yes. Do you think this meeting is coincidental? I know you think that it was your idea to have this meeting today, but that couldn't be further from the truth. Do you think it's chance that I knew about your meeting tonight?"

"I don't know what to think right now."

"You have much to do in the future, Archbishop, but you must prepare yourself for it. It will be a very hard journey and you will be tested many times, but there will always be help available if you ask for it."

He was silent for several minutes. He rose from the chair and walked over to his desk, sat down and shuffled some papers. He opened his top drawer, looked in and closed it. He came back and sat in the other chair.

"Arielle, I don't know whether to believe you or not. I hadn't really thought anything about our meeting. Oh, I thought it would be interesting to talk with you, but you have far exceeded any expectations I had. What are they saying will be expected of me in the future that I don't already know?"

"As I told you, you must prepare yourself first. If you do, I was told you would be made a Cardinal within four years. It will be your work to help reform the church and clergy, with the help of other Cardinals you will meet at the Vatican."

"Reform? At the Vatican? In what way?" He scratched his head. "This is too much."

"The church maintains its grip over its flock mostly by fear—fear of eternal damnation. It teaches if you don't follow this rule or obey that decree, or if you do things you're not supposed to, and you know what I'm talking about, you will go to hell for eternity if you die with those sins on your soul—no second chances. You excommunicate those who obtain a divorce or marriage outside of the church or don't come to church on special days. Does that do service to God? Is that gathering His flock? Do you really think He wants you to throw them out with the bathwater, or to guide and inspire them to reform their behavior? The church doesn't consistently enforce the notion that God loves them more than anything and wants to help them. He wants them to come to Him with their problems, their sorrows, and their joys. He doesn't push them away—only you do that. Can His church thrive in the future with this negative mixed message? Why do you have to scare people into coming to God? It doesn't have to be that way and it's time to change it."

"That's it?"

"No. Look at all the huge churches and the televangelists telling everyone how great they are. Are they meeting the needs of their congregations? How many of them cover up issues within their churches, cover up financials, and cover up morality shortfalls of their own? How many children have been hurt, been separated from ever knowing God because of these deceitful people within the churches? Is it the children's fault that they grow up hating religion or anyone connected to it?"

"Why doesn't He just send an angel to the Pope and tell him to change the church? Wouldn't that be the easiest way?"

"I don't pretend to know His ways, but I know things aren't always as they seem either. If He chooses to do it this way, there's a reason, a plan, but maybe it is not for us to know. I do know it is time for all preachers, rabbis, priests, pastors, bishops—even archbishops and cardinals, to start serving the people as the apostles did, instead of being their spiritual masters."

"You certainly don't speak like a twelve-year-old, Arielle. Where did you learn all this?"

Arielle shook her head. "You still don't understand what I've been telling you. I didn't *learn* or *know* anything I have passed on to you. I am simply revealing to you what the angels have told me to tell you, and they are just doing God's will."

"I have always thought I *was* doing His will."

"Do you think He wants His servants living in mansions and riding in luxury limousines while His children are starving in parts of the world, living in hurt and misery—even here where you live?

Are you not a priest to all His children? They're craving leadership, someone who will stand up to corrupt governments that want nothing but power and money.

Many people live under an illusion of freedom. They believe they are free because they can travel anywhere they want, or buy things that please them. But they live under an economic slavery. How free is a person who must give a part of their income to the federal government, a part to the state government, a part to the county government, then a part to the city government. On top of that, most churches demand a tithe, another percentage to belong to their church, all of this out of fear? They worry constantly of going to jail as mortals for not paying taxes, and going to hell in the afterlife for not giving enough to their church. Which is the greater evil? Religion cannot thrive under these requirements."

The archbishop shook his head. "I can't take on all you're giving me. You're asking me to give up what I have earned, which rightfully belong to the churches and me, and take on the Vatican and the governments? How can I do this? It's more than one man can possibly undertake."

Arielle again went over to him and held his hand in hers. "He will help you if you ask. He will give you the knowledge and the strength to accomplish what He asks, and more." She looked over at her mother. "It's time to go, Mom."

The archbishop rose from the chair and gave Arielle a hug. "I wish you the best. I still don't know whether you actually speak with angels, but you've given me much to think about. Go with God. I'll walk you to the door."

After formal goodbyes, Arielle and Rebecca were escorted back to the limousine and driven home.

CHAPTER 16

The Schoolyard

The bell rang signaling afternoon recess for the rambunctious sixth-graders. Spring had arrived early and it was hard to keep their attention. The warmth of the spring sun called to the students like a mother goose to her goslings to come outside and play.

Arielle and her friends had established a routine on many afternoons. They gathered on the playground bleachers to talk and discuss different family problems, the latest trends, and other schoolgirl gossip. It had started with just a couple of girls who were having troubles at home or with boyfriends, plus situations they didn't know how to deal with and weren't comfortable talking to adults about. Arielle had become their confidante and helped them through some difficult times with her sage advice. Nothing was too difficult, or too fun, to discuss.

On this day, eight girls gathered on the playground bleachers. Since no one was having any particular problems at home or school requiring discussion, the conversation turned to church—who went and who didn't, and what church they went to.

Of the girls present, one was a Catholic, one Presbyterian, one Jew, one Baptist, one Episcopalian, one nondenominational, and two did not belong to any church.

"My dad says that Catholics worship statues and that is against the word of God, it's idol worship," Annie said. "Statues aren't allowed in our synagogues."

"No, we don't," replied Mary, trying to defend her faith.

"No, Annie, that's not true," Arielle said with authority. "Catholics pray to whom the statue represents, like a middle man with God. If it's a statue of Mary, that is who they are praying to, if it's Joseph, one of the saints, or Jesus, that's who they are praying to, not the image itself. It's not really true idol worship unless you believe who or what you are praying to is a god or a deity."

"My parents lied to me?"

"No, I'm sure your parents didn't lie to you or try to give you bad information; they usually just don't understand because they haven't educated themselves about other religions. Most people don't. They're raised with one type of religious instruction and stay with that the rest of their lives. Ignorance and rumors are the primary causes of many people to have bad feelings for another's faith, and to have started many wars."

Arielle stopped and held up one finger. After she had everyone's attention she stated, "I want all of you to understand, there is only one God, and we all pray to Him. No matter what your faith, we all have the same God. The different faiths or religions may have differing practices on how to worship or pray to God, but there is only One, and we are all His children."

Katie was confused. "You mean we pray to the same God as the Jews?" She was a Presbyterian.

"Absolutely. The Jews have always been the chosen people and protected by God, but their God is the same God you pray to every day."

"My mom says Jews aren't Christians, that they don't believe in God," Jamie told Arielle.

"Well, she has it partially right," Arielle smiled. "Jews don't believe that Jesus is the Son of God. But they believe He was a great prophet. They do believe in God, the same God you believe in."

"So what is a Christian?" asked Jessica. She had never been to church like the others. There were a few giggles.

"Does anyone have the answer to that?" Arielle asked.

"It means you believe in Jesus Christ," Jamie answered.

"I've heard of Him," Jessica said, "but I don't know anything about Him."

"Don't be embarrassed, Jessica," Arielle said, "it's not your fault. We'll help teach you. You can also learn a lot yourself by reading the New Testament in the Bible."

"It means you follow the teachings of Christ and try to be like Him," Katie said resolutely.

"All of that and more," Arielle said. "It also means you believe in His love for man, that He is the Son of God, He was resurrected after dying and that He died for our sins."

"Girls," a raspy voice interrupted their discussion. They all turned to see Mrs. Dunnell, one of the sixth-grade teachers standing next to them with her hands on her bony hips. "What's going on here?" She peered down on the girls through black, horn-rimmed glasses that had slid down on her long nose, giving her the appearance of a cartoon stork.

Mrs. Dunnell taught algebra. She was a frumpy, middle-aged woman who always wore the same long, brown skirt with a colorless shirt, brown shoes, and knee-high brown hose, which sagged around her ankles. She wore her hair strangled high up in a tight bun, but usually missed many hairs, which stuck out like she had just inserted her finger in a light socket. Her permanent scowl emphasized the bleak mood she was routinely in.

"We're just talking, Mrs. Dunnell," Mary stammered as she started moving back away from the group.

"About what," she demanded.

"God," Mary said.

"Yeah, Arielle is telling us about Jesus and Christians," said Denise. "She knows more than my parents do."

"Oh, is that right?" Mrs. Dunnell cackled. She focused on Arielle with steely eyes, "Well, Miss Arielle, what makes you an authority on religion? Do you have a special landline to the Almighty?"

"Kind-a," replied Arielle as she lowered her head. She wasn't about to tell her teachers she talked to angels, least of all Mrs. Dunnell.

"And just what are you filling their heads with?"

"I'm just telling them that God loves each of them and they are all special in His eyes. We're talking about everyone's different beliefs and how they tend to separate all of us instead of bringing everyone together."

"Well, Miss Religious-Know-It-All, this is a public school, and religion is not allowed to be discussed here. It's against the law and against the school's rules. Stop it right now and all of you—on your way." She waved her arms to herd them away from the bleachers. "I have to report this to the principal."

"Are we in trouble?" Mary asked, worry highlighting her wide brown eyes.

Several of the girls scrambled to their feet; they didn't want to cross this teacher. Arielle didn't want any trouble either, but she didn't want to end their discussion when she was just starting to get through to her friends.

"No. Wait," Arielle said to the girls. She turned to the teacher. "Mrs. Dunnell, can't we talk among ourselves about God on our recess? We aren't bothering anyone. We aren't making anyone listen to us."

"I told you. This is a public school and it's against the rules. We can't have God, Jesus, Allah, or any religion discussed here or in the classrooms. Now, on your way," she demanded. "Everyone!"

Arielle was about to argue her point, but the bell rang indicating it was time to go back to class anyway. She decided to discuss it with her mother later.

CRSO

That afternoon, Arielle decided to walk home from school instead of taking the bus. As she left school, Jessica, one of the girls who had never attended church, caught up with her and asked if she could walk with her. Arielle eagerly agreed.

"Did you get into trouble this afternoon, Arielle?"

"No, but I'm sure we'll hear something about it. Maybe tomorrow."

"The old bat. She reminds me of a crow."

Arielle giggled. "You shouldn't say that."

"I know. But it's true." She hesitated. "Can I ask you something?"

"Sure. What?"

"I heard Peter say on the bus one morning that you talk to angels. Do you really?" Jessica asked as they waited for traffic to stop so they could cross the intersection.

Arielle thought for a moment about how she should reply. She knew she couldn't lie. "Yes, I do," she said.

"Well, I told my mother what Peter said, and she said you were crazy, that no one can talk to angels 'cause they don't exist."

Arielle's eyes grew large and she broke out in a large grin. "Oh, they do exist, Jessica. Just because you can't see something, doesn't mean it doesn't exist. You can't see electricity, but you know it's there. Look at the air," she said waving her arm with a flourish, "you can't see it, but you know it's there. And if you wave your arm hard enough, you can feel it. Just like the air, if you pray, you'll also feel God and know Him."

"Yeah, but Mom says..."

"Jessica, don't let others pollute your mind and soul. You study the Bible and think for yourself. God exists and He loves you. And angels exist. I know that for a fact. I wouldn't lie to you."

Jessica was silent for several minutes as they walked along the sidewalk.

"You still don't believe me, do you?" Arielle asked.

"It's hard, Arielle. Mom says one thing, you say another and my aunt tells me it's wrong to question the existence of God. She says it's blasphemy; I should have faith. It's so confusing. I don't know who to believe."

"First of all, your aunt shouldn't tell you that. God gave us free will, the capacity and the intelligence to examine and question everything. If he didn't want us to question His existence, wouldn't He just make us so we all knew He existed? Wouldn't He show Himself to all, so there would be no doubt? He wants us to study His word, search for the answers, and come to Him with an open heart and understanding. Use what He gave you," Arielle said pointing to Jessica's head. "What good would it be for you or anyone else to have blind faith? Faith without understanding and love is next to no faith at all."

Jessica tilted her head, her lips tightly pursed. "It's just..."

"I know. It's like I said this afternoon, your mom isn't lying to you, she was just telling you what she believes. But she doesn't know the truth; maybe she was never taught. Believe me, God knows and understands your doubts; after all, He created us. He's with you and in you."

Arielle stopped and paused for a moment. "Jessica, I was just told I could share a very big secret with you."

Jessica stopped and looked around. "What? There's no one here."

"I was told by an angel."

"An angel just spoke to you?"

"Yes, but you have to promise never to tell anyone. It will show you there *are* things in the spiritual world you can't see that actually do exist. It's a very rare gift few receive. When you pray to God, be sure to thank Him for it."

Jessica was excited. "Okay. I promise."

Arielle held out her hand and concentrated. Suddenly, the orbs appeared and glowed with a bright golden hue in the palm of her hand. For several moments Jessica's face lit up as they mesmerized her with their dazzling dance. Then, they gradually disappeared.

"*What were they*, Arielle?" Her eyes widening, her grin spread from ear to ear.

"I can't tell you what they are, but the angels tell me what to do with them. Someday you may find out, but you must always keep this a secret until the time is right."

"When is that?"

"I'm sure you'll know," she replied.

"I promise, Arielle. That was awesome!"

CRSO

For the rest of the afternoon Arielle thought about Mrs. Dunnell's orders. She was confused. Why would the teacher stop her group from talking about God on the playground? Were there actually people who didn't want her to talk about God, or to Him? Why? As soon as she arrived home, she went to her mother.

"Mom, can I ask you something?"

"Of course, honey, what is it?"

"I was talking about God and different religions this afternoon on the playground with some of my friends. We were by ourselves on the bleachers and weren't bothering anyone when one of the sixth-grade teachers, Mrs. Dunnell, came over and told us to stop talking about God. She was really rude."

"What? Why did she tell you to stop?"

"She said it was a public school and we weren't allowed to discuss religion or God on school property; it was against the rules. That can't be. She has to be wrong."

"That sounds ridiculous. I'll speak to the school principal tomorrow. Don't worry, honey, you didn't do anything wrong. I'll get it straightened out."

"Thanks, Mom. They won't listen to me, I'm just a kid."

Rebecca laughed. She knew Arielle was right. She thought back to when she herself was eleven years old and she witnessed a neighbor pocket an item in a local department store. When she told her mom and dad, they ignored her accusations. She always felt it was because of her age and if she had been older, they would have believed her.

CRStO

The next day, while on her lunch break, Rebecca called the school.

"This is Rebecca Price, Arielle Price's mother, may I please speak to the principal, Mrs. Holden?"

"I'll see if she is available." After a moment, Mrs. Holden answered.

"Yes, Mrs. Price. Thanks for calling. I had intentions of calling you today regarding your daughter. I think I know what you're calling about."

"Yes, I'm sure you do. Have you been able to resolve the situation yet?" Rebecca asked.

"Resolve?"

"Yes, I believe it was Mrs. Dunnell. Have you spoken to her and straightened this problem out?"

"Mrs. Price, I'm afraid there may be a misunderstanding here. I see nothing to straighten her out on. According to our policies, she was correct in admonishing the girls and stopping the discussion."

"Stopping the discussion? A few girls on recess talking about religion on the playground? Does that represent a threat to someone? The last time I checked, I was living in the United States; this isn't China or the old Soviet Union. Is the government going to fall if you don't stop this chat? What about their rights of free speech and assembly?"

"Mrs. Price, as she told the girls, this is a public school and according to policy, there shall be no discussions of religion or God on this property. That is our rule."

"Is that the school policy or your policy, Mrs. Holden?"

"That is the school policy."

"May I have a copy of it? I'd like my lawyer to take a look at it."

"Well, ah, it's not actually written anywhere—but it's always been the school's policy."

"Mrs. Holden, you have a whole binder containing hundreds of school policies in writing, but you say this one isn't. How can you enforce a policy that doesn't really exist? How is anyone supposed to know the policy if it isn't in your manual?"

"Mrs. Price, why don't you consider placing your child in a private, religious school. I know of several very good ones. I'm sure Arielle would be much happier in that atmosphere and she can discuss religion all she wants there."

"Why, that's very nice of you to offer to place Arielle in a private school. Which one do you think she should go to? I'm sure they'll want you to pay the tuition up front."

"No, no, Mrs. Price. I meant *you* should place her there. You would have to pay her tuition."

"Why should I have to pay for it? You're the one who wants her to change schools."

"I'm sorry, but we can't use public funds for a private school."

"You know, I would send her to a private school if you would pay for it. But, since I'm required to pay for her schooling here, why should I have to pay twice? If you and the teacher's unions didn't protest against school vouchers, Arielle could go to a private school and we would all be happy, wouldn't we?"

"If we did that for Arielle, Mrs. Price, we'd have to do it for everyone and the public school system would lose too much money. We'd have to cut back on everything, including the teacher's salaries. Then we wouldn't be able to attract the best teachers."

"What ever happened to 'what's best for the children'?"

"I have to go now, Mrs. Price. If you wish to discuss this issue further, you can attend the school board meeting tonight at six o'clock and speak to them."

Rebecca was furious, but she didn't want her emotions to get the best of her. And she surely didn't want the principal to know. "You can depend on my presence. Thank you."

CHAPTER 17

The School Board

Rebecca and Arielle were at the school board meeting twenty minutes before it started. Rebecca added her name to a list of those who wanted to address the board during the public forum. Hers was the second name on the sheet, and she listed the topic as *Free Speech*. They were each allowed two minutes to make their point. The boardroom was filled to capacity, with standing room only as the meeting was about to begin. The first person to address the board took only a minute and was finished. Rebecca was then called to the podium.

"Good evening, ladies and gentleman of the board, my name is Rebecca Price. I am here with my daughter Arielle, who is in sixth grade. She and some of her friends were on the playground during recess yesterday at Highland Elementary. They were discussing religion among themselves when a teacher came up and told them they were not allowed to discuss religion or God on public school grounds. The teacher broke the group up and told them to go on their way. I personally find this abhorrent. I had a conversation about this today with the principal, Mrs. Holden, and she sided with the teacher. She even went as far as suggesting I send my daughter to a private school. I was told it was school policy that God or religious matters may not be discussed at the school. I asked for a written copy of the policy and was educated to the fact that there is nothing in writing. I would like the school board to clarify this policy to the principal, the teacher and myself.

First of all, I don't believe this phantom policy exists, as the principal cannot produce a written copy, and second, if it does, I don't believe it would override my daughter's first amendment right of free speech and assembly. Lastly, I believe policy-making is the board's duty; have you a policy, or don't you?"

The seven members of the school board looked at each other, confusion etched on a few of their faces. One of the members opened a thick binder and started thumbing through the pages. The board president, Mr. Jeffries, covered his microphone and spoke to the members on each side of him.

"I'm sorry, Mrs. Price, if you'll give me a moment, I'm trying to obtain a clarification of the policy myself."

After discussions among themselves, the president addressed those in the room.

"May I have everyone's attention. We are going to go into executive session to obtain legal advice from our lawyer. I would ask that everybody please clear the room. We will notify you when you may return."

Every person filed out of the room into the corridors. The Boardroom doors were locked and the windows that opened into the room from the hallway were covered. Several people came over to Rebecca, introduced themselves and told her they supported her daughter's free speech. They were also curious to know what the board would have to say and how they would rule.

A half-hour later the doors were again opened and everyone invited back in. Rebecca was recalled to the podium and the school board president addressed her.

"Mrs. Price, frankly, I'm embarrassed that we don't have a written policy in force. The other members of the board have informed me that an unwritten policy has indeed been in place for many years. We've had extensive discussions on this very topic in which the board seems to be split as to whether the policy should stand. Our attorney has produced a written policy from another school's board that was approved years before, and it appears to mirror the unwritten policy at your daughter's school. To make it official we are going to take a public vote on it."

The board's lawyer then read the policy into the record. He then proceeded to further caution the board that numerous court cases have set a precedent on the policy they were about to vote on, and they should disregard the other school's written policy. He told them they should treat the religious matter as a free-speech issue as long as the children aren't causing a disruption in the school.

Without further discussion, the president then called for a motion and a vote. A motion was made and seconded to accept the other school's policy as their district-wide policy. The board voted four to three, with a majority voting for the written policy. There were noticeable groans and whispers from parents and students in attendance. Two individuals in the rear of the room applauded the vote.

"This is outrageous!" came one voice from the rear.

The school's legal counsel, who was seated next to the board, silently shook his head back and forth. "What am I doing here if you're not going to follow my advice?" he was heard to say.

"I'm sorry, Mrs. Price, the board has voted and the policy will stand," informed the president.

"I'm sorry, too," Rebecca replied. She was steamed, but was determined to keep her composure. "We'll see you in court. You can't gag people in this country simply because you don't agree with their beliefs—but thank you for your time."

Rebecca looked over at Mrs. Holden and Mrs. Dunnell who were sitting in the front row. They were smiling and whispering to each other, obviously pleased with the decision. Rebecca wondered if they had given a 'heads-up' to the board that she would be present at the meeting to complain, which resulted in a preordained decision.

As Rebecca and Arielle left the meeting, several people shook Rebecca's hand and patted Arielle on the shoulder, apparently indicating their support.

The next morning Rebecca read an article in the local newspaper describing the school board action, but it was only a small blurb mixed in with all the other agenda results.

CHAPTER 18

Lawsuit!

It was late evening, the night after the board meeting and Arielle was already sound asleep. Rebecca was watching television when the phone rang. She thought about letting it go to the answering machine as she was in the middle of a movie, but she stopped the video and answered it.

"I apologize for calling so late. Is this Rebecca Price?" asked the male voice on the other end.

"Yes, it is. Who is this?"

"My name is Alan Rabinowitz. I am the rabbi at the synagogue on Fourth Street."

"Yes, Rabbi, what can I do for you?"

"Rebecca, I obtained your name and phone number from Mrs. Weiss. Her daughter, Annie, goes to school with your daughter, Arielle. She informed me about what had occurred in school yesterday and I read about the results of last night's school board meeting in the newspaper. I think they are very wrong to do this to the children and would like to help."

"Help? In what way, Rabbi? I was going to have to drop the matter. I threatened to see them in court, but I can't afford a lawyer. I think they knew it was a hollow threat."

"This matter is too important to drop, Rebecca. I have a close friend who is a constitutional lawyer and he also attends our synagogue. I've already taken the liberty of calling him and explaining the situation. He says he would like to take the case *pro bono* and file a temporary injunction against the school in court tomorrow for you and Arielle, if you would agree. It would restrain the school from implementing the policy the board voted on yesterday until the case could be heard. From there he'll seek a permanent restraining order. He must see you and Arielle first to obtain the facts."

"Oh, Rabbi, that would be great! I've been praying for help."

The rabbi gave Rebecca the name, address and phone number of the attorney and told her he would be expecting her call at eight in the morning. She thanked the rabbi and hung up.

Rebecca was so excited at the prospect of seeing the principal and board in court, it took her over an hour to get to sleep.

CRSO

The next morning, Rebecca took the day off work. Arielle came to breakfast ready for school and her mother told her she would be late going to school this morning. She explained about the conversation she had the night before with the rabbi. At exactly eight o'clock she called the attorney, who asked them to be at his office at nine.

The appointment with David Sharon went well. He was a very pleasant man, unlike any lawyer Rebecca had ever met. After listening to their story and obtaining all the facts of the incident and the school board meeting, he was optimistic about their chances for a positive court challenge.

"I'm fairly confident that in the end we can win a restraining order, but don't be surprised if we lose the first couple of rounds and have to appeal a decision or two before this ends," David told them. "Judge Troy Davis is the judge who will be presiding over this case, and he is not known to be very friendly in regard to religious matters. We may have to wait until it gets to the Superior Court."

"Will we have to testify?" Rebecca asked.

"Arielle will probably have to," he replied. "It's up to us to establish our case. I'll put Arielle on the stand to give the facts as they happened."

"Are both of you up to it? Will either of you be too nervous to testify?" David asked.

Rebecca looked at Arielle. Smiling, she gave her mother a thumbs-up. "I'm a little nervous, but it looks like she's ready."

"Good. I'll get started right away."

"Everything will be all right," Arielle told Mr. Sharon. "The judge will need a little help, but he'll be convinced."

"Don't be too sure, Arielle," he said as he stacked papers on his desk. "He can be a tough nut to crack."

"Have faith, Mr. Sharon. He's on our side," Arielle said smiling, pointing upwards.

"I'm sure He is, Arielle."

Rebecca and Arielle got up to leave.

"I'll file the papers in the court today and have the school served. I'm hoping the judge will fast track the case. Don't be surprised if the newspapers and television stations pick up on it and have a few stories. If they contact you, just refer them to me. I'll handle the reporters."

As soon as the restraining order was filed, the local and national newspapers and television stations did pick up on the story. The headlines, "12 YEAR OLD SUES SCHOOL" and "SCHOOL SUED OVER RELIGIOUS FREEDOM" topped the newspapers. One television station interviewed David, their lawyer, and tried to imply Arielle was attempting to convert students at the school. He set them straight by stating the facts, that she was part of a discussion group, during recess, and that was the extent of it. Their case would be boiled down to one simple question; can students discuss religion or God as a group, by themselves on school property? David stated that the student's first amendment rights of freedom of discourse did not stop at the edge of school property, and a few anti-religious zealots at the school were not going to intimidate them.

The next day, with attorneys present for both sides, the judge set a hearing date for two weeks away. Within those two weeks, anti-religious and "civil rights" groups urging the court to find for the school had filed fourteen amicus or *friends of the court* briefs. They made their position very clear. They did not want any religious matters or the subject of God discussed on school property. On the other side, six briefs were also filed from other churches and religious groups, which supported Arielle's right to discuss God and religion on school grounds, on her own time, outside of the classroom.

☙❧

Their day in court came fast. All of Arielle's friends had wished their new celebrity good luck the day before. David had met with Arielle and Rebecca several times to prepare them for what they might encounter on the stand when, and if, they had to testify.

"Arielle, you seem to be a natural witness, you're not nervous and you're definitely not shy," David told her. "I wish I had people like you testifying in all of my cases."

Arielle smiled. "Thanks Mr. Sharon, it's exciting."

As they entered the courtroom, Arielle saw her principal, Mrs. Holden, the sixth grade teacher, Mrs. Dunnell, and the school board president, Mr. Jeffries. She smiled and waved at them. No one waved back.

"I have some good news, Rebecca," David stated as they walked up to the front of the courtroom. "I have two other young attorneys who are going to help me today. They're real eager and have been doing a lot of the research I needed. Some of the other churches have kicked in some funds and have agreed to help pay them. They'll be sitting up-front with us."

"Which churches decided to help?"

"Your church for one. Pastor Sherman was very generous. He said Arielle was his favorite Bible student. My synagogue donated, and one of the Catholic churches, a Father Joe Sherman said he talked the Archbishop into making a donation."

Rebecca nodded and smiled. Maybe all those meetings were helpful after all, she thought to herself.

Arielle and her mother sat right behind their lawyers in the first row of seats. Arielle looked all around the courtroom; there wasn't an empty seat to be had. Spectators and reporters with notepads filled every chair.

When Judge Troy Davis entered the courtroom, everyone stood up. After the case was announced, the judge told everyone to have a seat. He then spoke for several minutes setting his ground rules for the hearing. He stated that after the inquiry, he would study the testimony along with the submitted briefs and decide whether to grant a permanent restraining order. He would issue his decision the next day at ten in the morning.

The trial went all morning, with Arielle testifying first and the tape of the pertinent parts of the school board meeting played. After lunch recess, the teacher, Mrs. Dunnell and the principal took all afternoon testifying to their recollection of the facts. Very few things were in dispute. Just as their lawyer predicted, the hearing came down to the question as to whether the children could discuss God or religious beliefs on school property.

The lawyers for both sides took up the last two hours of the day arguing each side of the case to the judge, directing his attention to past court rulings. Rebecca thought the pointed questions the judge asked each of the lawyers seemed to favor the school.

As Judge Davis was about to end the session, he called Arielle to the stand again.

"Arielle, you know you are still under oath and must tell the truth, correct?"

"Yes, Sir."

"Did anyone tell you to preach or talk about God at school?"

"No, Sir."

"Did you try to get other children to come and listen to you?"

"No, Sir."

"Do you think your little group could find somewhere else to discuss God other than on the school grounds?"

"I suppose so, Sir. If we had to." She thought a second. "No, Sir. That's the only place we're all together."

The judge cleared his throat. "Do you have anything else to add to all this today?"

Arielle cupped her hand next to her mouth and leaned over to the judge. She whispered, "God will help you come to the right decision, Sir. You won't have to make it alone."

The judge appeared stunned by what he heard and drew back from her.

"You may step down, young lady."

One of the lawyers for the school wanted to know what Arielle told the judge, but the judge waved him off.

The attorney protested. "Your Honor, we have a right to know what this witness said to the court."

"I assure you, counselor, neither the court nor you were threatened," the judge stated.

There was laughter from those watching the proceedings. The judge banged his gavel and ordered silence. Red-faced, the lawyer sat down.

After about a minute, the judge cleared his throat again and addressed the courtroom.

"This case will not be difficult to decide. The question of whether a public school can legitimately keep a division between church and state has been decided on many occasions, but usually has been decided about adult activity. This case, however, seems to hinge on whether the children, themselves, can talk about or discuss God, or even proselytize on school property. Children are not usually entitled to every right that adults hold, but those rights cannot be abridged unless the state has a specific and legitimate reason. I'll deliver my decision in the morning."

With that statement, the judge adjourned for the day and left the bench.

"Well, how do you think it went?" Rebecca asked David.

"I don't know. I told you this judge isn't particularly open to religious issues. He's more a strict separatist—the separation of church and state. He thinks constitutional rights come secondary to those separations."

"How do you think he'll rule, Arielle?" asked David as he placed his paperwork in his briefcase. "You did really good today and I'm proud of the way you handled yourself. The judge seemed to show a deep interest in you."

"He'll decide in our favor, Mr. Sharon. He just doesn't know it yet."

David laughed and looked over at Rebecca, who shrugged her shoulders.

"She's predicted these types of things before."

"I hope she's right," he said.

CR&SO

On the way home Arielle and her mother discussed the hearing.

"Arielle, what did you tell the judge at the end that seemed to upset him? He seemed shocked by whatever it was."

"I told him that God would help him make the right decision."

"Did the angels tell you to tell him that?"

"Yes."

"Were they with you during the trial?"

"There were lots of them there today, Mom. They were everywhere. Most of them I've never seen before."

Rebecca watched as her daughter's attention was drawn somewhere else.

"Okay," Arielle finally said. Tears filled her eyes. With that, she held up her arm and blew across her palm. Rebecca watched as an orb left her hand and flew out of the car. She pulled the car over to the curb and stopped. "What was that for?"

"It went to help the judge. He's in a real bad situation right now, Mom. It'll keep him from harm."

"What kind of bad situation? What kind of harm?"

"I don't know. I was just told what to do to help him. They might tell me later."

CHAPTER 19

Revelation

Relaxing in his silver BMW on his way home from a long day in court, Judge Davis couldn't help thinking about the case he had just finished hearing. The child he questioned didn't seem like a religious zealot to him, just a little girl with strong convictions. The evidence showed they weren't bothering anyone on the playground and they weren't trying to convince, convert or otherwise participate in any religion. As a matter of fact, they were probably too young to proselytize and the teachers, staff and student body were certainly in no danger of twelve-year-olds wanting to discuss their religions within a group by themselves. How could he keep God off the playground and still uphold a person's right to free speech and association? And did free speech and association extend to minors at a public institution? Those were the hundred-dollar questions.

His cell phone rang. A text message appeared on his phone from his wife asking him to stop and pick up a gallon of milk and a loaf of bread on his way home. The judge rolled his eyes at the thought of stopping at a convenience store during the rush hour. He'd probably have to stand in line and he hated that. He didn't like running into lawyers who wanted to discuss a past case or decision he had rendered, and he certainly didn't want to run into any defendants he had sentenced or come before him over the years.

He pulled into the nearest gas station/convenience store and squeezed his car in next to two men just parking their black Kawasaki motorcycles in the crowded parking lot. Both men were dressed head to toe in black leather with matching black helmets with shaded front visors.

As the judge got out of his car, both men looked at him and he nodded a polite "hello." One of the men held up his arm to return the greeting, but the other man quickly turned to his friend and said something inaudible. The judge went into the store.

He found the milk in the cooler at the rear of the store and retrieved a half-gallon. They always put the milk farthest away, he thought. As he started to walk to the front of the store to get the bread, he heard a loud bang, like a firecracker, only louder. He looked up to see the two motorcycle riders robbing the store. He froze in the aisle, halfway up to the counter. Each biker had a gun in his hand. One stood guard at the door while the other went around the counter, opened the cash register and grabbed the cash. Another warning round was fired into the ceiling.

"Everyone down on the floor!" he yelled.

Six other customers immediately lay down on the floor. The judge went down to his knees, slowly starting to lie down.

"Not you, *Your Honor*," drawled the robber, pointing his gun at the judge. The hollow, muffled voice from inside the covered helmet sounded eerie. "I've got something special in mind for you." He calmly walked over to face the judge as he stashed the cash from the register into his pockets. "You enjoy convicting people and sending them to prison, don't you?"

Judge Davis stood up, his head held high. "I don't mind sending punks like you there when I get the chance."

The man grabbed the judge by the lapel of his coat, cocked the gun and stuck it in the judge's face.

"I just might send *you* somewhere *this* time."

"C'mon, Joe, hurry up. We haven't got time for this," yelled the man guarding the door.

"You idiot, don't use my name!"

Just then, a buzzer from the door being opened was heard and another customer entered the store with a small child.

"Get down on the floor!" the lookout at the door yelled to the new customer, sticking the gun in his face as he pulled the door shut. The man put one of his hands above his head while holding on to the toddler and lay down on the floor. The child began to cry.

"C'mon, there's too many people. Let's get out of here!"

"Shut that kid up. I've got some overdue business to attend to," Joe replied as he opened the visor on his helmet. "I'm going to send this one right to hell—where he belongs."

"You said no one was going to get hurt! You promised!" his partner yelled.

"Yes, I did," Joe said calmly. He was smiling. "But I wasn't planning on running into the judge here." Joe brought the gun down and pushed the revolver against the judge's chest, right near his heart. "You don't remember me, do you, Judge?"

"Even if I could, I try to forget about as many of you as I can. You're worthless to the human race. All you do is prey on others unable to defend themselves."

Joe's smile disappeared. "That's pretty courageous for someone who's about to die. Say goodbye, Your Honor," he drawled again.

"Hold on there a minute, Joe," a voice called from the rear of the store. A man in a dark gray trench coat and a gray fedora walked towards them.

"Who are you?" Joe asked.

"If I told you, would it matter?" the man asked.

Still holding the judge's lapel, Joe turned and pointed the gun at the stranger who continued to close the gap between them.

"Yeah, it does. Where'd you come from? Stop right there and get down," he yelled, "or you can join this one."

The stranger kept coming, looking into Joe's eyes, speaking directly to him. "If you're going to shoot someone, shoot me. This person hasn't harmed anyone."

He was almost upon Joe. "I said stop! Get down!" Joe screamed this time. His eyes wild, he aimed the gun back and forth between the stranger and the judge. "I'll waste you, old man!"

He came even closer.

"I'm going to pop you!" The gun was now pointed solely at the stranger.

He kept coming. Joe fired when the man was about three feet from him. He kept coming. Joe fired again, and again. The stranger never stopped, never even hesitated. He grabbed the gun by the barrel and held on to it. Joe could only stand and gawk with his mouth agape.

"I shot you. You should be dead," Joe sputtered.

"But I'm not. I'm giving you a second chance at life, Joe. Go now and don't hurt anyone else," he said.

The gunfire spurred Joe's compadre to flee out to his motorcycle, start it and race off without Joe.

As soon as the other customers saw that no one was guarding the door, some stood up and others crawled, but they all scrambled for the exit.

Joe pushed past them out the door at a fast run without his gun.

The stranger turned to the judge. "Your Honor, please hold out your hand."

"Who are you?"

"You don't know me. Please, hold out your hand," he repeated.

Slowly, the judge complied with the stranger's request. He held out his trembling hand, wondering how the stranger knew his profession.

"Here, use these as a reminder," the stranger said as he dropped three bullets, one at a time, into the judge's hand. "These are a gift from Arielle."

For once, Troy Davis couldn't speak.

The man with the fedora tipped his hat, said goodbye, and turned to walk out of the store.

"Arielle who?" the judge yelled from across the store.

The stranger turned around. "How many do you know?" he asked in reply. He smiled, tipped his hat again, and walked out the front door.

Minutes later the police arrived; one officer recognized the judge.

"Are you all right, Your Honor? The other customers said they heard one of the perps yelling he was going to shoot someone and then they heard three shots. Who was shot?"

Troy Davis was still in a daze, his whole body shaking. He felt drained. He slipped the bullets into his coat pocket, and then held up his hand to the officer, signaling to give him some space. He walked away to focus on how he was going to reply. He fingered the three bullets in his pocket. How could he tell the police that, yes, someone was shot three times but walked out the front door. Oh, and before he left, he handed him the three spent bullets he had been shot with. He scanned the store. He could see there were two video cameras pointed towards the cash register, but none pointed out into the merchandise area.

Could the guy in the gray coat have been wearing a bulletproof vest? The judge took the bullets out of his pocket and examined them. They were still perfectly formed, as if they hadn't hit a thing! In fact they were like brand new!

He knew if he told the truth they would immediately take him to a padded room and lock him up! All of his past cases would go under review and he would have to retire. He could see his future going up in smoke before his eyes! All because he stopped at a convenience store for milk and bread.

Returning to the officer, he apologized and said, "Yes, he fired three rounds, but I believe they were just to scare us. I don't think anyone was hit."

After several more questions, the judge asked if he could leave. The officers took his phone number and said they would be in contact the next day for a full statement and a photo lineup.

The judge decided to permanently keep what happened to himself. He couldn't even tell his wife; even she would have a hard time believing his story.

Outside the store, he observed several of the customers subjected to the robbery being interviewed by police officers.

As one of them was leaving, the judge cornered him. "Excuse me, did you happen to notice a man wearing a trench coat and hat come out of the store after those punks left?"

"No. No one came out after them," the witness stated.

"Well, how about in the store, did you see anyone with that description in there?"

"Look, the guy said to stay down, and that's what I did. I didn't see anyone."

The story was the same with every person. Each said they were so scared they never looked up.

Judge Troy Davis went home without his milk and bread. Later, he called the police station to speak with the investigating detectives. He asked if they had found anything. The detectives stated they went through the store with a fine-tooth comb looking for the five rounds that everyone stated had been fired. They found the two rounds which had been fired into the ceiling, but that was all. They were puzzled, but came to the only conclusion they could, the last three rounds had to have been blanks.

CHAPTER 20

The Verdict

The next morning, promptly at ten, Judge Davis appeared in the courtroom to render his decision. He looked tired. His eyelids were drooping and bags sagged under his eyes. He slumped in his chair, a sharp contrast in posture from the day before. After all the court formalities, he sat at the bench perusing everyone for several minutes. He then called both attorneys before him.

In a subdued voice, and with his hand over the microphone, he made a strange request. "I have a few more questions for the petitioner before I rule on this restraining order," he said, thumbing the thick pile of papers in front of him. "I would like to question Miss Arielle and her mother in my chambers, without any lawyers present, if there are no objections."

The lawyer representing the school started to object. "Your Honor..."

"And I hope there aren't," Judge Davis snapped, interrupting and staring directly at him.

The two attorneys looked at each other, shrugged their shoulders, and agreed to the judge's request. "We have no objections, Your Honor," they both stated.

After the judge recessed and left the bench, David told Rebecca and Arielle that the judge wanted to speak to them without counsel present.

"You mean without you?"

"Yes," David said.

"Why? What does he want?"

"He didn't say why or what he wanted to talk about. The judge just wants to talk to you and Arielle privately." He lowered his voice to a whisper. "This is unusual, but let's just go with it for now. See what happens."

Rebecca shrugged her shoulders. "Okay."

Arielle smiled at her mother.

"What do you know that I don't?" she asked her daughter.

She giggled. "Just wait. You'll see."

They followed David to the judge's chambers where he opened the door and ushered them in.

∞

The chambers smelled of leather and musky cologne, and exuded an air of power. The judge sat in an enormous, mahogany colored, leather chair behind a large oak desk, which sat in the middle of the room. Massive shelves filled with law books, some leather bound, flanked it. A large window, which looked out on the busy avenue below was framed with plush, royal blue draperies. A gold-colored chandelier hung from the ceiling with dozens of small lights; crystals sprinkled refracted light throughout the room.

"Good morning," the judge rose to greet them as they entered the room. "Please, have a seat," he said gesturing to two leather chairs facing his desk. Rebecca and Arielle sat down.

"Why have you asked us here?" Rebecca queried as the judge moved some papers around on his desk and took a sip from a glass of water. He kept glancing at Arielle. After clearing his throat several times, he started to speak.

"I had quite an experience yesterday evening, and I couldn't sleep all night. I still don't know what to think of it, but I believe it was extraordinary. A man told me the experience was a gift from Arielle. I asked him Arielle who. He then asked me how many I knew. I've searched my memory, and you are the only Arielle I can recollect having ever met. Can you enlighten me?"

Arielle smiled. "What would you like to know, Sir?"

"Who was the man who saved my life?"

Arielle thought a moment. "I've heard my mother say to her mother once, 'Don't ask a question if you really don't want to know the answer.'" Arielle hesitated. "Are you sure you want to know the answer?"

The judge stroked his chin for a moment. "I think I'm going to regret this, but yes, I believe I do."

Arielle smiled. "He was an angel."

"An angel?" The judge sat back in his chair and smiled. He waited a moment. "He couldn't have been. He was a real person. I spoke with him."

"He was an angel," she repeated.

"How do you know this person was an angel?"

Rebecca whispered to her daughter, "How come everyone gets to talk to your angels but me?"

"Mom, please," Arielle whispered back. "I helped send him," she stated to the judge.

"*You* sent him?" he asked. "*This is getting stranger by the minute,*" he said under his breath.

"I must ask you, why'd you send him? How did you know I was in trouble?"

"Angels told me you were in trouble. I did what I was asked to do."

The judge sat back in his chair and stared at Arielle. "This is really hard to digest, Arielle. I'm really confused."

She smiled again. "I asked if you really wanted to know."

"If I may, Judge. Maybe I can shed some light," Rebecca chimed in.

"Please. Please do. This is way beyond my reasoning or comprehension."

"Arielle has always said she talks to angels and they direct her to do certain things at certain times. She has helped several other people. I think you have been the recipient of one of those special occasions."

"But why me? Why now?"

Arielle smiled at the judge. "God wanted to assist you in making a decision that will affect many people for a long time. He wanted you to make the right decision. Now it is up to you to do that. He wants you to know that what you do will make a difference, and that He is with you and watching," she stated bluntly.

"But I've never believed..."

"He knows that. That is why He gave you the gift of a special visit, to let you know He is real and you need to do the right thing. Just as I know you can't tell anyone what really happened last night, I know you never will be able to tell anyone what is said in this conversation. That is the way it is. No one would believe you anyway."

The judge sat back in his chair for a moment nodding his head. "I see."

"Believe me, Sir, what you experienced last night was real. It was as real as I am sitting here before you," Arielle assured him.

Rebecca noticed his hand shaking as he picked up his glass of water and took a drink.

The judge got up and walked around the desk. "Thank you for your time, ladies. Would you please give me a few moments to myself?" He went to the door and opened it for them. "I'll see you back in the courtroom."

Arielle and Rebecca got up to leave. As Arielle was about to go through the door, she turned and said, "Judge, I was just instructed to tell you something."

"Yes. What is it?"

"You should keep the bullets in a glass on your bench. It will forever remind you of your real duties."

His eyes widened as he stared at Arielle.

"But I didn't tell you…" he stammered.

"I know." She smiled and followed her mother into the courtroom.

David rose from his seat as his clients came out of the judge's chambers. He seemed anxious to know why the judge had wanted an audience with them.

"What did he want?"

"He just went over some old stuff," Rebecca answered as she noticed the other attorneys listening to their conversation. She looked at Arielle and winked. "Please don't ask anymore," she whispered.

David nodded and sat down. "I hope it was good for us."

"I believe it will be."

 C R S O

It was another half hour before the judge came back into the courtroom. He sat looking over his glasses between Arielle and his paperwork for several minutes before uttering a word. Prior to speaking, he placed a small glass on the rail surrounding his bench. It contained the three bullets given to him by the angel. Arielle looked at her mother and smiled.

"What did you guys say to him?" David asked. He looks like a nervous wreck."

Rebecca looked down at Arielle and gave her another wink.

The judge took his glasses off. "I have thought long and hard about this case and have studied the briefs submitted, along with court decisions other judges have rendered. I realize my decision will have profound effects on many in the following years." There was an extended pause; the judge did not look up.

"I can find no harm in the school children discussing God or religion on school grounds, nor anything that prohibits it. I find they were not promoting nor trying to reach out to other students. Merely, they were holding their own discussion group outside the earshot of anyone else. I further find that as a matter of factual record, they were trying to keep to themselves. The separation of church and state does not mean there can be no God in our schools; it means the schools may not promote any religion. I find the school personnel and the school board acted improperly and I am granting the permanent restraining order so requested. This court stands adjourned." The judge slammed the gavel down, got up and retreated to his chambers.

A temporary hush in the courtroom gave way to cheers from the spectators sitting behind Arielle and Rebecca. David jumped from his chair and hugged them both. Reporters bolted from their seats and rushed the door. Rebecca thanked the other lawyers who had helped, and Arielle gave each of them a kiss on the cheek, which they gladly accepted as a bonus for their services.

Long, somber looks came from the lawyers, principal and teachers of Arielle's school as they filed out of the courtroom. Out in the hallway, the lawyers for the school were being pelted with questions from the teachers and principal. They wanted to know if the attorneys were going to appeal the judge's decision.

"I'll appeal the decision if the board wishes, but if you recall, I had already cautioned them to disregard the policies. It's the board's decision whether to spend more of the school's money on further appeals."

David recognized the tension and said in a voice loud enough for everyone to hear, "If you have any problems at school, Arielle, you give me a call and I'll speak to the judge. I don't think he'll take too approvingly to any violations of his order."

Rebecca nodded approval as she heard the school lawyers inform the teachers and principal not to cause any problems or seek retribution against Arielle and her friends. He also told them any breach of the restraining order could be cause for jail time, heavy fines, or termination.

CHAPTER 21

Missing

Summer had arrived and Tommy was up early most mornings to get his chores done. He liked to have them out of the way so he could play the rest of the day. He pulled on his favorite jeans, a clean white t-shirt and a pair of sneakers. After a quick breakfast of cereal and bananas, he had to make his bed, clean his room, take out the trash, and water his mother's vegetable garden. He didn't mind watering the garden; he loved helping his mother take care of all the plants, watching them grow from seeds, stronger and taller each day. But, like every other eight-year-old boy, he hated making his bed and cleaning his room. He would do that last.

His mother was still sound asleep. She had worked until midnight, waiting tables at a local restaurant. She often slept in until nine o'clock because she usually couldn't go to bed until she unwound, that being around two in the morning.

After his regular chores, Tommy would watch television or go play at one of his friend's houses. If he went anywhere, his mother told him to always leave a note on the kitchen table to let her know where he would be. That was the agreement between them and it had always worked out for both. He usually returned home around noon when his mother would have lunch ready.

Today, Tommy hurried to get everything done. He had a baseball game at ten and the coach had asked them to come an hour early for some practice. This was his first year playing in the league and he and his friend, Billy, were going to ride their bikes to the ball field together.

He finished his chores and left a note on the table letting his mother know where he was going. He rushed out the door to his black and silver mountain bike lying on the lawn, but as he was leaving, he thought he heard the phone ring. Not wanting it to wake his mother, he ran back inside to answer it.

"Hello," he said, out of breath.

"Good morning Tommy, this is Nana."

"Hi, Nana. I was just going to my baseball game."

"Oh, I hope you win! Is your mother up yet?"

"No. She said not to wake her this morning. I think she got home late."

"I need a big favor, Tommy, I'm not feeling too well. Could you tell your mother I need the medicine she picked up for me at the pharmacy yesterday? I accidentally dropped my last pill in the sink and it went down the drain. "

"Okay, Nana. I'll leave her a note."

"Thank you. Have fun and good luck at your game today."

They said their goodbyes. Tommy started to write another note to his mother but the pen ran out of ink. He looked for another, searching the kitchen and living room, but couldn't find one. He decided he would tell his mother after the game. He ran outside, hopped on his bicycle and began pedaling to Billy's house.

Tommy had second thoughts—he wanted to get to practice, but he also dearly loved his nana. He felt bad and was afraid something awful might happen to her if she didn't have her pills. Tommy thought if he hurried, he could take the shortcut through the state forest bordering his home, and still make the baseball game. He had taken the route before with his mother. He would miss part of the practice session, he didn't mind that, but he would be on time for the game. Nana needed her medicine. His mom would approve of that. He turned around.

Tommy went back into the house and found Nana's drugs in his mom's purse. He called Billy and told him he had something he had to do, would be late for practice, and not to wait for him.

Tommy entered the woods on foot. He knew the path. He started out with a jog, and then dropped to a fast walk. After about twenty minutes, his pace slowed. He wished the path was smooth enough to ride his bike over. He knew he was still on the right trail, but the trees, bushes and other vegetation looked much different in the summer from when they walked it the last time. Then, his mom had been with him, it was late fall and the trees were practically barren.

Spots of sunlight peeked through the leaves, casting dappled light everywhere. The birds, crickets, frogs, and other animals of the forest blended their voices for a melody that only the mind of an eight-year-old could hear and understand.

As he hiked through the forest, Tommy suddenly remembered he had heard grown-ups talk about a bear that roamed the woods, although no one had seen it recently. Everyone thought it had migrated to another part of the forest. Even so, he decided to keep his eyes open in case it had taken up residence nearby again. He picked up two large sticks he found along the path to make himself look bigger and create noise in case he ran into the bear. Maybe he could even poke the bear in the eye.

⁂

Tommy's mother, Carol, awoke earlier than usual, right after Tommy left, unable to sleep any longer. Once the morning fog cleared her head, she realized something bothered her, but she couldn't put her finger on it. She went to the kitchen and started a fresh pot of coffee. As she sat down at the kitchen table, she read Tommy's note, *gone baseball*. Oh, yeah, she thought, he had a game this morning. Maybe she would go watch.

C02800

Tommy thought he was almost to his grandmother's as he dragged the sticks along the ground, but the trail seemed much longer this time. He was feeling proud of himself, delivering the medicine and still making the game. Walking briskly, he thought about how he was going to be the catcher today, the coach had promised. He would catch every pitch. Nothing would get by him. He had been watching and studying the catchers on the big-league teams and he knew just what to do.

A noise in the brush off to his left startled him out of his daydreams. He froze. At first, it was just a little rustle in the brush. Maybe a squirrel, he thought. He continued on. Up ahead, Tommy remembered a log lay on the path and then there was supposed to be a small stream he had to cross. The stream would be high today after the rains they had the past few days, and he definitely did not want to get his new baseball shoes wet. Downstream, he knew where a fallen tree formed a narrow footbridge across the water; his mother had shown him.

The continuing noises behind him now made him anxious. He kept looking over his shoulder, but couldn't see anything. A low growl froze Tommy in his tracks. Turning around, he raised the two sticks he was carrying, preparing to meet the bear. If it came at him, he knew he wasn't supposed to run, but now his mind was a blank; he couldn't remember what he *was* supposed to do.

The noises stopped. Nothing appeared. The forest seemed eerily quiet. The adrenaline that had built up in his body made his hands shake. He felt a chill travel down his back and he shivered.

He knew after he crossed the stream up ahead, the path veered sharply to the right. Maybe if he took a shortcut and got off the path the bear would quit following him.

He decided to take the shortcut. The woods were darker here; the tree canopy was so thick, hardly any sunshine made it through, but then there wasn't as much brush either. He could see farther in case the bear did try to sneak up on him.

The growling in the distance returned. Something *was* following him. Tommy picked up his pace. *Where was the stream? It had to be close!* He had to get across.

He turned around and walked backwards hoping to spot anything moving behind him. There it was—he saw it! Movement about fifty yards behind him. It was moving at the same speed he was. He stopped. It stopped, too.

A patch of sunlight breaking through the canopy lit up the predators—a pack of wild dogs, the lead dog showing his fangs. They had been shadowing him through the woods and now they had their prey within striking distance. They came rushing at him at a full run. Tommy threw his sticks in the direction of the dogs and ran. He had nowhere to go but up a tree. He saw a fir tree with some low limbs and ran towards it. Grasping the lowest branch, he pulled himself up and climbed as fast as he could. He wasn't fast enough. The dogs surrounded the base of the tree growling, barking and snapping at him; one jumped and caught the heel of Tommy's shoe in his teeth, the dog hanging in mid-air. Tommy screamed and shook his leg violently. His shoe fell off and the dog dropped with it to the ground. Several dogs fought over the hard-won trophy. Tommy thought his heart was going to jump out of his chest. He screamed at the dogs, hoping they would leave. They didn't.

The predators continued circling the tree, patiently waiting for their prey. One rose up on its hind legs, stretching out as high as it could, scratching at the tree and barking at Tommy. It had white froth spewing from its mouth, its eyes dark and wild. There was nothing Tommy could do now but wait for help, or wait for them to leave.

CB§O

Carol swallowed her first cup of coffee and went for a second. As she looked out the window, she saw Tommy's bicycle lying on the lawn. That was odd, she thought. He usually rode it to the baseball diamond. Oh yeah, he was going with Billy today, she remembered, maybe Billy's father had taken them. She decided to surprise Tommy and show up at his game. It had been a while since she had been able to watch one of his games and he would be thrilled to have his mom watch him play.

Carol finished her second cup of coffee and was ready for the world. She showered, dressed, and drove to the baseball field. The game was just about to start. Coach Dan saw Carol and came over to see her.

"Hey, Carol, where's Tommy? Doesn't he know we're starting soon?"

"Isn't he here? He left me a note. It said he went to play baseball."

"He never showed up here, even for practice. I've been waiting for him. He was going to catch today and I wanted him to have some practice."

Carol was now in a panic. "There's Billy. He always rides here with Tommy. Ask him where he is."

The coach called Billy over to him.

"Son, do you know where Tommy is?"

"No. He called me and said he was going to be late for practice and not to wait for him."

"His bicycle was still in the yard. I thought your father picked him up," Carol said.

"I rode my bike here," Billy stated. "Dad's at work."

"Oh, my God!" Carol yelled. She looked around the ball field. "Where is he? What happened to him?"

"Do you have any idea at all where he might have gone?" Dan asked Billy.

"No, Sir. He said he had something he had to do and sounded like he was in a hurry."

"I've got to call the police," Carol said. She dialed 9-1-1 on her cell phone.

Carol met the police at her home and told them what she knew. She had been calling all of Tommy's friends to see if anyone had seen him; they hadn't. She gave the officers his class picture from school.

"We'll drive around the neighborhood and see if we can locate him, Ma'am," stated one of the officers.

The officers scoured the neighborhood, stopping every child and adult they saw, asking if anyone had seen Tommy.

⚬⚬⚬

As they passed Rebecca's house, Arielle was playing a board game on the front stairs with some of her friends. The officers inquired about Tommy; none of the girls had seen him. Arielle and her friends decided to walk around the neighborhood to see if they could find him. She told her mother where they were going and why. After a thorough search of places they thought he might be, they returned to Arielle's home. Rebecca found Carol's phone number and called her. She told Carol the girls had looked around, but didn't find him, and to call her if he hadn't been found in a couple of hours.

CRITER

By noon, Carol was terrified something dreadful had happened to Tommy. Maybe he'd even been abducted. She called her mother.

"Mom, have you heard from Tommy? He's missing and no one's seen him."

"Missing? I spoke with Tommy this morning. I asked him to tell you I needed the pills you picked up for me yesterday. I've been expecting you to come over with them all morning.

"I'll bring it over this afternoon, Mom, but I need to find Tommy first."

"Of course, dear. Let me know if you can't come over, I'll find someone to pick them up."

Carol looked in her purse and then all over the house and in her car for the medication, but couldn't find it. The thought crossed her mind that Tommy might try to take it to his grandmother through the forest, but she dismissed it.

The police officers returned in a couple hours.

"I'm sorry, Ma'am, but we couldn't find him. Perhaps he's at a friend's house," the officer explained.

"No, no. I've called all his friends and no one has seen him."

"We'll put a report in, but unless we have something to go on we have to assume he's a runaway or just somewhere you're not aware of. If he hasn't shown up by tomorrow, we can gather the troops and start searching for him."

"Something's wrong. Something is terribly wrong. Tommy always leaves a note to let me know where he's going or tells me. He missed his baseball game. He would never do that. We have to start looking for him now."

"Let me contact the station. I'll see if they want to start a search party now." The officer went to his car and radioed information to the station. He came back to Carol.

"They're contacting volunteers at the Civil Defense and the city's search and rescue teams. They should be here within the hour."

"Oh, bless you, thank you."

⌘

Later that afternoon, neighbors started gravitating to Carol's house after seeing all the official vehicles parking in front of her house. Everyone was anxious to volunteer to help find Tommy. Even school officials arrived. They called many parents of Tommy's classmates, asking first if they had seen him, then asking if they would help find him.

⌘

Later that day, Carol called Rebecca and let her know a search party was being organized. Rebecca volunteered herself and Arielle to help. They hastily changed into their hiking clothes and stopped at a convenience store to purchase bottles of water and a couple of energy snacks. As they drove the last few blocks to Tommy's house, Rebecca saw Arielle wipe a tear from her eye and send another orb.

"Where did that one go?"

"It went to help Tommy."

"Is he okay now?"

"No, but he's safe. He's still lost."

"Well, where is he?"

"He's lost out in the forest somewhere."

"Can't you help him find his way home?"

"No. I can only make him safe. He's being chased by a pack of dogs."

"A pack of dogs! Why can't you help him?"

"He has to be found by searching, Mom. There are bigger things going on."

"Bigger things? What do you mean?"

"I'm not sure. All I know is it's going to be a busy evening."

CHAPTER 22

The Search

It was close to five o'clock when Arielle and her mother arrived at Tommy's house. The sunny sky had darkened under gray cumulus clouds. A volunteer greeted them as they approached the house and instructed them to check in with the search and rescue group's command center—a small tent station set up in the driveway.

Inside the command post, two individuals with official looking badges sat at a small table, occupying the only chairs in the confined space. They registered the names of all the volunteers and assigned them to a group leader. Rebecca and Arielle were assigned to Bart Williams, a local Boy Scout Troop leader.

Bart was pointed out and they reported to him.

"Good to have both of you. We're assigned to the forest. There's a rumor Tommy liked to play out there. I hope you're okay with that," Bart said.

"That's where you'll find him," Arielle said as she walked toward another group of people who had gathered down the driveway.

"What'd she mean by that?" Bart asked Rebecca.

"She seems to think Tommy is lost in the woods," Rebecca replied.

"What makes her think he's out there?"

"I don't know. She said on the way over here she thought he might have gone into the forest."

"Has she played with him out there before?"

"Not that I know of. She's not even his age."

Arielle came back to her mother. "Is it all right if I go with Jessica's group, Mom? Her stepfather is with the group and you can still go with Mr. Williams and search the forest."

"Where're they going? I'd rather you stay with me."

"They're searching the fields down the road back to the river."

"But you said Tommy's likely in the forest. Why would you want to search the fields if you know he's not there?"

"I have to go with her, Mom. Please." Arielle's serious look gave Rebecca pause.

"Let me meet Jessica's stepfather first."

They went over to where the group had gathered and Rebecca introduced herself to Arthur Stevens. He was a thin man, about six-feet tall, light reddish-brown, thinning hair, and very white, almost albino skin color. She asked if it was all right for Arielle to accompany them. He assured her it was fine.

"Come over here for a minute," Rebecca said to Arielle.

Rebecca walked a short distance with her daughter, out of earshot of everyone else. "Is this something you were told to do?"

"Yes, but I don't know why yet."

"I don't know these people, Arielle. I don't like you going off with people I don't know anything about."

"I'll be okay, Mom."

Rebecca knew better than to argue with Arielle's angel. She also knew Arielle would be with several adults and there shouldn't be any problems.

"Okay, but you stay with the adults and when it starts to get dark, or if it starts to rain, you guys get back here. And be careful."

"Thanks, Mom. I will."

CR80

A half hour later a team of ten, including Arielle, Jessica and Arthur, were pushing through waist-high brush. The field, rocky and sloped, was hard to walk in. The team spread out so that each person was about forty feet from the other. Arielle, Jessica and Arthur were on the west end of the line that backed up to a thickly wooded area.

After thirty minutes of walking and searching, the team stopped for a rest. Arielle pulled out her water bottle and one of her energy bars, sharing them with Jessica.

After they finished their snack and drank half the water, Arielle tucked the wrapper into her pocket. They got up and walked a short distance from Arthur. Sitting down together on a large boulder amid blooming sunflowers, they pulled briars and stickers out of their pants.

"Jessica, I know what your stepfather has been doing to you. I'm going to tell him that I know and he's got to stop."

"What do you know? What do you mean?"

"I know he's been molesting you for a while now. It's not right. He's a bad person for doing those things to you, and it's not your fault."

Jessica was silent for several minutes. Arielle could see the pain in her eyes and the toll of years of abuse reflected on her face.

"He always tells me he loves me. He said he'd never hurt me. But it does hurt, Arielle. It hurts everyday."

Arielle hugged Jessica as she started crying.

"What are you two doing?" Arthur called out.

Between sobs, Jessica pleaded with Arielle. "Please don't say anything. He'll get angry and we'll both be in big trouble."

"I have to, Jessica. It's something I have to do."

"Why? How did you find out?" She wiped her tears away with her shirtsleeve.

"Do you remember the lights I showed you when we walked home that day?"

Jessica nodded. "Yes."

"Remember I told you angels talk to me?"

She nodded again.

"Well, that's how I know. They told me what your step dad is doing to you and also told me to confront him to make him stop. Beyond that, I'm not sure what will happen."

They watched Arthur get up from his resting spot. "Come on, we need to catch up with the rest of the group," Arthur yelled. "They're already ahead of us."

They began walking back towards Jessica's stepfather. "You still talk to angels?" Jessica asked.

"Yes, but most people don't believe me. They think I'm nuts or something like that. I've been told I'm delusional, whatever that means."

"Why are they telling you to help me?"

"I don't know, Jessica," Arielle whispered, "but you must be special. They don't tell me everything, just what they want me to know at the time. They've never let me down, so if they tell me to do something, it's always worked out."

They arrived back at Arthur's side. "What are you two up to?" he asked with a suspicious smile.

"Nothing," Jessica said. She lowered her head. "We want to walk together instead of being so far apart."

"And why is that?"

Arielle had a blank stare as she looked at Jessica. "Arielle's afraid of snakes. She's scared to walk alone."

Arielle's eyes widened. If Arthur asked if that were true, Arielle would have to deny it. She couldn't lie, and that would definitely get Jessica in trouble.

Arthur eyed Arielle. He laughed.

"Well, okay, but keep up."

Arielle and Jessica pushed through the harsh brush, back to the edge of the wooded area.

"Jessica, you shouldn't tell lies like that. I'm not afraid of snakes and I would have had to tell the truth if your stepfather asked."

"But I couldn't think of anything else at the time."

"How about, 'we both just wanted to walk together'?"

"He'd wonder why. He's very distrustful of who I talk to and what I talk about."

"I guess I would be too if I were doing what he is," Arielle said.

"How are you going to stop him from hurting me? What are you going to say?"

"I don't know yet. I've only been told I have to tell him certain things."

"By the angels?"

"Yes." A couple minutes later Arielle told Jessica, "I'll be right back."

"Where are you going?"

"To talk to your stepfather."

"I'm scared, Arielle. You don't know him. He can blow up in a matter of seconds. I don't want you to get hurt."

"I'm scared, too. But don't worry. God is watching over us. He'll protect us."

"I hope so."

Arielle cut across the field to where Arthur was searching. He saw her coming when she was about halfway to him and stopped to wait for her.

"Hi, Arielle, what's up?"

"Hi, Mr. Stevens. I have to talk to you."

They started slowly walking again, Arielle just to the left of Arthur, at arm's length. She wanted to be able to run if he tried to grab her.

"What about? What's on your mind?"

Arielle was hesitant and definitely nervous. She didn't know how Arthur was going to react. She summoned all the courage she could muster and blurted out, "I know what you're doing to Jessica and you have to stop it, now."

"Well, little lady, just what are you talking about?"

"You know what I'm talking about, Mr. Stevens. You've been molesting her for a long time. You're hurting her and you've got to stop it or I'm going to tell the police."

Arthur stopped and faced Arielle. "Listen, I don't know what Jessica has been telling you, but she's been known to tell some pretty tall tales, and this one, this is detestable."

"She didn't tell me, Mr. Stevens. You can't blame this on her."

"Well, I don't care who told you. It's simply not true and you're going to mind your own business. Who filled your head with these crazy ideas anyway?"

Arielle hesitated and looking Arthur in the eye, she said, "An angel told me. And he said to tell you to stop."

Arthur busted out laughing. "You tell the police anything you want. Who's going to believe a twelve-year-old who got her information from some fantasy angel?"

"They'll believe me, Mr. Stevens. You'll get caught and it will be by your own hand. God is giving you a chance to stop. He still loves you and he loves Jessica, but He doesn't want you to harm her anymore. She's been hurt enough."

"Well, you tell your angel he's crazy. I haven't done anything to Jessica. I love her too, and I wouldn't ever do something that would hurt her."

Arielle could see the veins throbbing in his neck—he swallowed hard several times. She could tell he was desperately trying to suppress his anger.

"Don't say you weren't warned, Mr. Stevens. I hope you repent and stop hurting her." Shaking, she left Arthur standing in the field and walked briskly back through the thick brush to Jessica.

Jessica's questions came out rapid-fire. "What happened? What did he say? Is he going to stop?" Her eyes locked onto Arielle's, hoping for good news.

"I don't know what's going to happen. He denied everything, just like I thought he would."

"Oh, Arielle, he's going to be so mad! He's going to think I told you everything and he'll beat me!"

"I told him you didn't tell me."

"It doesn't matter, he's not going to believe you! He's going to blame me for this whole thing!"

"Have some faith, Jessica. The angels and God are watching over us."

"They may help you, Arielle, but they've never helped me before."

"Don't say that! How do you know they haven't helped you before? They're helping you now and you don't even realize it."

By this time the three of them were several hundred yards behind the other searchers in their group. Dusk was settling in and a chill was in the air. Arielle looked up and saw Arthur coming across the field toward them as they plodded through the tall grass.

"Here he comes. We're in for it now," Jessica whispered.

"Don't worry. We're in good hands."

Arthur was within ten feet of the girls. "They told us to check the old Baker homestead," he said pointing to an opening in the forested area off the field. "It's over there through those trees. Let's go."

Arielle threw Jessica a glance.

"We better go with him," Jessica whispered.

"I don't like it," Arielle whispered back. "I'm getting a creepy feeling."

"You two quit your whispering. It isn't polite."

They followed Arthur along a path through the breach in the forest. Keeping a distance behind Arthur, Arielle crumpled the energy bar wrapper in her pocket, and then dropped it on the ground behind her. About two hundred yards later, they came upon a clearing where the remains of an old concrete foundation stood, surrounded by small trees. Weeds, saplings, and flowers grew up waist high through cracks in the floor. Pieces of charred wood surrounded the foundation.

As they entered the area that was once a house, Arielle saw a rusted doorknob and several hinges lying on the ground. Broken and melted glass was scattered about the area and crunched under foot.

"This is the old Baker homestead. It burned to the ground about twenty years ago. The fire department couldn't get to it and had to let it burn," Arthur told the girls.

"It's getting dark out," Arielle said. "My mom said we had to get back before dark."

"We'll get back. We have to check the root cellar first. Make sure Tommy isn't trapped in there."

"He's not here," Arielle said.

"How do you know? You know where he's at?" he asked rapid-fire. He sounded perturbed.

"Yes."

"Well, where is he then?" he asked with a scowl on his face.

"He's in the forest, in the back of his house."

"And just how do you know that? Are you a psychic or something?"

"No. The angels told me."

"Yeah, right. We're going to check."

Arthur walked over to the far side of the foundation. The girls followed close behind. He bent down and raised a large metal door. The hinges groaned as he folded it back. A set of partially rotted, wooden steps led down into the dark hole.

"You two stay up here while I go down and have a look around."

"Sounds good to me," Jessica said looking over to Arielle. "It looks pretty spooky down there."

Arthur carefully climbed down the steps into the darkness. The two girls watched from above as he lit a match and walked out of view. The light from the match went out.

"Owww! My leg!" came howls from the dark abyss. "Help me!"

The girls looked into the cellar, but Arielle couldn't see a thing.

"Help me! I think I broke my leg!"

"We have to help him," Jessica said.

"Something's wrong," Arielle whispered. "Maybe we should go get a grown-up."

"Both of you. Come down here and help me. I can't get up," he yelled.

"I'll go and get an adult, Mr. Stevens. I'll be back in a few minutes," Arielle yelled back.

"No, no. It's too dark. You might get lost. If you'll just come down here and give me a hand I can pull myself up the stairs."

"Something's not right, Jessica," Arielle whispered again.

"We have to go down and help him, Arielle. It's getting late."

She thought for a moment. "Okay, but I don't like it. He's lying to us. I just know it."

Step by step, the girls slowly made their way down into the root cellar, one after another, with Jessica leading the way. They felt their way as they inched along. The dampness, combined with a dank smell, made Arielle's skin crawl with goose bumps. Finally, at the bottom of the stairs, they hung on to each other.

"Light another match, Mr. Stevens, so we can see where you are," Arielle said.

"I'm right here," he said. Arielle felt a shove and fell to the ground. As her eyes adjusted to the darkness she could now make him out, standing at the foot of the stairs in the dim light.

"So you think you're going to report me to the police, do you? You little snob. You're not going to say a word to anyone."

"Arthur, what are you doing?" Jessica cried. She went over and hovered over Arielle.

"Arielle, are you alright?"

"I'm okay. My knee hurts."

Arthur picked Jessica up by her shirt. Arielle heard a slap. "I loved you, Jessica, and this is how you repay me. I begged you not to tell anyone and you had to go tell this little twit. Now you can stay here with her."

"Arthur, pleeese!" Jessica pleaded. "I'll do what you want. Don't hurt us."

"It's too late!" He threw her up against the wall. Arielle heard a hollow thud as she hit.

"Ohhh." Her groan sounded weak.

"Jessica, are you all right?"

A faint voice replied. "But I didn't tell her. The angel did."

"Angel, my butt. Both of you. You can stay here till you rot." Arthur climbed the stairs. "See if your angel will get you out of here."

Arielle watched the square of dusk swallowed up as the rusted metal door slammed shut. Total darkness enveloped them.

"Let us out of here!" Arielle yelled. Her pleas went unheeded.

Scraping sounds and loud thuds on the trap door above them told Arielle things were being piled on top of it.

Minutes later she could hear his faint footfalls receding further and further away.

"Jessica, are you okay?"

"I don't know. My head hurts. I think I hit a rock."

CHAPTER 23

Rescue

"I can't see anything, Arielle. What're we going to do?"

"I don't know yet. Just be calm and wait. Someone will rescue us."

"But no one knows where we are."

"They will. It'll just take a little time."

"Are you sure?"

"I think so."

"You *think* so?"

"Think about it, Jessica. What is your step dad going to tell everyone? He lost us? We ran away? One minute we were there and the next we were gone? No one's going to believe him. My mom will be all over him like bees on pollen."

"I hope so."

"Jessica, he can't get away with this. What he's been doing to you is bad enough, but now he's trying to kill us."

"I'm sorry for getting you into this, Arielle. I feel so bad."

"Don't be sorry, you didn't get me into this. It's not your fault. Your stepfather was given a choice and he chose the wrong path. Now he has to pay for it. God will protect us."

"I'm hungry."

"Me too. I've only got one energy bar left, but I think we ought to save it for awhile."

"Can I have a drink of water?" Jessica's voice sounded weaker.

Arielle passed her the bottle. "Only take a swallow. We have to save as much as we can. We don't know how long we'll be in here."

"My head really hurts."

"Let me feel it."

The back of her head was wet and sticky.

"You'll be okay." Arielle could tell Jessica's injury was serious. She would need a doctor, and soon.

⚘

Arthur hurriedly caught up with the rest of the search group.

Feigning concern he asked, "Has anyone seen the girls?"

"The last I saw them, they were sitting on a rock way back in the field," stated one woman.

"I thought they were with you guys," Arthur said. He borrowed a pair of binoculars and started looking around in the dimming light. "I don't see them."

"Maybe they got tired and started back to Tommy's house," another man said. "You know how kids are."

"Yeah, maybe they did," Arthur responded. "I'm going back to check. Maybe I'll see them on the way."

"Okay. We'll continue the search here for a few more minutes. We have to return soon," the group leader said. "It's getting too dark."

Arthur walked back to Tommy's house, in no particular hurry. The sun had gone down and a chill was blanketing the air. Rebecca's group had already come back from the forest. They hadn't found Tommy. She saw Arthur as he returned and walked over to see him.

"Hi Arthur. How'd the girls do?"

He hesitated before answering. "Just fine."

Rebecca questioned his hesitation. "Do you know where Arielle is?"

Arthur hesitated. "I was hoping you knew where the girls are."

"What do you mean?" she demanded.

"I twisted my ankle and had to sit down for awhile. I thought the girls were with the main group, but no one has seen them. I thought they might have come back here."

"What? Are you telling me you don't know where they are? They're still out there somewhere? How could you do that? I trusted you to take care of them!"

"Calm down, Mrs. Price. They have to be around here somewhere. We'll find them."

"Calm down, my butt! It's dark out. The girls are lost and you don't seem to give a rat's behind. If Jessica was your daughter, I guarantee you'd be out there looking for her right now!"

"Now just hold on a minute. I assure you, I love Jessica as much as you love your daughter."

"You don't show it."

Rebecca hurried over to the rescue headquarters tent. Inside, staffers were drinking coffee, eating cookies, and getting ready to pack it up for the night as soon as all the teams reported in.

"My daughter and her friend are missing. They were on one of the search teams. They haven't come back."

"What's your name?" asked one of the coordinators as he sorted through the team rosters.

Carol walked into the tent as he was asking. "Her name is Rebecca Price. What's wrong, Rebecca?"

"Arielle and Jessica are missing. They went out with a group with Jessica's step dad. He came back. They didn't."

"What did he say?"

"He said he thought they came back here by themselves."

"Mrs. Price, I'll round up a team and send them out right now to look," said the staffer.

"Please hurry. And I'm going with them."

The other members of Arielle's team had just arrived as Rebecca exited the tent. She asked each one if they had seen Arielle or Jessica.

"The last time I saw Arielle was when she was sitting with Jessica by the tree line. Arthur was close by them but not with them," one of the female searchers stated. She volunteered to go with the new team to show them where.

Rebecca sought out Arthur again. She found him relaxing on a chair and munching on a cookie from one of the trays of food the neighbors had supplied. "You don't seem too concerned about finding Jessica. Have you called her mother yet?"

"You're overreacting, Mrs. Price, but to answer your question, no, I haven't. I don't want to needlessly alarm her. She's working and doesn't get off until midnight. I'll tell her then if they're still lost or missing. Right now, I'm hungry. If we're going out again, I need something to replenish my energy."

"I'm not overreacting and we're leaving now. You need to come and show us exactly where you last saw them."

"I'm coming." He popped the last bite of his snack into his mouth and followed Rebecca to the new team of searchers.

Everyone was issued flashlights with extra batteries. Two of the search and rescue individuals had radios. The rescuers piled into several vehicles.

As they were about to leave, shouting and cheers could be heard coming from the rear of Carol's house. Rebecca bolted out of the truck and ran toward the house to see what the yelling was about. She hoped it was the girls returning.

Seconds later, Carol appeared in the front of her house with Tommy. Carol was on her knees hugging and kissing her son. She thanked everyone for helping search for him. When she saw Rebecca heading back to the truck, she ran over to her, grabbing her by the arm.

"Rebecca, I wish I could go and help you search for Arielle..."

Rebecca turned to Carol. "It's all right," she said in a reassuring voice. "I understand. You go take care of Tommy. We'll find Arielle and Jessica." She strode back to the pickup. In the rear of the truck was a large, black dog.

"Who's dog?" Rebecca asked the other riders in the truck.

"He's mine," stated the driver. "I'm Roger." He nodded at her in a greeting.

"Is he a tracking dog?"

"No, just a pet. I figured he could use some exercise."

"Oh. I was going to get something of Arielle's for him to smell and track."

"Sorry. We'll bring in tracking dogs tomorrow if we can't find the girls tonight."

"We'd better find them tonight," Rebecca said glaring at Arthur.

Rebecca was silent the rest of the way to the field. Something was bugging her, but she couldn't figure it out. *Why wasn't Arthur more concerned? Why didn't she make Arielle stay with her and go to the forest?*

"Over there. That's where I last saw them," Arthur pointed out as they approached the field.

The driver pulled the truck over onto a grassy area of the field and parked. The other trucks followed. Everyone piled out and turned on their flashlights. Roger dropped the tailgate and released his dog from the bed of the truck.

"Everyone stay within fifty feet of each other. We don't want anyone else getting lost," Roger said. "Let's spread out across the field. Be careful and stay in line."

Rebecca chose a spot between Arthur and Roger. After a few minutes, Roger yelled to Arthur, "Are you familiar with this area?"

"No, never been here before today."

"I want to find out if there are any wells or open pits in the area," Roger said to Rebecca. "They have to be around here somewhere. I can't see them going into the forest by themselves."

Rebecca walked over closer to Roger. "That's what bothers me," she said. "Arielle's extremely responsible. She wouldn't have done anything like that without an adult. Arthur is the one I left her with, and I don't particularly trust him anymore."

"He seems like an odd bird, but we'll find her, Mrs. Price. If one of the girls got hurt, the other would probably stay with her."

The flashlights' beams pierced the night like a laser show. Many of the searchers were calling the girls' names. The pace of the search was painfully slow in the uneven, rocky terrain. A slight wind kicked up causing even more of a chill in the air.

⊗℧℥

Arielle felt around the cellar trying to find another way out. All she could feel was cold stone and dirt. There was no other way.

"Arielle, Arielle, are you still there?" Jessica's voice was weak, broken.

"I'm here."

"I need some water."

Arielle felt around for her friend. Jessica was lying on the cold ground, her body limp. She sat down next to her, picked up her friend's head and cradled it in her arm. Again, she felt the warm, sticky fluid on the back of Jessica's head. It was still bleeding.

"Here, just take a sip."

"My head hurts, Arielle. I think I'm going to go back to sleep now."

"No, Jessica. Stay awake with me. Please don't go to sleep."

Minutes later, tears flowed down Arielle's cheeks as she rocked a sleeping Jessica in her arm. She held her hand up and concentrated on the orbs. They gradually radiated a strong enough light for her to see around the room. She looked down at her arm, which cradled Jessica's head. It was covered with blood. A pool of thick blood also coated the ground where her head had been lying on the dirt floor. She laid Jessica's head on her lap. The orbs extinguished their heavenly light.

"Oh, God, help her," Arielle cried. "This is my fault. Why did you have me help her? Why did this have to happen?"

A brilliant white light lit up the cellar. A light so bright Arielle had to shade her eyes with her hand. Three angels appeared.

"Arielle, why do you doubt your task at hand?" Jacob asked.

"Jacob, this wasn't supposed to happen. I don't want her to die."

"How do you know what was supposed to happen? You are a handmaiden to our Lord. His will, will be done."

Through sobs, Arielle questioned the angels. "But does she have to die? I thought I was supposed to help her."

"You are helping her."

"Who are you talking to, Arielle? Is someone here?" Jessica's eyes fluttered opened. She blinked several times, lifted her head slightly, looked around the room, and then looked up at Arielle.

"Go back to sleep, Jessica. Everything will be all right."

"Who are they?"

"They're angels. They're our friends. They're here to help us."

"Okay." Jessica said softly. She closed her eyes and appeared to immediately fall back to sleep.

"Send an orb, Arielle, as we have shown you in the past. Everything will be put in order," Jacob said.

The angels disappeared and the pit was again enveloped in total darkness. Arielle raised her hand and blew softly across her palm. She watched as a golden orb flew off her hand and passed through the steel trap door.

∽

"I don't know how much more we can search tonight, Mrs. Price. Everyone is tired and cold, and our batteries are about gone. I think we should pack it in before someone gets hurt," Roger said.

Rebecca was silent. She didn't want to give up if it took all night. But she knew Roger was right. She didn't want anyone getting hurt either and she was already using her spare batteries.

"I suppose," she replied.

Roger whistled for his dog. "Max. Come on, Max." Roger couldn't see him in the darkness.

"What kind of dog is he?" Rebecca asked.

Roger smiled. "I usually tell everyone he's a Curbstone Setter, but he's a Lab-shepherd mix." He whistled for Max again. They waited, but the dog didn't show.

"Where'd he go?" Rebecca asked.

"He was running back and forth up ahead of us. Probably searching for birds to flush." Roger spotted Max running towards him. "Here he comes."

Max had something in his mouth he was playing with—throwing it up in the air, letting it fall, and then retrieving. He was taking his time coming back, having fun.

"Max, what have you got?" Roger demanded. He picked it up. "What am I going to do with you? You pick up more trash."

Roger put the paper in his jacket pocket to throw away later. Rebecca caught a glimpse of the item as he took it from the dog.

"Can I see that?" she asked.

"Yeah. It's just a candy wrapper. The smell probably attracted him."

Rebecca looked at the wrapper. "This was Arielle's. This is one of the energy bars we bought on the way to Tommy's house." She pulled another out of her pocket. "See, it's the same as this one."

Roger examined the wrapper and the new bar together with his flashlight. "They're the same. Look, they even have the same lot numbers stamped on them."

"Where did the dog come from? Which direction?" Rebecca asked, urgency in her voice.

Roger blew a whistle, the signal for everyone to come in. The flashlights, which were dimmer now, started bobbing in his direction. In a few minutes everyone was gathered around.

Holding up the energy bar wrapper, he said, "Max picked this up somewhere in the field. Did anyone see where he got it or did anyone see him with it?"

"I saw him with it way back where we started," Arthur volunteered, "in the field."

Rebecca eyed him suspiciously.

"I saw him with it over there by the trees," Tricia stated while pointing towards the forest.

"Did you see him with it earlier?" Roger asked.

"No. Just a few minutes ago; when you were calling him. He caught my attention. He was playing with it, throwing it up and chasing it. I really didn't think anything of it. He looked like he was having a good time."

"What about it?" asked another searcher.

Roger explained the significance of the wrapper to the group.

"I need a volunteer to go and get more batteries. You can take my truck," Roger said. "I'll radio in ahead that you're coming. Anyone else who needs to go back or is too tired to go on can go back too."

Everyone chose to stay. Roger picked Bill to retrieve the batteries and tossed him the keys.

"Let's stay together until he gets back. Half of you shut your lights off so we can conserve what we have. Let's start looking where the dog was last seen. Tricia, you lead the way."

They followed her across the field to the edge of the forest where she had last seen Max playing with the wrapper. As they walked along the edge of the tree line, an opening came into view.

"Where does that go? Rebecca asked.

No one seemed to know.

"I checked that area earlier," Arthur said. "I didn't find anything."

Roger swept the ground with his flashlight. "Seems to be a lot of grass pushed down around here. Maybe we should recheck it." He winked at Rebecca. She nodded.

"Probably just animals. Maybe deer or the dog," Arthur suggested.

"Still, let's have a look," Roger said. "Half of you go back along the tree line where Arthur said he last saw Max. The other half stay with me."

"Roger, my light just died," Tricia said. "Maybe we should stay here and wait for the batteries."

Roger looked towards the sky. Not a single star could be seen, it was still pitch black.

"Okay, let's take ten and wait. Turn your lights off until Bill gets back."

After a short wait, the pinprick of headlights could be seen in the distance. Roger recognized the rumble of his truck's muffler and knew Bill was on the way. He turned on his light and flashed it on and off so Bill could find them. Several minutes later everyone was replenished with fresh batteries and the team was ready to continue the search.

"Okay, split up like we decided before. Watch for anymore candy or food wrappers," Roger said.

Rebecca eyed Arthur as he left with the group to search the tree line by the field. He kept looking back at her.

They entered the cutout in the forest, walking slowly, searching for anything out of place.

"There sure is a lot of grass matted down for just Arthur to have been here," Roger said.

"I still don't trust him," Rebecca said. "I think he's hiding something."

As they walked, the five of them took turns calling out the two girls' names.

After about a hundred and fifty yards into the cutout, Roger stopped.

"Quiet!" he said. "Did you hear anything?"

They all stopped and waited silently.

"I know I heard something," Roger said. "It sounded like a faint voice."

At first, all Rebecca heard was the breeze rustling the leaves of the trees. Then they all nodded their heads, indicating they heard the muffled voice also.

Rebecca cupped her hands to her mouth breaking the silence. "Arielle! Where are you?"

Again, a muffled voice sounded from the distance.

They walked deeper into the clearing of the forest.

"Arielle, keep yelling!"

"Look, up ahead. What is that?" Tricia asked. Beyond the beams of their flashlights, in the shadows, something could be seen ahead, but no one could make it out.

They walked faster. The voice seemed to be getting closer.

"Where's it coming from?" Rebecca asked.

"Slow down. It sounds like she's down in a hole or something," Roger said. "Maybe an old well." Then he yelled out, "Watch out for a well. Walk slowly and be careful."

Everyone was spreading out. The lights from the flashlights darted around the black night.

"It looks like an old foundation or something," Roger said.

"Arielle, where are you?" Rebecca cried out. They had surrounded the foundation.

"We're down here, in the cellar," came the faint voice.

Roger had followed the voice to the far corner of the foundation.

"Look for a metal door," the voice said.

"Over here! This is it!" Roger yelled.

Everyone gathered around him and Rebecca. He began pushing large rocks and a couple of cinder blocks off the metal cover. Pulling up on the old, rusty cover, the hinges creaked as he hoisted the heavy piece of metal back.

"Mommy!"

"Arielle!"

Her eyes were temporarily blinded by the brightness of the flashlights shining into the cellar onto her face. She shielded her eyes with her hand.

Arielle was still cradling Jessica's head in her lap. In the beams of light, Rebecca saw the blood covering Arielle's arms. "Arielle, you're bleeding! Are you hurt?" Rebecca cried.

"I'm okay, Mom, but Jessica's hurt real bad. She needs a doctor."

Roger carefully stepped down the steep, dilapidated stairs. When he got to the bottom he tried to wake Jessica, shaking her softly. He removed his jacket and placed it under her head.

"Tricia, catch my radio." He tossed the radio up and out of the cellar. "Call for an ambulance and a medical chopper. She's lost a lot of blood."

Arielle climbed the stairs out of the pit. Her mother picked her up and hugged her. "Oh, honey, I was so scared."

"Arthur did this, Mom. He hurt Jessica real bad."

Looking at all the blood, Rebecca asked, "Are you sure you're okay?" She pushed her back and passed the beam of her flashlight all over her.

"It's all Jessica's blood, Mom. I only cut my arm when he pushed me down."

"We'll take care of Arthur," Rebecca said. "Let me look at your wound."

Roger mounted the stairs. "I don't think we ought to move her. I can't pick her up and get up the stairs at the same time without possibly hurting her more."

"Roger, Arielle says that Arthur did this to them," Rebecca said through clenched teeth. She was so mad she could hardly talk. "Why would he do this?"

Roger spoke with Arielle. She detailed everything that happened to them and how they were injured. She didn't tell him why.

Roger went over to Tricia and pulled her aside. "Who's got a radio in the other group?" he asked.

"Peter," Tricia responded.

He relayed to Tricia what Arielle had told them. "See if you can get Peter. Tell him to go out of earshot of the others. When he is, ask if Arthur is still with them."

Tricia did what Roger asked and reported back. "Peter says Arthur left after we split up. He told them he had a headache and was going back."

"Okay. Call headquarters and notify them about him, and tell them we need the police out here also. They can catch up with him later. Jessica is our priority right now."

About ten minutes later the police and ambulance arrived. The paramedics prepped Jessica for an air ambulance ride. They wrapped her head with bandages, attached a collar and strapped her to a backboard. Fluids were started after they carefully lifted her from the cellar. She was carried to the open field where the helicopter landed and took her to the hospital.

Arielle rode to the hospital in the police car with her mother and the officer took her statement when they arrived in the emergency room.

೧೫೦

"Mom, is Jessica going to be all right?" Arielle was sitting on an exam table in one of the emergency room partitions.

"I'm sure she is, honey. They are working on her now. She has a bad cut and bump on her head. She might have a concussion."

"Arthur is a bad person, Mom."

"Why did you have to go with her?"

Arielle hesitated. "I guess everyone needs to know now. Arthur's been molesting her for a long time. I told him he needed to stop it. He said we could rot in the cellar so we couldn't tell anyone."

"He's molesting her?"

"Yes."

"Why didn't she say anything to anyone?"

"She was so scared, Mom. She didn't even want me to say anything to him. She was afraid he would beat her."

"Why didn't you tell the police about this when you gave them a statement?"

"I wanted Jessica to say something first. I didn't want them to ask me how I knew."

"What a horrible man," Rebecca said. "I hope they catch him, lock him up, and throw away the key."

A doctor and nurse came in to the room and examined Arielle thoroughly.

"I understand you've been through a pretty scary day, young lady," the doctor said as he gave Arielle a shot in the arm.

"Yes, Sir." Arielle agreed.

"I just gave you a tetanus shot and it looks like you'll be needing a few stitches. I have to numb your arm so I can sew you up," he said as he nodded to the nurse to give him a syringe.

Arielle scrunched her face. "Another one? I hate shots." She turned her head as the doctor injected the lidocaine. After the numbing agent took effect, he closed the gash with seven stitches. The nurse applied an antibiotic ointment, gauze and tape.

"Is Jessica going to be okay?" Arielle asked the doctor.

"She's going to be just fine. We're going to hold her overnight to watch her though," he said. She has a nasty cut and a large bump on her head."

Arielle sighed as though releasing a massive weight. "I was really afraid she was going to die when we were trapped in the cellar."

"Well, you're a couple of lucky girls. They found you just in time. Another few hours and it may have been a different story," the doctor replied. "She's lost a lot of blood."

"Can I see her?"

"When they're finished with her. They took her up to x-ray, but as soon as she comes down, and *if* she's okay, I'm sure it'll be fine," the nurse said. "You stay here for a few more minutes."

"Has anyone notified Jessica's mother yet?" Rebecca asked the nurse.

"I don't think so. You'll have to talk with admissions."

Rebecca checked with them on an in-house phone. She was told they had only been given a home phone number and no one was answering. Rebecca told them Jessica's mother was working until midnight and she would find a number for them.

She called several people, waking a few, and finally found that Jessica's mother, Betty, worked at a local convenience store. She called her and found she was about to get off shift and would be right over to the hospital. Rebecca didn't tell her any of the dark circumstances surrounding the events.

CR80

"Oh, my baby!" sobbed Betty as she hurried into Jessica's room. Jessica was awake, but she had a tube for I.V. fluids in her arm and wires connected to her, monitoring her vital statistics. Her head was wrapped in a bandage. "What happened to you?"

"It was Arthur, Momma. He did it. He hurt Arielle, too."

"He what? He couldn't have."

"I think he tried to kill us."

Rebecca entered the room. She put her hand on Betty's shoulder. "I'll explain it all to you. The important thing is they're both safe now."

"Momma, I saw angels," Jessica whispered not too quietly to her mother.

"You did?" Betty was trying to pacify her. "When?"

"In the cellar. They were talking to Arielle. She said they were our friends and would help us."

"Maybe they did," Rebecca said.

"Please don't encourage her," Betty said, throwing a quick glance to Rebecca.

"Honey, you've hit your head really hard. Maybe you were dreaming."

"Oh, no, Mom. It was real. I saw them."

"I'm sure you did, honey." Betty kissed her daughter on her check and patted her head. "You get some sleep now. I'll be back in a little while."

Jessica turned to Rebecca. "Where's Arielle? I want to see her."

"I'll see if they've finished with her," Rebecca said. "She wanted to see you, too."

Betty and Rebecca went down a hallway to a waiting room. Rebecca filled Betty in on everything that Arielle had told her about the abduction.

"But why, why, would he do that? He's really been such a great stepfather to Jessica."

"I've got more to tell you, Betty." She took a deep breath. "I'm afraid he's been molesting her for quite a while."

Betty looked into Rebecca's eyes and gasped, the color drained from her face. She clutched her chest. "*No, no. He couldn't have*," Betty cried as she fell down in a chair. "Not my baby!"

"I'm afraid so," Rebecca said, putting her arm around her. She rocked with her for several minutes.

"She's going to need a lot of therapy," Rebecca softly said. "Arielle told me Jessica thinks it's all her fault, so you're going to need to talk with her. I can recommend a real good therapist if you want me to."

Betty wiped the tears from her eyes and stood up. "I'll tell the doctor and the police right now," she said. "She needs to be examined and he needs to pay for this."

CR80

Arielle ran into Jessica's room and hopped up on her bed. She was all smiles. "How are you feeling?"

"I'm okay. My head still hurts. What happened?" she asked pointing to the bandage wrapped around Arielle's arm.

"It's all right—just a few stitches. I told you everything would be okay!"

"Arielle, I don't think Momma believes me. I told her I saw the angels."

"Don't worry about that. Grown-ups never believe me when I tell them either—and I've told a bunch of them. They just kind of look at me funny and smile. Some have even patted me on the head!"

Jessica laughed. "Yeah, that's what Momma did!"

"Do you remember our secret?"

"Yes, of course I do! I've never told anyone! You said someday I may find out what they were."

"Well, the angels that you saw in the cellar had me use one of those lights to save us. The lights are to help people, and one of them helped us. We've experienced a miracle from God."

"Arielle, I'm so excited just to have seen the angels. I want to tell everybody now."

"Your mother may not believe in Him, but you can be different. Just keep what happened about the angels to yourself and always remember it. When you're older, you can tell your children of your experience and let them know about angels. Someday you might be called on to help others. Always have faith in God and do what's right. You may not know it, and you may not see them, but angels will be there to help you if you ask for it."

"I will."

CHAPTER 24

Disaster!

"He decided to take the deal, Mrs. Price. Arielle won't have to testify," Ted Brandish, the district attorney said. He had asked Rebecca to step outside the witness waiting room where Arielle was watching television. As the district attorney spoke to her, she saw Jessica come from the courtroom and go into the witness room with Arielle. "You won't be seeing Arthur around for a long while—twenty years to be exact," he said.

"That takes a load off my mind," Rebecca said. "Arielle wouldn't have minded testifying, but it's just as well."

"I know, but to tell you the truth, I was more than a little worried that Arielle would have to tell her story about how she knew Jessica was being assaulted. The jury might think the whole account was fabricated."

"Well, I'm glad it's over."

Ted laughed. "After Jessica finished testifying, Arthur's attorney couldn't get a deal fast enough. You should have seen the looks on the juror's faces! If this was the Wild West, I think they would have adjourned the trial, taken him to the nearest tree and stretched his neck."

"I hope he becomes Bubba's girlfriend for the next twenty years," Rebecca said, shaking her head. "What he did to those girls, especially Jessica, was reprehensible."

"The girls have had several months to adjust. I hope Jessica continues with her therapy and the girls can get on with their lives."

CRSO

As Jessica entered the witness waiting room, a broad grin stretched across her face. Her face glowed with excitement as she nearly danced with joy. "Arielle! It's over!"

"Over?"

"Yes, they said we can go home. He's going to jail."

"That's great! How'd you do on the witness stand? Were you scared?"

"At first I was. Then I remembered what you told me and asked the angels for help. I didn't feel scared after that. I think they helped me, even when Arthur kept staring at me. He looked real mad."

Arielle gave her a hug. "Always remember."

"I will."

CRSO

Rebecca went back into the room. "C'mon, Arielle, we're all done here. Let's go have some lunch. Arthur pled guilty, so it's over."

"I knew he would, Mom."

"The angels?"

"Yep." Arielle collected her things.

"I still wish they would talk to me."

"They will soon enough, Mom."

Rebecca wondered what she meant.

They had lunch at a local fast-food restaurant, and were almost finished when Arielle asked, "Can we go now? The angels want to talk to me."

"Now?"

"Please, Mom."

"Why do we have to go home? Can't they speak to you here?"

"They said they had a lot to tell me and want my full attention. That would be hard here."

Rebecca finished the rest of her sandwich, tossing the remainder of her fries and drink. Arielle was silent the whole trip home.

"What do they want to talk to you about?" Rebecca asked as they pulled into the driveway.

"I don't know yet. They said we have a little time but it would have to be soon."

"Do you think they'll mind if I stay with you and watch?"

"No. They don't care."

Rebecca thought this would be a good opportunity to really observe her daughter talking with angels. Arielle went into her bedroom and sat on her bed. Rebecca stood in the doorway.

"Will they answer questions from me?" Rebecca asked.

"Maybe. I don't know why not, they answered questions from the priests and ministers." Arielle turned to her mother. "You still don't believe me, do you?"

"I think I do, Arielle, but I'd still like to see them or have them talk to me."

Arielle put her hand up towards her mother, indicating for her to stop talking. She sat calmly for several minutes, looking straight ahead. "Yes." she finally said. "How many?" Silence. "But why? How come so many?" Tears formed in Arielle's eyes. "Only one? Three?" Silence. "How soon?"

Arielle raised her right hand and softly blew across her palm. Rebecca watched as a golden orb flew off her hand and out of the room through the outside wall. Arielle sobbed softly as she hung her head. "Why so many?" she repeated.

"What is it, Arielle? What's wrong?"

Arielle looked at the clock on her nightstand. It was two-thirty in the afternoon. "I'm not allowed to say yet,

Mom. But you can probably see it on the six o'clock news tonight."

"How will I know?"

"You'll know. It's really heartbreaking."

CRSO

The Woo family were simple farmers in Sichuan Province, China. The three children consisted of two girls, Tu, seven years old, Liu, thirteen years old, and a boy, Ai, nine years old. Tu was a cousin to Ai. Her mother had died in childbirth and they took her in when her father suffocated in a mine collapse. Ai's parents adopted Liu when they found her as an infant in a forest close to them. She had been left to die at birth. It was not unusual to find female babies abandoned, as Chinese law allowed parents to only have one child. Most want a male, so as to carry on the family name and take care of them in their old age.

They all lived simply in a three-room mud-brick house on the edge of town.

Fuxin Number 2 Primary was the children's school. Each school day at seven-thirty in the morning they would walk together approximately a half-mile to attend.

As they walked to school on this May twelfth, there was still a nip in the air and Liu was looking forward to summer. In June she would be attending a class for gifted children in Beijing. She would be away from her family for a month and was looking forward to the new experience. She had already been chosen by the Communist Party to attend Beijing University after high school.

"I wonder where all the other kids are," she stated to her brother as they walked along the narrow dirt road. The usual flurry of activity was missing; normally scores of children converged on their way to school as they entered the city.

Ai looked around. "Yeah, where is everyone?"

Tan, a friend and classmate of Ai's, came running up behind the three, his backpack slung over his shoulder. "Oh, good! I won't be the only one late to school."

"What do you mean, late?" Liu asked as he kicked a rock down the street.

"We're all going to be in trouble. The headmaster will probably make us stay after school," Tan said.

"What do you mean, late?" Liu asked again.

"We're late. School started five minutes ago. Don't you look at your watch? Don't you have a clock at home?"

"Of course we have a clock. We left at the same time we do everyday. School shouldn't start for about fifteen more minutes."

Liu looked at her wrist. "I forgot my watch."

"You better get a new clock, Liu. It's five after eight. Like I said, we're late! Why do you think there aren't any other students walking to school this morning?"

The school was now within viewing distance. "See, no one else is around," Tan said as he spun around.

Ai felt a vibration under his feet. He stopped. "What's that?"

"What's what?" Liu asked, looking behind her at Ai. "Come on. We have to get to school."

"I felt something in the ground."

"I feel it, too," Tan said.

Gradually, the ground began shaking violently. In the distance, a rolling of the ground could be seen. They could see the earth rise and fall, a destructive roller coaster uprooting every tree, and trashing every building in its path, the street splitting, leaving gaping chasms. Other buildings were swaying, coming apart with the tides of the quake. Liu huddled the kids together in the street.

"Run!" Tan yelled. "It's an earthquake!"

"No, stay here!" Liu ordered as she watched several more buildings collapse. "This is the safest place."

Tan ran down the street towards the school, but stopped and came back to the others. The quake was so violent, it knocked them all off their feet as the earth shook and rolled. Everyone was screaming. Buildings fell, houses crumbled on their foundations. Thick clouds of dust and dirt swirled and hung in the air, coating the city in a heavy blanket of brown. People ran from their homes and businesses, yelling and screaming. Confusion and turmoil ricocheted all around them as their unbelieving eyes surveyed the damage.

After several minutes, the earth's convulsions subsided. The children picked themselves up off the ground where they were huddled together, holding on to one another. They coughed and choked on the dust cloud as they tried to breathe.

"Use your shirt to breathe through," Liu told the other children.

Ai looked toward their school, trying to make out the three-story structure through the cloud of dust. "Where'd our school go?"

They walked slowly down the broken, littered street toward their school, stepping over piles of debris. Bricks, stones and pieces of broken wood were strewn all over. Most of the homes and businesses they passed were completely obliterated. Screams, wailing, and crying were heard from everywhere.

"Where *is* our school?" Liu repeated.

☙❧

Rebecca turned on the six o'clock news and sat down with a cup of coffee. As she stirred the hot liquid, she called out for her daughter to join her.

"Arielle, the news is on. Let's see if your story will be told."

The lead news story was broadcast with few pictures. "A massive earthquake leveled parts of Sichuan Province in China, today. Sources are scarce at the moment, but reports coming out of China are saying tens of thousands of people are dead or missing and millions are homeless. The government is sending in troops to help look for survivors. The school day had just begun when the earthquake struck. It is feared the greatest toll will be the loss of thousands of children. Many schools have reportedly collapsed, pancaking the floors on top of each other. Aftershocks continue to rock the area."

Arielle came from her room in the middle of the broadcast. She had tears in her eyes again.

"Honey, is this what you were talking to the angels about?"

Arielle nodded. "But it's worse than they are saying. They just don't know how bad it is yet. Over eight thousand children died in schools, Mom. It's horrible. After the counts, if the government tells the truth, over ninety thousand people have died and over five million will be homeless."

"So what did the angels have you do? How could you save anyone from that type of destruction?"

"I didn't save anyone, Mom. I told you that before. Only God can direct the gifts and create the miracles. I am simply His helper. I helped save some special children."

"Miracles? Who said anything about miracles?"

Arielle hesitated. "What did you think they were?"

"What are you talking about?"

"The lights, Mom."

"I don't understand. Why would God need someone to do His miracles? Can't He do them on his own?"

Arielle sat down next to her mother. "Yes, He can. Let me try to explain it like this. Imagine yourself on the top of a ten-story building. You're looking down over the corner of a busy intersection. You see two cars speeding toward each other from a right angle. The two cars can't see each other because the building you are looking down from blocks their view. The stoplight malfunctions. Both the cars have a green light. You can see what is going to happen, but you can't do anything about it."

"Okay. I know what's going to happen. The cars are going to crash into each other."

"That's where I come in."

"How?"

"Suppose you saw someone below you knew, and you could call them and tell them there is going to be a terrible accident. Suppose you told that person to stop one of the cars before the crash happens."

"Okay..."

"That person you are calling is me."

"God calls on you and tells you what to do?"

"No, Mom. The angels do. They're God's messengers. Sometimes people need to see some type of divine intervention. Most people don't believe in what they don't see—and many times, they still don't believe even after they see. Angels are seen sometimes, but not often. There has to be something really special for an angel to appear."

"Like a big miracle?"

"Miracles happen everyday, Mom—but they usually happen in *natural* ways most people wouldn't give a second consideration to. No one thought anything about the van Christina was in, running into the police car after it had a blowout. She was just lucky. No one thought anything about the dog playing with the energy bar wrapper. He was just having fun with something that smelled good to him. And no one will think anything about the kid's alarm clock in China being ten minutes late. Power outages happen all the time there."

"Is that what happened? Is that how those kids were saved? A power outage?"

"Yes."

Rebecca folded her arms and leaned back on the couch. "So who was it you helped?"

"There's a girl, about my age. She's very special. We had to make sure she wasn't in the destruction of the earthquake."

"She's special? How?"

"She's very intelligent. Many years from now she'll be the one person that makes a difference between a possible world war and peace. I don't know anymore than that."

"How do you know what she's going to do so far in advance? Are you saying everything is pre-destined?"

"It's not that I know what is going to happen. I was told because I asked."

"I still don't understand."

"Think about those two streets that intersect I just told you about."

"Okay."

"Well, visualize those streets extending a long, long way... out to infinity."

"Arielle, how do you do all this? I mean, why?"

"Why what, Mom?"

"Why were you chosen for all this? Why do you have the lights? Why were you given to me? Why can you talk to angels?"

"I was chosen just as you were. I don't know why. The angels only tell me so much."

"I was chosen?"

"You were. Like I told you before, there are some things I can't tell you. But they did tell me you would know all the answers someday soon."

"Someday. I wish it were today," Rebecca retorted shaking her head.

"No you don't. Don't say that."

"Why not? I wish I knew the answers now."

"Because when my mission is finished..." Arielle stopped.

"Your mission?"

"Yes."

"What is it?"

"The rest—I don't know yet. I'm not told anything until it is time."

CHAPTER 25

The Pastor's Request

Many months had passed since the earthquake in China, and Rebecca hadn't noticed any special activity by her daughter, whether talking to angels, or sending orbs of light from the palm of her hand. She had noticed, however, that the number of lights Arielle now possessed had diminished.

This Saturday would be Arielle's fourteenth birthday and Rebecca planned a surprise party, secretly inviting many of Arielle's friends. She covertly bought all the food, drinks, and party favors, storing them over at her mother's house.

Rebecca smiled as she thought back to the day she found the little infant on her doorstep swathed in a pink blanket, all bundled up in a wicker basket. It seemed so long ago, and it seemed like yesterday. Her little girl had grown up. Arielle had become a wonderful young lady. She was so proud of her and wished her husband could be here with them, enjoying the happiness and trials of parenthood.

Rebecca didn't really know the exact date of Arielle's birth. She had picked October fifteenth as her birthday; that was the day she had worked the overtime shift in pediatrics and was able to sneak in the paperwork for a birth certificate.

In the end, it had all worked out so well; no one had ever suspected Arielle wasn't her child or her cousin's child, whichever little fib she stretched at the time. And now, fourteen years later, Arielle *was* her daughter, and no one could ever take her away.

Fifteen teenagers and three adults showed up to celebrate, including Arielle's grandmother. The party went off without a hitch, and lasted well into the evening. Rebecca surprised Arielle with an "angel food" cake she baked for the occasion. She received gifts of clothes, jewelry, a few books on angels and added several figurines to her angel collection.

When the party was over, one by one, parents picked up their teenage prodigy. Even Peter, the pastor's son, who had become a real gentleman, warmly informed Arielle as he was leaving that he had a good time.

"I'll see you in church tomorrow," he said.

As he was about to leave, his father appeared at the door.

"Happy birthday, Arielle!" he said through the screen door.

"Thank you, Pastor. I'm glad Peter was able to come. We had a good time."

"That's great." He turned to Peter. "Would you wait for me at the car, please. I have to speak to Arielle for a moment about another matter."

Peter left and the pastor stepped in and took Arielle aside.

"Is anything wrong?" she asked with concern.

"Is there somewhere we can speak privately for a moment?"

Scanning the living room, there was still a group of people standing around talking.

She led him to the den.

"I have a request of you, Arielle. Something very unusual has come to my attention and I would like you to help me, if you would."

"Of course. What is it?"

"I would rather not tell you ahead of time, but rather have you hear it first-hand."

Arielle smiled. "Sounds ominous."

"Not ominous, but very strange—though I hope not to you. Could you stay after service tomorrow and meet me in my office again?"

"I'm sure Mom won't mind. I'll see you then."

CR⊱SO

The next day after service, Arielle and her mother were leaving the church.

"I'm hungry. I hope your grandma has everything ready," Rebecca said.

"Mom, I forgot to tell you."

"Tell me what?"

"The Pastor asked me to stay after this morning to help him with something. I'm supposed to meet him in his office."

"But we're expected at Grandma's for lunch."

"I know. I have to go to the meeting; I promised. I'll call you when we're done and you can pick me up. Tell Grandma I'm sorry. Hopefully, it won't take too long."

"What's it about?"

"I don't know. He said he didn't want me to know about it ahead of time."

"Okay, I'll keep my cell phone on. Give me a call."

"I will."

Arielle reentered the church and went to the pastor's office. No one was present yet. She walked around the office, examining all the books crammed into the bookshelf on the far wall. There had been so many meetings here it was beginning to feel like a second home. She noticed several titles in one area near the pastor's desk that appeared to be very new. She pulled a couple of them off the shelf and giggled as she read the covers. They were all about angels.

CR&O

As she put the last book back, the pastor arrived with a young man. He was tall, well built with olive skin and thick black hair. Arielle guessed his age to be around eighteen years old.

"Good morning, Arielle."

"Good morning, Pastor. I enjoyed your sermon today."

"Thank you." He turned toward the young man and said, "Arielle, I'd like you to meet someone new in our congregation, meet Jason."

"Hi," Arielle said hesitantly.

"Hello, Arielle," Jason said. His voice sounded pleasant, but possessed an underlying chill. He held out his hand, but she remained across the room.

The pastor noticed Arielle's unusual demeanor. She didn't even walk over to greet the new boy, to shake his hand. Normally, she was bubbly and congenial. He could sense something was very wrong.

"Is everything all right, Arielle?"

"Yes, I'm fine, Pastor."

The pastor still wasn't certain. "Are you sure?"

"Yes." She hesitated for a few seconds. "Why'd you ask me here?"

"To meet Jason."

As the pastor walked around to his desk, he offered Jason a seat in front of his desk and a seat to Arielle on the couch.

"Thank you, Pastor, but I think I'll stay here," she said curtly.

"Very well. Jason claims that he speaks to angels and to God also. He says he has a history of predicting certain events and according to some of my sources, has done some pretty amazing things. Since both of you claim to speak to angels, I thought it would be interesting for you two to meet. You told me there are others who speak to angels, but you haven't met any yet."

"I'm glad you asked me here, Pastor," she said.

"So you speak to angels too?" Jason asked. He seemed surprised at the statement. He looked over at the pastor. "This is an interesting development."

Arielle looked up at the ceiling for a few seconds and nodded her head.

"I didn't think so," she said softly, barely audible to the others.

"Didn't think what?" asked the pastor.

"Jason is not who he says he is, Pastor."

"What?"

Arielle looked even more serious. "He does not speak to God, nor to angels."

Jason interjected. "What makes you say that, Arielle?" he asked calmly.

"Angels just told me, and confirmed my suspicions as to who you really are."

"Is that so? Then who am I?" he asked getting up from his seat.

"You aren't who you pretend to be. You aren't Jason."

"Arielle, what's going on?" the pastor asked.

Arielle walked across the floor to the other end of the office. "Please close the doors, Pastor."

"I don't think..."

"*Trust me* this one time, Pastor. *Please close the doors*," she repeated, only more demanding this time. "No one needs to see or hear this."

"See what?"

Arielle didn't answer.

As the pastor slowly rose from his desk and walked across the room, the doors of the office suddenly slammed shut. Jason was staring at Arielle, a wicked grin plastered on his face. His eyes were dark; his pupils pin-pricked.

"You wanted the doors closed. They're closed. So you think you know who I am?" Jason smirked as the pastor returned to his desk and almost fell into his chair. "*You think you know me?*" he yelled.

"Yes. I do. I've encountered many like you through my time."

"What...?" the pastor asked.

A large book from the pastor's desk flew unaided across the room, directly at Arielle. She held up her hand. It dropped to the floor several feet in front of her. "You'll have to do better than that."

"Very good, very good. And just who are you?" he asked, his smile having faded, his eyes on fire. "Try this," he said under his breath as he turned his back to Arielle.

Another book and a letter opener again flew off the desk toward her, the letter opener aimed directly at her face. Again she put her hand up and the items fell to the floor in front of her. The pastor's eyes were as wide as oranges. He couldn't believe or understand what was taking place in front of him. He made the sign of the cross.

"I'm a servant of the Lord. You must leave this soul and return from where you came."

"Ha. Sure you are. Where do you derive your power?"

"I'm an angel of the Lord. You cannot hurt me. In the name of Jesus Christ, I demand that whoever you are, leave the body of this boy, Jason."

"I'm not going anywhere!" Jason growled.

The lights in the office started flickering. A foul smell of rotting garbage and the stench of burnt flesh permeated the air. Thick smoke appeared from out of nowhere. The pastor watched in horror as warts slowly appeared on both his own hands and arms. He felt his face as sores welled, then exploded, oozing white pus down his cheeks.

"What's happening? Look at me!" the frightened pastor screamed. "It burns!" The pastor writhed in pain.

A boisterous, evil laugh erupted from Jason.

"Pray to the Lord, God," Arielle said. "He will protect you from this demon."

The pastor dropped to his knees and started praying *The Lord's Prayer* out loud.

"Pray all you want!" Jason yelled to the pastor. "He can't help you. I know all about you. Every evil deed, every thought that makes you mine!"

Without warning, everything from the walls—hundreds of books, pictures, and framed certificates—came flying at her. She held out her arm, and again, all the items crashed to the floor feet in front of her.

"Again, I command you in the name of Jesus Christ to leave this young man," shouted Arielle.

"Go ahead and demand. You haven't yet experienced my power," Jason spat. He waved his arm in circles.

The pastor's desk rose into the air and levitated about two feet off the ground. The closet door repeatedly flew open and slammed shut. The lights still flickered on and off like a strobe light. The few remaining books flew off the shelves and dropped to the floor. The room temperature plummeted to freezing. The fog of their breaths hung in the air. Pounding thundered from the walls and ceiling. The noise was deafening. The stench became overwhelming, gagging the pastor who used his shirttails to cover his nose. The pastor levitated off his knees and was thrown against the wall like a stuffed toy, where he slumped to the floor.

"Nor you, mine," Arielle whispered with a smile. A sudden beam of white light filled the room, blinding the pastor. Dazed, he tried to stand up, groping around for something to hold onto.

She walked over to the pastor, helping him to his feet.

"You must have faith in the Lord," she said to him.

He was shaking. "I do," he replied. "I do!"

"A real, unhindered faith, Pastor. Behold His power," she told him, "and forever bear *silent* witness."

She turned to Jason. "Demon, be gone!"

Arielle lifted her arm and softly blew across the palm of her hand. The pastor opened his eyes and watched as a golden orb appeared and left Arielle's hand, racing across the room to Jason. It encircled him, racing around and around at a rate of speed too fast for the eye to see, enveloping him in a bright golden shroud. The shroud glowed a brilliant sun-kissed hue for several minutes. Jason was frozen in time.

The smoke cleared from the room, the lights ceased flickering. Warmth gradually returned and the putrid smells dissipated. A deafening silence fell on the room. The warts on the pastor's skin faded away as fast as they had developed. The glowing cocoon around Jason finally subsided.

"Thank the Lord! Thank the Lord! And... *it's true!*" the pastor exclaimed. "Peter... and your mother... and you; all were telling me the truth!"

"What's true?" Arielle asked as she turned to him, wiping tears from her eyes.

"The lights in your hand. I saw them."

"Of course it's true. Mom wouldn't lie."

"Arielle, what was it I just witnessed? What happened?"

"Jason was possessed by a demon posing as a prophet. I have seen several of them before. I asked the other angels here and they confirmed my suspicion."

"In your time? What is your time?"

"Never mind," she said turning away.

"So, is Jason going to be all right now?"

"He'll be fine, though he won't remember anything about being possessed."

"And I heard you tell the demon something I have to know. You said you're an angel. Is that true or were you just...?"

"Yes, it's true."

The pastor went around to his desk and sat down, with his head in his hands, shaking his head. "I'm such a fool," he cried.

"Don't be so hard on yourself, Pastor. You're no different from anyone else. It's hard to believe what you cannot see."

"But I'm not supposed to be like everyone else."

"You must never tell anyone about what you have seen here," Arielle stated.

"Why is that? This is so miraculous. I've witnessed a miracle and I can't tell anyone?"

"No, you can't. Jason would be irreparably harmed by any revelation that he was possessed by a demon. Everyone would always look at him suspiciously and would never trust him. He is a good soul and must be allowed to have a normal life. He will be needed someday."

"What about you? Shouldn't I bear witness and tell everyone you are an angel so you can help those who are in need? Wouldn't it help people's faith if they saw and met an angel of God?"

"First, how many would believe you? I could never confirm your story and you would become the laughing stock of the city. Is that what you want? And most importantly, Pastor, is that faith? Is faith about seeing and knowing?"

He thought a moment. "I suppose not."

"Pastor, I have been sent here to complete specific missions. You are the only person on earth who knows who and what I really am. I still have work to do and won't be able to accomplish my tasks if those trying to constantly disprove me, inundate me with their foolishness, and believe me, there would be many. Please keep this to yourself. That is why I told you to bear *silent* witness to the miracle. Consider what you have witnessed as a gift from our Lord."

"You mean your mother doesn't even know?"

"No, she has no idea. Even though she has witnessed many miracles, like most people, she is determined to consider the ones who have been helped as just very lucky. Even though I think she now believes I speak to angels, she doesn't know who I really am. You remain the sole person with that knowledge."

"What about Jason?"

"Don't worry about him, he'll be fine. He won't even know why he was here, nor will he remember anything he did while he was possessed. He surely won't remember me. You will have to give him a reason why he was here, and be convincing without lying. That will be your task."

The pastor shook his head. "May I ask you something, Arielle?"

"Of course."

"Have you seen heaven, actually been there?"

Arielle paused and smiled. "Yes, of course."

"What's it like? Can you tell me?"

She thought for a moment. "I wish I could. It is so wonderful and exhilarating, but there aren't really any words to describe it. It would be like your greatest fantasy. When you're there, you don't want to be anywhere else; there just isn't anything on earth to compare it with and nothing in our language to describe it."

"Oh. I was hoping you could tell me about it." He sounded deflated.

Arielle thought for a moment. "Pastor, close your eyes."

He blinked several times, and then closed his eyes.

"Now, without using any colors, tell me how you would describe the color blue to a blind person."

He thought for a moment. "I can't."

"If I were to describe a color that was not visible to the human eye, what color would it be?"

The pastor was silent.

"Describe the taste of an orange to a person who can't taste or explain what the shade of a tree feels like to a person who has never been outside under the hot sun."

He opened his eyes. "I guess I see your point. I just wish..."

Arielle smiled at him. "Someday, Pastor, someday." She walked over to his desk. "May I use your phone, please?" she asked.

"Of course," he said with a smile. "How can I refuse a request from an angel?" She returned the smile as she dialed a number.

"Hi, Mom. I'm done here." After hanging up she looked around the office. "Would you like me to help you clean up your office?"

"Not unless you can wave your arm or send another light like you did, and everything fixes itself," he said with a wink.

She smiled again. "Sorry, Pastor. It doesn't work that way."

"I didn't think so."

Arielle helped pick books off the floor until a car horn sounded from outside the church.

"Mom's here. I have to go now. When you're ready with a good story, give Jason a shake and he'll come out of his trance."

"Okay. Thank you for everything, Arielle. I've learned a lot today."

"Remember, never a word to anyone. I wouldn't be able to confirm anything you say, and most people usually won't believe you anyway. You'll save yourself many headaches."

The pastor held up his hand. "I promise."

Arielle went outside to where her mother was waiting and got in the passenger seat.

"Well, what was the big secret about? How'd it go?"

"The pastor thought he had found another person who talked to angels."

"Well?"

"Turns out he wasn't telling the truth. I set him straight."

"Well, I guess if anyone can, it's you! Let's get to Grandma's. She's waiting to serve lunch and I'm starving!"

"Me, too!"

CHAPTER 26

Arielle's Decision

A week before Christmas, as they ate supper, Rebecca could see there was only one orb left in Arielle's hand. The lone orb rotated in its own orbit in her palm.

"Arielle, how come you only have one light left?"

"I've used all the others."

"When did you use them?"

"Different times, Mom. You know, when I was told to."

"What happens when they are all gone?

"Then my mission will be finished."

"Will you get more?"

"I don't know. It's not up to me."

"Maybe we can have another talk with the pastor. He seems to think pretty highly of you these days."

"He's a good person, Mom. And Peter has really changed. He used to be a brat."

Rebecca laughed. "He's a boy. He's probably just discovering girls." Arielle giggled.

That night Rebecca watched television as Arielle did her homework. Around seven o'clock Arielle set her homework aside and went to her mom.

"I'm going to bed, Mom. I don't feel so good."

"It's still early. What's the matter?"

"I just feel real achy, and I have a headache."

Rebecca felt her head. "You are a little warm. Go on to bed and we'll see how you feel in the morning. Take a couple of acetaminophen; it'll help the fever. I hope you're not coming down with the flu."

"Okay, I will. Goodnight, Mom. I love you."

"Love you, too." Both gave each other a peck on the cheek. "Don't give me whatever you have."

Arielle smiled. "Don't worry. I won't."

CRLSO

It was eleven o'clock when Rebecca turned the television off and headed to bed. She stopped in to check on Arielle and felt her forehead again.

"Oh my God! You're burning up!" she yelled. She tried to wake her, but couldn't.

She pulled the covers back and tried to pick Arielle up, struggling to half carry and half drag her to the bathroom. Arielle's pajamas were soaked with sweat. She was shocked to see her hands and feet were shades of purple. Rebecca held her the best she could as she plugged the bathtub and started the cold water running, mixing in a little hot to get it lukewarm. She gently splashed water on Arielle's face, calling her name, trying to wake her up.

With great effort, and as gently as she could, she propped Arielle in the tub and went for a phone. She grabbed the closest one from her bedroom and brought it with her into the bathroom. She checked on her daughter while dialing 9-1-1. She was still unconscious. Four, five rings. It seemed to take forever for someone to answer.

Not again! Please don't put me on hold, Rebecca thought as a recording answered.

An operator cut into the recording, "9-1-1 operator, what is your emergency?"

"This is Rebecca Price at 3679 Ridgewood Drive. I'm a registered nurse and have a medical emergency. I need an ambulance immediately. My daughter is unconscious and has a high fever."

"Standby, please."

After what seemed like an eternity, the operator returned.

"An ambulance has been dispatched, would you like me to stay on the line with you?"

"No. I'll take it from here. Thank you." She hung up.

Rebecca knew she had to unlock and open the front door for the paramedics. There was only a few inches of water in the tub, so she turned the faucets off, ran to the front door, unlocked and opened it, then ran back to her daughter.

As she returned, Arielle's body stiffened and convulsed, contorting her body. Struggling, Rebecca pulled her from the tub and laid her on the floor. Soon, the spasms subsided. She cradled Arielle's head in her arms.

"What's wrong with you?" she cried as she rocked her back and forth.

Several minutes later, the doorbell rang.

"Come in. We're down the hall in the bathroom," Rebecca yelled.

The paramedics entered and found their way to the bathroom, medical equipment in hand. Rebecca told them she was a registered nurse and filled them in on what had transpired up to that point. They started oxygen and an I.V. and took her temperature.

"Wow, she is high!" stated one of the paramedics. "Let's get her ready to go."

Arielle came to as the paramedics prepped her for transport. She opened her eyes and closed them again. She tried blinking several times. "Where am I? Mom?"

Rebecca bent over her as she wiped a tear from her eye. "You're still at home, honey," she said holding back more tears. "They're getting you ready to go to the hospital."

"But why? What's going on? Ohh, I feel so hot." She was groggy and confused.

"You've had some convulsions and your temperature is very high. We need to get your fever down," one of the paramedics said. "We have some ice packs in the ambulance."

"My neck and back hurt."

The paramedic looked at Rebecca, concern in his eyes. She knew what the look meant and the gravity of Arielle's potential illness—the possibility of meningitis or encephalitis.

Rebecca rode with Arielle in the ambulance to the hospital. She could always call on her mother to pick her up and take her home if needed. Normally, her drive to work was about fifteen minutes. Tonight, even though they were in an ambulance and traveling above the speed limit, the ride seemed to take forever.

At the hospital emergency room, a doctor immediately examined Arielle. She was prepped for a spinal tap right away. The doctor told Arielle to curl up into a fetal position. A large needle was inserted into her back at the base of her spine to extract the fluid for testing. Arielle screamed and cried as her mother helped hold her tight. Three vials were extracted.

The doctor visually inspected the fluid he'd removed. Rebecca saw it was clear, which was good, but the doctor's facial expression didn't indicate he was pleased.

"What is it?" she asked.

"The viscosity seems a little thicker than it should be," he said shaking one of the vials. "We'll get it to the lab. They'll check for excess protein."

Arielle fell back to sleep after the procedure was completed.

Rebecca went to the nurse's lounge after the spinal tap, while her daughter slept, but couldn't sit still. She walked the corridors. As she looked around and watched the various activities, the sights and smells of the hospital she was so familiar with seemed different. Tonight, the other patients' problems seemed trivial, the smells of the hospital offended her; the lights were too bright, the halls too quiet.

After checking on Arielle, Rebecca decided to call her mother. It was late, but she would be upset if she weren't told. After waking her mom up and telling her what had happened, she wanted to immediately come to the hospital.

"No, Mom, stay home. There's nothing you can do. She's resting now, but her temperature hasn't come down. The doctor was concerned about the fluid he took from her spine. It could possibly be meningitis. Just pray it isn't a bacterial meningitis."

"Why, is that bad?"

"Bacterial can be deadly," she responded slowly. "But most meningitis is viral, and if it is, she'll be better in a few days. But what bothers me is her temperature won't come down and she's disoriented. That could point to other things. It may be bacterial."

"Are you sure you don't want me to come down there?"

"I'm sure, Mom."

"I'll pray for her, Becca, but I'll be down in the morning. You still need to get some sleep."

"I'll sack out in the nurse's lounge for a while. I want to stay near her. She's been quarantined into an isolation room for now until they know exactly what she has."

At two-thirty in the morning, Rebecca lay down and tried to sleep. It was fitful, and she kept waking up in the dark room, wondering where she was.

At five in the morning, a nurse from the emergency room came in and shook her lightly, waking her up.

"Betsy, what... what's the matter?"

"I'm sorry to wake you, Becca. You'd better come."

"Why? What...?"

Betsy spoke with concern in her voice. "I went and checked in on Arielle. She's getting worse and nothing the doctors have tried is helping. She's had more convulsions."

Rebecca got up slowly, shaking out the cobwebs, trying to think what could be so wrong with her daughter. What had she overlooked? All the training she had, all the years in school, all the other people she helped save, and she couldn't help her daughter. She walked up the stairs to the quarantined room with Betsy, her mind in a daze. They put facemasks on before entering to protect against anything contagious Arielle might have. Rebecca pulled the chart at the end of the bed and examined it. Arielle's temperature had gone up to a hundred and six. Ice packs were lined up alongside her overheated body.

"Arielle, what is wrong with you?" Rebecca cried, tenderly holding her hand.

"I'll leave you two alone," Betsy said. She put her arm around Rebecca. "I'm sorry, Becca. If there's anything..."

Rebecca sat down on a chair next to the bed in the darkened room. The monitors threw a soft green light on Arielle as they quietly beeped and buzzed, calling out and recording their different readings. The oxygen hissed. Rebecca had never listened to these noises before. She never heard them; they had always been just background sounds. Now she listened to them like they were something new to her, something she had to pay strict attention to. She held Arielle's hand and gently stroked it. She could feel the heat radiating from Arielle's soft skin and could also see the lone orb left in the palm of her hand. It glowed with an unusual golden sheen. If only someone else could see it too.

"Arielle, if you can hear me," she whispered, choking back tears. "I need you. Don't go anywhere, honey. I can't bear to... to lose another child. You're my life. I love you."

Tears flowed down her cheeks as she cried, dripping onto her shirt. She stood to get some tissues from a box on the opposite side of the bed. As she came back around and sat down, Betsy came into the room.

"There's a priest outside the room. He says he is Cardinal Scanlon and that Arielle is a friend of his. He wants to see her."

"He's here? Please, let him come in."

Betsy went back out and gave the Cardinal a face-mask. "Please wear this. We don't know what she has yet and it may be contagious."

He put it on and entered the room. Rebecca greeted him, tears in her eyes. "Cardinal Scanlon, it's good to see you again," she whispered.

"I wish it were under better circumstances," he said. "I just arrived from Rome, but when I heard about Arielle, I had to come."

"Pray for her, please," Rebecca pleaded.

"I would pray for her and give her Last Rites, but I believe she's closer to Him than I am."

The Cardinal knelt down beside Arielle's bed and closed his eyes. With folded hands, he bowed his head and started to pray. Rebecca sat down on a chair behind him. Several minutes later he rose and put his hand on Arielle's, giving her a blessing. He left a rosary wrapped around her hand.

"I wish I could do more for her, Rebecca. I have to go now, but I will keep praying for her recovery."

"How did you know she was in the hospital so fast?" she asked. "No one except my mother knows she was here."

The Cardinal didn't answer at first. He just stood there. "Let's just say..." He stopped. "I would prefer not to say."

"I think I understand." Rebecca thanked him and he left. She still wondered how he heard about Arielle, but then thought back to Arielle's prophecy to him when he was an Archbishop. She knew there would be no direct answer forthcoming.

CRSO

As she sat back down and held Arielle's hand, a bright light effervesced from above Arielle and lit her up in a soft brilliance.

"Who's doing that? What's going on?" Rebecca asked quietly, looking around the room. She got up and walked back around the bed to see if she could find the source of the light.

"We thank you, Rebecca. You've been a good mother to our little sister, Arielle," a gentle voice said, coming from somewhere in the room.

Rebecca looked around. She slid the mask off her mouth. "Your sister? Where are you? Who are you?"

"We are here. We have been here all along."

Six figures gradually appeared on the other side of Arielle, backlit in the same shimmering light as was illuminating Arielle.

She gasped, her eyes wide with astonishment. "Who are you?"

"We are the angels Arielle has been conversing with over the years."

"Angels?" Rebecca stammered. "Oh my God! What..., why are you talking to me now? What is happening to Arielle? Can you save her?"

"She doesn't need saving. It is time for her to come home with us. Her work is done here."

"But..., she can't!" Rebecca pleaded. She put her hands together in prayer. "Please, please, don't take her!"

"It is not, and never has been, our decision. Arielle knew her time was upon her. That was the one thing she couldn't tell you. She did tell you there would be a time when we would talk to you and answer any of your questions."

"I didn't know it would be like this. I didn't know it would be when she is dying."

"She cautioned you not to wish for this day," one of the other angels said.

"What day? What are you talking about?"

"The day you would speak with us."

"Who is she? Why was she brought to me?"

"Arielle is an angel of our Lord."

"She's an angel?"

"Yes, she is. Do you remember when she told you that you were also chosen?"

"I remember. But chosen for what?"

"The Lord chose you to raise Arielle after you came to Him."

Rebecca didn't understand. "After I came to Him?"

"Yes, she was your gift from Him. After your son died, you asked for God's forgiveness for cursing Him. You asked for His help."

Rebecca lowered her head. "And He heard me?"

"He hears all pleas for forgiveness and help."

"Will he hear me now?"

"Of course, but her destiny has been set in motion. Only He can change it."

Rebecca knelt down. "Please, I'm begging."

"Look in your right hand," the angel said.

Rebecca turned her right hand in toward her. "What...?"

"He has given you Arielle's last gift as a reward for raising and taking care of her. Use it wisely, as you wish. Use it as she did."

"May I use it now?"

"Yes."

"And I can use it how I want?"

"Yes."

Rebecca slowly turned toward Arielle and hesitated. Her inclination to immediately send the orb to Arielle was tempered by thoughts of her comatose husband. She could send the orb to him and he would be cured, or, she could save her daughter, who was an angel. It was a heart-wrenching choice. *Sophie's Choice* came to mind. How could she make such a decision?

She blew across her palm. The orb glowed brightly for several seconds, but did not leave her hand.

She stared at the orb. She blew on it again, it just hovered above her palm. "Why won't it leave?" she cried. She shook her hand, trying to get it to leave. "You said..."

"Your wish and love has been heard," another one of the angels said, moving forward. "He has given the decision of staying on earth or coming home to Arielle. It is now up to her."

The first angel spoke again. "I must tell you, if she decides to stay, she will no longer be able to speak to us while she is on the earthly plane, as her mission is complete. For all intents, she will be just like everyone else. She won't be helping anyone through us anymore."

"She won't be an angel anymore?"

"She'll always be an angel, but without angelic powers, knowledge and gifts until she returns to us. She will be giving up very much to stay with you in your world."

"I hope she knows how much I love her."

"She does. She will make her decision soon."

"How..., when will I know?"

"You will know."

The angels faded away and the bright light dimmed to darkness, punctuated only by the green glow of the machines. Rebecca was left alone in the darkened room, watching her daughter, wondering what she had just witnessed. A miracle? A hallucination?

She sat back down in the chair and stared at the lone orb still glowing in her hand. It was the only thing left that confirmed to her she hadn't lost her mind and the visitors she had were real. She made a wish and raised her arm, blowing softly across her palm. To her surprise, the orb sped off through the wall and disappeared. She smiled. *Let's see if I'm not totally insane yet.* She half expected to see men with the little white jackets come marching through the door.

A half hour later, Betsy entered the room with her facemask on. "I have to take Arielle's temperature and change her drips, Becca," she said softly. "You should put your mask on. We still don't know what she has yet."

Rebecca nodded, and pulled up her mask. When Betsy was finished, she wrote on Arielle's chart, brought it over and showed it to Rebecca. At first she just glanced at the writing, then she grabbed the chart and looked at it again. She jumped up, giving Betsy a hug.

"Oh, thank God!" Rebecca said.

"The antibiotics seem to be working. I'll let the doctor know her temperature has come down."

⋘⋙

Rebecca went down to the hospital chapel and prayed for an hour, thanking God for his gift for allowing Arielle to return to her. Exhausted, she dragged herself down to the cafeteria for some breakfast. Sucking down three cups of four-hour old coffee, she also forced herself to swallow some cold bacon and eggs with burnt toast.

She desperately wanted to go back to the nurse's room and curl up in a little ball and go to sleep. Partially re-energized from the caffeine, she went back to Arielle's room to tell her goodnight and thank her for deciding to stay. As she entered the room, she was about to put her facemask back on, but was surprised to see her daughter awake and sitting up in bed.

"Arielle, you're awake! You've come back!"

"Yes, Mom. How could I not? Don't you know how much I love you, too?"

She ran over to Arielle and they hugged each other tightly. "How do you feel? Are you all right?"

Arielle had a big smile on her face. "I'm still a little achy, but I'll be okay. You don't have to fuss over me."

Just then, Betsy entered the room. She stopped when she saw Arielle sitting up in bed. "This has to be the fastest recovery in the record books. You lay back down now, young lady. You're not completely healed yet."

Arielle winked at her mom and slunk back down under the sheets. Betsy took her temperature again. When she pulled the thermometer out of her mouth, she walked over to Rebecca.

"Look at this. It's impossible! She is completely normal. Ninety-eight point six."

"Miracles do happen," Rebecca said. She winked back at her daughter.

Betsy stared at Arielle for a moment. "Are you sure you were even sick?" she asked with a smile. "You weren't faking it, were you?"

Betsy turned to Rebecca. "I completely forgot what I came in here for!" She grabbed Rebecca's arm and pulled her over to the door.

"You're not going to believe this," she whispered looking back and forth between Rebecca and Arielle. "The hospital just received a call from your husband's nursing home. *Craig woke up, Becca! He woke up!* After all these years, he's back, and he wants to see you!"

"Oh, my God!" Rebecca screamed. She leaped off the floor at Betsy who caught her in mid-air and spun her around. They hugged each other for several minutes, Rebecca with tears streaming down her face again. Arielle was watching, her face beaming.

Rebecca finally let Betsy go. "Oh, no," she sighed.

"What is it?" Betsy asked.

"Now I have to tell Craig about Arielle. How am I going to do that? Should I tell him right away, or wait until I see how much memory he has?" Rebecca was staring intently into Betsy's eyes, waiting for an answer.

"Oh, yeah, that's right, he doesn't know about her." Betsy held her hand to the side of her face, hiding a grin. "I completely forgot that you made him a father—without his knowledge."

"You know?" There was terror on Rebecca's face.

"Of course I know. You told me. Don't you remember?" Betsy asked.

"What'd I tell you?"

"That you adopted Arielle before Craig's accident and he doesn't know he's a father yet."

Thank God! For a minute I thought she knew about the birth certificate!

Betsy couldn't contain herself any longer. She let go with a howl, which turned into a belly laugh.

"What are you laughing about?" Rebecca admonished.

"I didn't tell you yet," she said with a sheepish grin. "Craig already knows about Arielle. He asks that you bring her too."

"How'd he know?"

"I don't know, maybe the staff at the nursing home told him."

Rebecca looked over at Arielle who was smiling and nodding her head. A smile broke out on her face. "I know how," Rebecca said, wagging her finger.

CHAPTER 27

Continuum

Sarah was almost ready for work. It was hard to prepare herself today after almost four months of vacation, rehabilitation, and counseling. She still had to take things slow–her normal routine for work in spite of all the therapy, was painful. Her hip was not quite back to normal, and she felt the stiffness in her knee. She was told her limp would eventually diminish and go away.

Sarah's six-month old son, Christopher, and her husband, Ben, had been killed in a terrible car accident; a head-on collision with a teenage driver, high on drugs and alcohol. She had also been seriously injured, requiring an extensive hospital stay and over a month of physical and occupational therapy. The sounds of crunching metal and terrified screams forever echoed in her memory.

Their new car had been totaled, but the airbags had saved her life. Her supervisor told her that her job as an executive secretary at the automobile assembly plant would be waiting for her when she was ready to return. She hadn't even been able to attend the memorial or burial services for her son and husband. Her depression and grieving had started only two weeks ago; her doctor told her she was probably still in a state of shock up to that point. She didn't know what to believe.

It was a cool spring morning as she left her mother's home. She had to give up the house her family had been renting before the accident; it was a multi-level and she had been in a wheelchair for several weeks after her release from the hospital, and then on crutches for the next month. She had needed extensive help with daily activities and had taken her mother up on her offer to move in with her, at least until she could be on her own again and back at work. That was on her mind this morning as she slowly ambled to her car, parked on the street in front of the house. She opened the driver's door and got in.

Something was odd. She was sure she had locked the door the night before, but here it was, unlocked. She looked around the front interior. Everything looked okay. A strange sight met her eyes as she looked in the backseat through the rearview mirror. A wicker basket!

She got back out of the car and opened the rear door, pulling the basket over to her. It felt heavy. "What in the world is in this?" she asked aloud. It contained a loose blue blanket bulging out of the top with a note pinned to it. She opened the safety pin, releasing the note. In beautiful script handwriting, it read: *SARAH, I AM A GIFT FROM GOD. PLEASE TAKE CARE OF ME.*

She carefully pulled back the blanket. Sound asleep was a naked little baby boy.

61808893R00159

Made in the USA
Columbia, SC
27 June 2019